DOUBLE IDENTITY

It was difficult for Luke to think clearly with that gun aimed at Isabella's heart. He was afraid to push it until he had her out of range. Too many damn memories. He was getting it right this time. No screwups.

But he also needed to know what he was up against. "Who were you talking to?" he asked their captor.

Who knew Adam Fie had been found? Jesus. *He'd been found.*

Instinct told him to kick ass and bolt. To disappear again. But Isabella had to be safe first. He couldn't leave her behind. Had to get her safe first.

But it wasn't so easy anymore. Because Adam Fie was a wanted man, and his presence would bring all hell down on anyone associated with him.

Other books by Stephanie Rowe:

ICE
IF THE SHOE FITS
UNBECOMING BEHAVIOR
SHOP 'TIL YULE DROP (Anthology)

CHILL

STEPHANIE ROWE

LOVE SPELL NEW YORK CITY

For Ariana, my dearest love and greatest joy

LOVE SPELL®

December 2009

Published by

Dorchester Publishing Co., Inc.
200 Madison Avenue
New York, NY 10016

ISBN 10: 0-505-52776-6
ISBN 13: 978-0-505-52776-9
E-ISBN: 978-1-4285-0784-5

The name "Love Spell" and its logo are trademarks of Dorchester Publishing Co., Inc.

Printed in the United States of America.

10 9 8 7 6 5 4 3 2 1

Visit us online at www.dorchesterpub.com.

ACKNOWLEDGMENTS

Thank you to my fantastic editor, Leah Hultenschmidt, for all her support, and to my family and friends, who make my life richer every day simply by being a part of it.

CHILL

CHAPTER ONE

Luke Webber swore as the swollen, angry river fought to grab the wheels of his low-flying bush plane. The liquid fury roared its need to snatch him out of the air and suck him down into a hellish death at the mercy of Black River.

Water sprayed up over his windshield, killing his visibility. The wind buffeted the small plane like paper in a hurricane. Whitecaps lashed out at the wheels. The rapids smashed over rocks.

"Hell, Luke." His radio crackled with static as his partner, Cort McClaine, made contact. "I'm ten minutes away, and this storm is getting worse by the minute. What does it look like there?"

Through the blinding rain, Luke caught a glimpse of the island he'd been fighting to reach. Three shadowy figures were waving frantically, marooned on the small strip of sand alongside the raging river. Hot damn. He'd dropped off the scientists four days ago so they could research a rare species of plant. Thank God they were still alive.

But his relief faded as he took in the grim reality of the situation. The beach was a third of the size it had been, the island . . . shit . . . it was almost underwater.

The woodsy area was often submerged during big

storms, especially in the spring, but the forecast had been clear when he'd dropped them off. However, like many weather fronts in Alaska, this storm had formed in a matter of hours, and she was a raging fury.

Luke had been in the air the minute he'd realized what would be going down at the research site, and it looked like he was still too late.

There wasn't enough beach left to handle the plane. The island would be underwater within hours. His clients, drowned.

"Luke." Cort's voice came over the radio again. "Talk to me. What's going on?"

"I might be able to land, but no way I could get back up. There's not enough beach."

Cort swore. "What about me?"

Luke knew Cort wasn't questioning his ability to fly. After eight years as a bush pilot, Luke was as skilled as his business partner, who'd been piloting his own rides since he was seven.

Difference was, Luke was sane and Cort wasn't. Not when it came to making choices in the air. Yet even Cort wouldn't touch down now, not in Luke's plane. But Cort was flying a smaller plane that needed less distance to get aloft. He still had a window to get down and get up.

"I'm over the river now," Cort said. "How much beach is left?"

"Not enough for my plane." Luke pulled up, aborting the landing attempt, and panic broke out on the beach. The men jumped up and down and gesticulated wildly. Luke could taste their desperation as they realized he wasn't going to land. He gritted his teeth as they chased the plane down the beach. Luke knew they could hear death's laughter in the howling wind as they watched their only hope to live abandon them.

Luke ground his jaw as he left the island behind. Cort's plane was too small to carry all three men in one load. And by the time Cort came back for a return trip, the island would be underwater.

Which meant at least one or maybe two scientists would die if Luke didn't get his ass down there and back up again. For Luke to leave those men to die . . . it was akin to murder.

And murder was no longer a part of his life.

He'd sworn long ago no one else would die because of him. Leaving those men behind to save his own ass . . . that was something his dad would do. Fuck that.

With a loud shout, he banked the plane and circled back around toward the island. He narrowed his focus on that small strip of gray beach. He ignored the voice in his head shouting that he would die along with them.

Cort's voice came back. "Jesus, Luke! What are you doing? I can see you now, and there's no way you can take off from that beach! Leave it for me!"

Cort was the most daring bush pilot Luke knew, and the smartest. If Cort thought Luke had any chance of making it, he'd never call him off, not when lives were at stake.

Luke rubbed his thumb over the brand his father had burned into his wrist when he was eight. The brand that forever marked him as Marcus Fie's son.

"I'm not your son," Luke snarled. Then he sat back, gripped the controls and headed right for that slip of sodden earth.

The plane hit easily, and Luke hauled her to a stop

with room to spare. But entry wasn't the problem, and he knew it.

He also knew it could be the last landing he'd ever make.

But when he taxied around and saw his clients running toward him, stumbling over the rocks and shouting for help, he knew he'd make the same choice again. If he failed, at least he'd die trying to do the right thing.

A claim his father would never be able to make.

Marcus Fie's sixtieth birthday party reminded Isabella Kopas of the night her mother had been murdered.

The sultry live music. The dark lighting casting shadows over the ornate decor of Marcus's ballroom. The high-end cigar smoke drifting through the three-hundred-thousand-dollar crystal chandeliers. The clink of the finest champagne glasses.

The muted hum of cultured male voices. They all had refined way of speaking that didn't quite mask the violence rolling beneath the surface . . . by intent, Isabella was certain.

Despite the similarities, though, this night wasn't the same.

Tonight Isabella's seven-thousand-dollar scarlet gown hadn't come at the price of her body or her morals . . . at least, not in the way her mother's had.

This evening Isabella's date was a handsome art dealer who had brought her two dozen roses and a matching corsage, not a cash payment up front.

At eleven o'clock, she wouldn't be cradling her mother's battered body in her lap, waiting for an ambulance to save the life of the five-hundred-dollar-a-night escort no one cared about.

No one except one seventeen-year-old daughter.

"You can't possibly give *this* to Marcus." Roseann Martin held out the platinum-and-diamond bracelet Isabella had just handed her.

Isabella pulled her gaze off the tuxedo-clad orchestra playing muted jazz on the glittery ballroom stage. "Of course I can." She lifted the bracelet from her best friend's palm. The diamonds set sparsely in the heavyset links were masculine and tasteful. She draped it over the back of her hand, so it slid across her scarlet fingernails. The light from the chandeliers made the stones glitter, as if they were dancing. "He'll love it."

Her friend shook her head. "Isa—"

"Roseann!" One of the kitchen staff leaned out the door and beckoned to her. It was a young man, one of the new hires in the constantly rotating door of Marcus's household staff.

Roseann turned to go, but Isabella set her hand on Roseann's shoulder. "She'll be right there," Isabella called back.

The youth hesitated, then ducked back inside, clearly not senior enough to realize that the fact that Isabella lived in Marcus's house and was his most valued professional asset didn't translate to having any authority whatsoever in the management of his household.

Neither woman bothered to waste the brief respite they'd been given. "It's not the bracelet that's the problem," Roseann said. "It's the engraving."

As the orchestra struck up a new tune, Isabella turned the bracelet over. The bass reverberated in her chest and her ears began to ring. The dim lighting made it difficult to read the beautiful script, but she'd spent hours laboring over the right words and knew exactly what it said.

To Marcus, the father I never had. I love you, Isabella.
I love you.

She'd never said those words to Marcus, not even once in the six years since she'd come to work for him, or in the five years she'd been living in his house. He'd moved her into his lair so she'd be available to him 24/7. It was common for him to wake her up at three in the morning to inspect an antiquity that had just arrived under the veil of night. He never accepted an item until he'd gotten her expert take on its value, its history, its origins and most importantly, its authenticity.

In all that time, Marcus Fie had never uttered the words "I love you." Marcus Fie didn't believe in love.

But she didn't buy it.

Everyone needed love.

Isabella closed her hand over the bracelet. "I think it's perfect. I think it's exactly what he needs." She hoped it would finally break through the cold veil he had over his heart, to allow him to finally accept he needed her in his life for more than the value she could add to his already immense coffers. It was time for him to accept that he had become the family she'd yearned for her whole life.

She was nervous about giving it to him. Yes, she loved him, and she was sure he loved her, beneath the icy veneer he carried, but if she were wrong . . . and he reacted badly . . . Was she really so entrenched in his life he wouldn't eject her for trying to get closer than he wanted?

Isabella closed her fist around the bracelet, and a sudden chill reverberated down her arms. Would it be better to simply accept the half-life he'd offered her instead of risking losing it all? But she couldn't live like that anymore, pretending not to care when he ignored her, or having to hide her feelings. For her, personal connection to those she cared about was as necessary as breathing, and he was all she had.

"Isa." Roseann's blonde hair was coiffed in a tight bun on top of her head, per Marcus's strict dress code. "Marcus Fie is not a man you love. He's a man you fear. He—"

"You're wrong." Isabella held up her hand to silence her friend. "I know what people say, but they don't know him like I do—"

"No!" Roseann was the one who interrupted this time. "God, Isa, I'm so worried about you! Don't you see what you've become? He's drawn you into his spell. You can't do this to yourself. Ever since that whole thing with Daniel, you've retreated into—"

"I don't want to talk about Daniel." At the mention of her ex-fiancé's name, a heavy weight settled in Isabella's chest.

"Fine, but the point is, you're emotionally unhealthy right now. You have to get out. Start dating."

"I am dating. Zack brought me flowers tonight—"

"Zack is using you to get to Marcus." Roseann pointed behind Isabella. "Look at him."

Isabella turned to see Zack in deep conversation in a shadowed corner. He wasn't talking to Marcus, but his head was bent next to the grayed coif of Simon Fuentes, one of Marcus's clients, a man who had a long list of rare and difficult-to-obtain antiquities he wanted for his personal collection. He didn't care how he got them, and he paid well.

There was something about Simon that made Isabella uncomfortable, and she made a point of never being in the same room with him unless there was someone else present. Why was Zack talking to him? It wasn't as if he could do business with Simon, who bought only from Marcus. Simon's paranoid nature didn't allow him to trust anyone but the world-renowned Marcus Fie to provide him with the real deal and not a fake.

And the reason the world trusted Marcus Fie to get only the real thing?

Because of the talents of his Harvard PhD antiquities expert, Isabella Kopas, who had never, ever made a mistake in the six years she'd been working for him. Marcus knew it, and so did everyone in his line of business.

The job offers came in regularly, but she'd never considered accepting.

She didn't want more money.

She wanted roots, and Marcus had given her the chance to plant some.

"Zack doesn't love you," Roseann said. "And neither does Marcus. They aren't the type of men who can love or give you a home—"

"This place is my home." Isabella picked up the jewelry box she'd set on a nearby marble table.

Roseann sighed. "Oh, Isa, you feel like this place is home only because you don't know what a real home is like. If your mom was still alive—"

"She's not." Isabella laid the bracelet across the velvet interior and snapped the box shut. Her index finger pinched in the hinge, and she winced. "But you are, and you're a part of this place, too."

"Isa." Roseann slipped her arm around Isabella's shoulders. "I need to tell you something."

God, it felt good to have an arm wrapped around her in comfort. Marcus never touched, and Daniel had been aloof as well. But her mom had been so touchy, and Isabella missed being held so much. She leaned her head on her friend's shoulder. "What?"

"Tonight is my last night working for Marcus."

Isabella whirled around, her chest tightening in panic. "What? You're leaving? You can't!" Tears stung at her eyes, and she blinked hard to get them back. "Why?"

"Because I'm pregnant."

Isabella stared at her friend in shock, and her throat was suddenly so clogged she could barely talk. "You are? You're going to have a real family?" The words were a whisper, all she could manage.

Roseann nodded, and set her hand on her slightly curved stomach. "Irving and I agreed we have to cut our connection to Marcus, now that we're going to have a baby. It's too dangerous to have a child this close to Marcus Fie."

Isabella fought against tears, the desperation, the anguish ripping at her heart. The loss. "What are you talking about? He'd never hurt your baby."

"Oh, come on, Isa. You've heard the stories about Marcus and his son."

Isabella pressed her lips together. "Those have to be exaggerated—"

"Do they? What else would prompt a man to walk away from his own father, from all this money and privilege? You've heard about the hate between them before his son took off. You think that kind of hatred can happen in vacuum?"

Isabella winced at the sudden roiling in her stomach. "It can't be true." Yes, she knew Marcus had a side he hid from her. She knew there were aspects to his business that were a little sordid, and she was well aware of the undercurrent of violence that pervaded

Marcus's life. But he'd also given her a golden ring to grasp when she'd had nothing else. He'd saved her life, and given her a future. He was her friend, her savior and her only roots, regardless of everything else that went on around them.

"And even if only a few of the rumors about his son are true?" Roseann shook her head. "Still awful. You think I'd risk my child?" Roseann grasped Isabella's shoulders, her dark eyes vibrant with health and joy Isabella had never seen in her friend's face. A happiness Isabella had never felt, despite all her efforts to find it. "Come with us. We're going to move back to Florida to be near my family. You can stay with us until you get a job. This is your chance to start over, Isa, to leave this world behind and start fresh. New life, new love, a chance at all the things you want—"

"No." Isabella wrenched herself away from Roseann. "I can't leave him. He's my only family. He's all I have."

"He's not your father, Isa! He's your boss, and he's going to get himself killed someday by pushing it with the wrong people one too many times." She gestured at the room full of tuxedos and glittering ball gowns.

As Isabel watched, Marcus's right hand, Leon Pareil, walked up to Zack and said something. Even from here, she could see the bulge of Leon's gun. He was Marcus's enforcer, his best retriever, and the one man who knew every one of Marcus's secrets and hidden chambers.

Leon was the one Marcus had always told her to go to if something happened to him, and she agreed. He was one of the few people on Marcus's staff she felt comfortable with. But she knew he was deadly. There was an element of ruthlessness about him that made her shiver.

"This isn't a home," Roseann said, drawing Isabella's attention back to her. "And this isn't what you want."

"It's all I have," Isabella said.

Leon looked her way and winked, and she waved back. His gaze flickered to her throat, and his face became utterly unreadable when he noticed the necklace she was wearing. Frowning, she turned back toward Roseann. "Marcus takes care of me. He keeps me safe." From poverty. From being alone. From the ugliness her life would have been without him.

Roseann shook her head in dismay. "Oh, Isa, the last thing Marcus does is keep you safe."

"Roseann!" The head of the kitchen staff, Opal Mascow, glared at Roseann from the doorway of the kitchen. Her black hair was pulled back so tightly she looked as if she were being tortured, and her thick hands were clenched by her sides.

"Gotta go." Roseann threw her arms around Isabella and clung to her. "I love you, Isa. I'll miss you so much."

Isabella bit her lip to hold back the tears. "I love you, too."

Roseann released her and ran for the kitchen, without looking back.

Isabella stared after her friend, grief welling in her chest. God, how could she let Roseann go? Roseann was like a sister. What if she went to Florida with Roseann? But the thought made her chest hurt. This was her home, the only place she was secure enough to believe she would never lose her place—

"Isabella."

Oh, God. It was time.

CHAPTER TWO

She stiffened her spine as Marcus walked up to her. She brushed her hand across her cheeks to wipe off any evidence of the near tears. Marcus abhorred weakness, and tears at his birthday party would infuriate him. "Happy birthday, Marcus."

"Thank you." He didn't smile, but he brushed his lips politely past her cheek, not quite touching. He never touched her. Ever.

With his jet-black hair, he was absolutely riveting in his tuxedo. His jaw was hard, his body lean, his eyes a vibrant blue, his posture erect. Marcus Fie resonated with wealth and power, with a ruthlessness that made people crumple before him. A few strands of silver at his temples were his only concession to age.

He nodded at the necklace dangling between her breasts. "I'm glad you're wearing that."

The jewelry had arrived at the office earlier in the day, and Isabella hadn't had time to research it. Marcus had told her to wear it tonight, so she had. It had a large red stone in it, probably a ruby, and it was set in a swirl of gold tendrils cradling dozens of smaller stones of assorted brilliant colors, mixed with dozens of large diamonds. She was very curious as to its origin, and she was itching to have some time to research it. It was rare for Marcus to go public with any of his acquisitions, and she wondered what was so special about this one to have prompted its display.

Then his eyes narrowed as they fell on her other necklace. "I told you not to wear that tonight. It's not appropriate for someone on my staff."

Isabella stiffened as she automatically covered her jewelry with her hand. The small turquoise pendant encased in engraved silver was battered and scratched from three generations of wear. It was the only thing she had left from her mother, and she hadn't taken it off since she was seventeen. Not even for Marcus. "Yes, you did, but you know how I feel about it."

He gave her a hard look. "Let go of the past, Isabella. You aren't the girl you were when you came here." He gestured at it. "That's not you anymore."

Her fingers clamped protectively over it, and she took a step backward.

His face immediately softened. "Hell, Isabella, don't give me that look. I'm not going to forcibly remove it from your neck. Keep the damn thing if it makes you happy." His blue eyes filled with the affection she was accustomed to seeing when he interacted with her. "I forget how emotional you are sometimes," he said.

She knew he was thinking about the time he'd had the photo of her mother taken out of its original frame and reframed in a beautiful, expensive setting that had wrenched her heart from her chest. The frame and photo had been a gift from her mother, and Isabella had been devastated by the loss.

It had been the first and only time she'd ever seen Marcus apologize to anyone for anything, and he'd sent out his top retriever to find an old battered frame like the one he'd had thrown out. He'd found almost an exact replica of the one she'd had, and he'd even had her mother's name carved in the back, like her frame had had.

His efforts hadn't healed the hole in her heart, but it had shown her a side of Marcus she'd never forgotten.

Marcus cleared his throat. "How is your research on my son going?"

She brightened. "I've found him. He changed his name to—"

"No!" Marcus held up his hand to silence her. "I told you, I don't want to know the details. I just want you to be able to tell me that he's okay."

She sighed. Why wouldn't he want to know how his son was? "He seems to be fine. He runs his own business."

Marcus smiled. "Of course he would. Adam's too stubborn to work for anyone else." He nodded at the necklace. "He would appreciate that I finally found that. It was one of his special projects."

Isabella narrowed her eyes at his direct comment. It felt forced. "Really? You want me to tell him we have it?"

Marcus laughed softly. "I would like to see his reaction to that news." His smile faded and his eyes became sharp. "Has anyone else asked you for information on him? Have you told anyone about him?"

Isabella dropped her hand from her turquoise pendant, relieved Marcus had moved on to a new subject. "No, of course not. You asked me to keep it confidential."

Marcus relaxed visibly. "Excellent. I knew I could trust you." Then he tensed again. "You haven't done any of the work on your computer, have you?"

"I haven't saved anything," she said. "But I've used

my computer to do some research, of course." She frowned. "You think someone's going to break into my computer and look for the trail?"

Marcus rubbed his jaw. "You use all the security safeguards, don't you?"

"Of course I do." What was wrong with him? He was always careful, but bordering on paranoia wasn't his thing.

He nodded. "Okay, that should be fine. But you let me know if anyone asks."

Isabella began to tense up at his concern. "What's going on? What are you worried about?"

He stiffened. "I'm not worried," he snapped. "Everything is under control. I have someone I'd like you to meet. Be in my office in fifteen minutes."

"Okay." Obviously, now wasn't the time to press him. She'd save that for later. "Fifteen minutes?" She checked the time on the diamond-crusted watch Marcus had given her for her twenty-ninth birthday. It was only the second occasion she'd had to wear it, and she cherished it. "I'll be there."

Marcus did business whenever the opportunity presented itself, and it wasn't a surprise he was using his birthday celebration to make a new deal.

"Excellent." He started to turn away, and she touched his arm.

He looked down at her hand, and she dropped her hand, her cheeks flushing. "Sorry." She took a breath, then handed him the jewelry box. "Happy birthday, Marcus."

He smiled as he took the box, his blue eyes gentling ever so slightly. Her heart ached for more. He was a tease to her heart, hinting at softer feelings, but so rarely sharing them. "Ah, Isabella, you probably bought that months ago, didn't you?" His tone was softer now, the warm tenor reserved for late nights when they were alone and his guard was down.

The Marcus she alone knew, who no one else saw.

She smiled. "Maybe."

"You would have liked my wife," he said as he opened the box. "She always took such care buying presents for me."

Isabella caught her breath, startled by his statement. He almost never talked about his deceased wife or their son, who'd taken off and disappeared so thoroughly eight years ago. "I'm sure I would have enjoyed her very much," she said softly, desperate to open the door he'd suddenly cracked. "Do you miss her?"

Marcus said nothing. He was staring down at the bracelet.

Isabella peeked at the box. The inscription was facing up so he could read it.

She waited, her heart hammering.

A muscle ticked in his cheek, and he slowly traced his index finger over the words, as if breathing them in through his skin. There was pain in his brilliant blue eyes.

Raw, emotional pain.

The kind she had to chase down every morning when she first woke up and her defenses were down. The kind she'd sensed in him so many times but never actually seen. She lifted her hand to touch his shoulder. "Oh, Marcus—"

He snapped the box shut and handed it back to her. "In my office. Fifteen minutes. Don't be late."

Then he turned and walked away.

Leaving the gift in her hands.

Stunned, she stared after him as he walked up to

Zack and gestured toward her. Did he want her to hold on to it for him? Or was that a rejection?

As Zack began to walk toward her, Marcus turned to look at her.

His eyes had become icy blue. Cold. Hard. Ruthless.

Never once had he turned that look toward her.

Never until now.

Dear God, what had she done?

Luke jumped out of the plane almost before he'd stopped it. The minute he stepped out, the freezing rain pummeled him. He had to hunch his shoulders against the wind to keep from getting knocked over. The roar of the river was deafening, and the black rapids were hammering at the edge of the beach.

Shit.

Sam Friedman, a client Luke had been flying for eight years, grabbed Luke in a big-ass bear hug. "Jesus, I've never been so glad to see your ugly mug, Webber." His face was ruddy and drenched. His gray hair was plastered to his head, and his lips were blue with cold.

Luke managed a grim smile. "Yeah, well, don't thank me yet." He shot a grimace at the stack of equipment piled up on the beach. After spending twelve years as a scientist traipsing around the world doing research, Luke knew how important that equipment was to these men. But any additional weight would add distance to how long it took to get airborne.

A plane roared overhead as Cort came in for a landing. He left maybe twelve inches of clearance between the planes. Crazy fuck. With all of Luke's money hidden . . . or tied up . . . in their business, he hated when Cort pulled shit like that.

Cort stopped next to Luke and leapt out. He was bundled up in rain gear, and his black hat was tight around his head. He was saturated within seconds. He didn't bother to ride Luke's ass for landing. Right now was about survival.

"Can you take two?" Luke asked. The three scientists had fallen silent, as if they'd figured out their rescue didn't mean shit until they were in the air.

Cort glanced down the beach, and Luke could see his partner calculating the weight of the two passengers and the length of the beach, the speed of the rising waters and the odds of being able to come back in time for a second rescue. "Yeah."

"Then do it. I'll take the equipment." Luke snapped his fingers at the scientists. "Six minutes to load the plane and then we're going airborne. If you can live without it, leave it. Every pound counts."

His clients were already running for their stash of equipment by the time Luke finished talking. Cort jogged over to help them while Luke jerked open the baggage compartment of his plane.

The rain was horizontal now, slicing through his pants like thousands of miniature daggers. Hail hammered into his cheeks. Luke leapt into the plane and grabbed the first box as one of the scientists handed it up.

The men worked in silence, hauling ass across the drenched beach.

Luke turned down three machines he knew would drag them to their death. Too damn heavy. One he knew was worth a couple hundred grand.

But his client had merely shot Luke a grim look and set it aside. Cort appeared and handed up a box. "Water's getting higher."

Luke nodded. "We have to call it."

Cort gave him a nod and gestured to the scientists to climb on board. "You take off first," he said. "You need the distance, and every minute steals you more space."

Luke shook his head. "With two passengers, you'll need more room as well. You've got two lives counting on you. I've got one. You first."

Cort gave him a hard look, but then he nodded. "Done." He turned and sprinted back toward his plane, shouting at his passengers to buckle up.

Luke swung down and latched the door, well aware of how lucky he was to have Cort as a partner. They'd both made the right decision for the clients, and there'd been no time wasted with asinine posturing about who should be the martyr and go last.

The job came first, not ego or accolades.

It was one of the things Luke liked about Alaska: people were too focused on survival and doing their jobs to be bothered with crap like killing each other off for financial gain. It was a world of basic humanity, of raw earth and honesty, and the kind of integrity that came with depending on others for food, water, companionship and survival.

He settled into his seat and began to strap himself in.

"Are we going to make it?"

Luke looked over at Sam, who had apparently chosen to put his lot with Luke. Of course he would. Sam was that kind of guy. Loyal. Luke appreciated that trait in a person. "Odds are on."

Sam raised his brows as Luke began to taxi toward the end of the beach, following Cort's SuperCub. "You ever lie to a client?"

"No." Luke flexed his jaw. "Liars piss me off."

Sam nodded and settled back in his harness. "Good. Let's do it then."

Luke flashed his friend a glance. Yeah, any wonder he liked this job? Scientists were too into their work to bother with anything but doing their jobs, and they comprised most of the lot he carted around. In addition, being in the air gave Luke freedom. If his past ever came after him, he could simply take to the air before they could track him, before they could try to leverage him by taking out the people he cared about.

Which was no one.

His job made it easy to live a life without connections. Cort was his partner, and he liked the guy, but he'd intentionally kept a distance between them. To protect Cort, and to protect himself.

If Luke had no ties, no one could be killed because of him, and he couldn't be forced to do anything in the effort to keep them safe. Not that he expected anyone from his past or his dad's circles to find him in Alaska. He'd made damn sure there was no way to find him, and after eight years of silence from that lifetime, he was pretty confident he was officially lost.

Cort's engine roared, and the little plane took off down the sand. Luke circled around at the top of the beach, and he and Sam watched intently as the little plane rumbled down the inadequate runway. Closer and closer to the rock outcropping at the end of it—

And then it was in the air, the wheels barely skimming over the whitecaps. The plane was low, so low, but it was airborne and starting to climb.

Luke let out a breath. He knew Cort had been pushing it to take two passengers, but even with two bodies, his odds were still better than Luke with one passenger. Sam had flown enough to know the bigger plane was the riskier ride, and yet he'd still chosen Luke's plane.

Why? Because he'd put the safety of his younger teammates at a higher priority than his own, and Luke appreciated that.

Luke positioned the plane at the very end of the beach, so his rear wheel was actually in the water. Every last inch could make a difference.

"Want me to unload more stuff?" Sam asked suddenly.

"No time. Gotta go." And then Luke gunned it.

The plane rumbled down the beach. The sand was rutted from the two landings and Cort's takeoff, but it was hard from all the wind and rain, and Luke could feel the tires gripping.

"Come on, baby." He pushed her harder, and the end of the beach was close, too close.

"We're not going to make it!" Sam shouted. "Stop and try again!"

"Too late." There was no going back now. Do-or-die time now. "Come on!" They were pushing hard, but the wheels were still entrenched in the sand. The raging river was less than thirty yards ahead.

Twenty yards.

Ten yards.

"Fuck!" Luke gave the plane everything he had, and then he couldn't see beach ahead of him. He could see only water—

He braced himself for the lurch of the plane hitting the water, of the wheels getting sucked down—

But there was no abrupt stop.

Just sudden smoothness . . . relatively speaking.

Hot damn. "We're up."

The plane began to tug against him, and Luke knew the wheels were grazing the top of the river. One big wave and they were done. A gust of wind tossed the plane sideways, and Sam sucked in his breath. Luke swore as he felt his wing dip. If the tip caught water, the likelihood of recovery was minimal.

He wrenched the plane back upright again, and then the plane relaxed slightly, and he knew the wheels were out of the water.

Inches of clearance, but they were climbing now.

They were clear.

Sam made a gasping noise in his throat and let his head fall back against the seat. "You're a crazy fucker for doing this for a living."

Luke grinned over at his old friend and former colleague. "Wouldn't go back to my old life for anything, my friend."

And that was the truth, no matter what that choice had cost him.

CHAPTER THREE

Marcus looked at the jewelry box still clutched in Isabella's hands, and his mouth tightened before he turned away.

"Marcus!" She broke into a run, suddenly certain he wanted the gift but just didn't know how to cope with it.

"Isabella." Zack caught her arm as she stepped onto the dance floor. "Dance with me, my dear."

She tried to pull away. "I have to talk to Marcus—"

"He's in a meeting." Zack nodded toward Marcus, who was walking shoulder to shoulder with Simon.

She groaned, knowing it would be a mistake to interrupt business. She would have to wait. Frustrated, she clutched the box. "I have to take this upstairs."

"I'll hold it for you." Zack plucked the box from her hand and slipped it inside his jacket pocket.

"No." She turned on him. "Please give that back to me. It's very important."

Zack gave her a mischievous grin. "After you dance with me, my dear."

Fine. He was her date, after all. With a sigh, Isabella allowed him to pull her close and lead the dance. His hand slid down her lower back and she tensed, suddenly wishing she hadn't agreed to Zack's invite to the party.

All she could think of was Daniel—how she'd trusted him and how it had ended. She'd thought she was getting the family she'd wanted, only to discover Daniel rooting through Marcus's display of antiquities one evening. His love had been a lie, and she'd believed it.

She'd been too desperate for security. She wouldn't make the same mistake again. Daniel had helped her appreciate Marcus and his intense loyalty toward her, even if he couched it in terms of her being a professional asset. He never promised more than he gave her, and she appreciated that.

She'd learned her lesson long ago about men who promised more than they were willing to give, and Daniel had been a big reminder. Marcus's approach of promising nothing and delivering much suited her better, even if it was frustrating.

Zack bent his head to brush his lips over her neck, and Isabella's stomach roiled.

"You look beautiful tonight, Isabella. I—"

"I'm sorry, Zack." She pulled back, out of his grasp. "I can't do this."

He frowned. "Do what?"

"Dance. I'm just . . . it's too soon."

His brow furrowed, and then softened in understanding. "Ah, your old boyfriend. Ended badly?"

She gave a slight nod. "I'm just not comfortable. Dancing is intimate. I'm not ready for that."

Zack smiled. "It's no problem." His voice was easy, not offended. "Why don't we just grab a glass of champagne and head out to the terrace?"

She stiffened. "I don't think—"

"I'm not going to try anything. I just want to get to know you." He winked at her. "Marcus would shoot me if I did anything to you, and we both know it."

Isabella almost laughed at his comment. He *was* right. Having a date know she was under Marcus's protection kept her absolutely safe.

Zack grinned. "Ah, there's that smile. Come on, let's go. I'll be good." He tucked his hand around her elbow, and Isabella allowed him to guide her off the dance floor.

His grip was light and unthreatening, but she still wanted to pull away. Maybe Roseann was right. Maybe she was more of a mess than she thought she was. God, what was she going to do without Roseann?

"Out here." Zack pushed open one of the patio doors and led her outside. There were a number of guests enjoying the balmy September evening, and Isabella relaxed when she saw how populated the terrace was.

Zack led her to the railing and she leaned on it, surveying the expansive gardens so rare in the city. They were an architectural masterpiece on which Marcus prided himself. She inhaled the fresh scent of nature, of warm air, closing her eyes to get the full sensation.

"I like your new necklace," Zack said, startling her. "Family heirloom?"

Isabella immediately tensed at Zack's casual tone. It was too casual. Too intentional. "No." She heard the shuffle of feet behind her, and then realized she couldn't hear any conversations anymore.

Were they alone?

Fifteen people vanished in less than a minute?

Isabella didn't dare to turn around and acknowledge that she'd noticed the patio had been cleared, but dread began to creep down her arms.

"Where did you get it? It's quite unusual." Again, the question was too casual.

She turned her head slightly to look at him. He immediately gave her a warm smile, but it didn't reach his eyes. No. They were like the eyes of so many people in Marcus's business. Cold. Calculating.

He wanted the necklace.

God, she should have known better than to listen to Marcus and advertise something she didn't understand. What was the necklace? She had to warn Marcus. She licked her suddenly dry lips. "May I have my champagne?"

"Of course." Zack handed her a glass, and she took it, careful not to let her fingers brush against his.

She took a small sip, as she frantically tried to think of a way to get back inside. Zack was between her and the building.

"Isabella." Zack moved closer, and she felt the threat in his pose. "Tell me about the necklace."

Her fingers tightened around the stem of her glass. "It was Marcus's wife's," she lied. "He brought it out for me to wear."

Zack narrowed his eyes. "Was it?" His voice was soft, too soft.

He knew she was lying. "I'm getting cold. Let's go inside."

"No." He grabbed her arm, and this time his fingers were digging in. "Let's go for a ride, sweetness. I need that brain of yours and that necklace."

The pain shooting up her arm triggered something inside Isabella that hadn't been alive for a long time. Terror.

For an instant, she went numb, unable to resist as he started dragging her across the patio.

But he stepped off the stones onto the grass, the stark reality snapped her back into focus. He was stealing her from her *home!*

"No!" She whirled on him suddenly and smashed her champagne glass into his face.

He howled with agony and released her to cradle his face as blood trickled through his fingers.

Isabella whirled and sprinted into the house. She kicked off her heels and ran toward Marcus's office. He had to be there. It was almost time for their meeting. And if he weren't, at least Leon would be there and—

Marcus flew out of the doorway to his office and crashed into the wall. He let out a groan and slumped to the ground.

Isabella skidded to a stop and dove back around the corner, out of sight. Dear God! What was going on?

Marcus grunted with pain, and she peeked around the corner, her heart pounding.

Leon was striding down the hall toward them from the other direction, and she sagged with relief. Leon would save him—

"We lost the girl," Leon said. "We need to find her." Then he turned toward Marcus, and hauled him to his feet. "Is she wearing the real thing, or a fake?"

Marcus just leveled a cold stare at his best man. "Fuck off."

Leon scowled and slammed his gun into Marcus's stomach.

Isabella sucked in her breath. Leon was involved? He was the only one she trusted and—

Footsteps raced down the hall toward her, and she whirled around. *Shit!* She ducked into the room and pressed the door shut as someone ran past.

"Did she come this way?" Zack barked. "She was heading for Marcus's office."

"No," Leon answered. "Get Marcus to the car while

we find Isabella. Don't shoot him yet. We need him alive until we find the necklace and Isabella."

Don't shoot Marcus *yet?* Dear God, what was going on? Isabella raced toward the window and unlocked it. She popped the screen and stuck her head out. No one was around. She slipped outside and ran down the patio stairs toward the kitchen.

She sneaked inside the kitchen, and then froze when she heard screams.

"Where the hell did she go?"

She recognized the voice of another of Marcus's men, and Isabella moved behind a shelf, wanting to see who else she couldn't trust. She peeked through the boxes of flour in time to see Nate Sampson, one of Marcus's top retrievers, raise his gun and point it across the room. "Tell me where she is."

"I don't know! I swear I don't know!"

Isabella gasped at the sound of Roseann's voice. Her friend was huddled against the wall, her eyes wide with terror.

She couldn't let them hurt Roseann and the baby! Isabella leapt to her feet to run around the shelf.

"Then you're useless."

"Wait! I'm right here!" Her shout was drowned out by the explosion of a gun going off, and then Roseann was sprawled on the kitchen floor, a red stain oozing out from under her upper body.

Isabella gasped and went down on her knees, unable to stand. *Oh, God. Oh, God. Oh, God.*

"Isabella has to be around here somewhere," Nate said. "Find her."

A man moved past the shelf, mere feet away, jerking Isabella out of her stupor. She lurched to her feet and backed toward the door, unable to take her gaze off the slumped figure of her best friend. Her only friend.

She heard another gunshot in the distance and more screaming. From the party guests.

More dead?

She had to get away. Escape. Find help.

There was only one way to get out. One hope. A dead end if Leon thought about it and got there first.

She slipped through the kitchen door, hoisted up her dress, and broke into a frantic run toward the south garage. Did Leon know about the SUV Marcus kept in bay five? Did he know she knew about it?

She was deep in the gardens when she heard a shout. "She's in the yard! Get out there!"

Isabella ran harder, her bare feet getting sliced on the sharp rocks. Her dress caught on a bench and she went down hard on her knees. Shouts echoed behind her, and then the gardens were flooded with light.

She ducked beneath the thick foliage and scurried along behind the shadows. Less than two hundred feet from her destination.

"She's heading toward the garage!"

Isabella abandoned hiding and broke into a run again. Her lungs were burning, and she heard more shouts. No guns, though. They needed to keep her alive so they could ask her about the necklace, she realized.

She yanked open the heavy door and ran inside, then threw the deadbolt. She only needed a moment. A fraction of a second to disappear.

She ran across the polished floor. Something slammed into the door she'd just locked. Angry shouts. The door rattled again.

The tool cabinet was up ahead. She grabbed the drill and two screwdrivers and jammed them into holes in the side of the cabinet exactly how Marcus had showed her.

A gunshot made her jump, and they rattled the door again. Shooting off the lock. Two more shots would do it. That was what Marcus had told her. Three shots to get through it and then she'd be out of time.

She wiggled the screwdriver in the hole, but nothing happened. *Crud!*

Another gunshot. Metal on metal.

They tried the door again.

"Come on!" She wiggled the screwdriver again, and this time the bottom eighteen inches of the back wall of the storage cabinet slid away. "Yes!"

She dropped to her knees and shoved tools aside.

The third shot rang out.

She wiggled past the paint cans and squeezed through the opening. The door rattled, and Isabella reached into the cabinet to return the tools.

The door opened, and she leapt back and slid the back wall of the cabinet back into place.

There was a faint light in the cavernous garage, and she could see the outline of the SUV Marcus had stashed here. He'd said it was loaded with everything she would need to get away. The car was unlocked, and the keys were in the ignition, just as Marcus had said they would be.

But as the engine roared to life and the steel garage door rolled open behind her, she was filled with a sudden sense of wrongness. She dropped her head to the steering wheel, her chest too tight to breathe. How could she leave Marcus and Roseann behind? What would happen to them? What—

The cabinet slammed open and Leon's head emerged. They stared at each other for a long moment.

The man Marcus had trusted with her life and his own.

He smiled, a special smile she recognized from so many shared jokes. "Isa," he called out. "It's all okay now. I've taken care of them. Are you okay?"

Isabella's heart lurched. God, to have it be over . . . "Leon—" Then she saw his right hand was hidden, out of sight.

He'd never hidden his gun from her before.

He was lying.

She jammed the truck into reverse and slammed her foot on the accelerator. The truck flew backward up the ramp. Leon shouted. He whipped out his gun and fired. A bullet bounced off the hood of the SUV.

And another.

And another.

Then she was outside, in the dark silence of early morning in Boston.

She threw the gearshift into drive as Leon raced up the ramp toward her. He raised his gun and aimed right for her. A lethal shot.

The truck lurched forward, the passenger window shattered, and pain ricocheted up her shoulder. Isabella gasped at the agony, and the truck careened across the road.

"Come on!" She grabbed for the steering wheel, yanked the truck back toward the yellow line and floored the accelerator.

She didn't wait to see how long it would take for them to run around the house to their cars parked out front.

She just gunned it and raced for her life.

CHAPTER FOUR

Isabella tensed as the Hummer skidded around the sharp turn of the highway on-ramp. The truck's rear slid out and its front end careened straight toward the guardrail. She hauled the steering wheel to left, the truck bounced back up on the road and she slammed on the brakes, skidding to a stop in the breakdown lane.

She was shaking so badly she could barely get the gearshift into park. She draped her arms over the steering wheel and dropped her forehead to the cool leather, trying to calm down.

But despair and grief welled up and burst free. She pressed her palms to her eyes, rocking back and forth as the sobs shattered her defenses. Was Marcus dead? Was Roseann? What about her baby? Were Leon and Nate after her?

Of course they were.

She couldn't stop. It wasn't over. She needed to get help. But where? Whom could she turn to?

Not Leon.

Not the police. She knew enough about Marcus's business to know she couldn't bring the police in.

She had to pull it together. Focus.

Who would help her? Who could she trust?

Isabella looked down at the necklace. Answers were in there. She quickly started the truck and drove a half mile to the service area ahead, hiding her vehicle behind an eighteen-wheeler.

She put the cark in park, then turned her attention to the necklace. Her hands were trembling so much it took three tries to unfasten it. She turned on the interior light and began to inspect it. She needed to know what was so important about the piece that Leon would shoot her.

God. He'd *shot* her. Her shoulder was throbbing, but she forced herself to ignore it. No time to be hurt.

Instead, she carefully assessed the jewels, but found nothing unusual. She flipped the necklace over . . . and found a little mark by the clasp.

Please, God, don't let it be what I think it is.

Her hand trembling, she looked more closely at the necklace. The etching was a double X, carved in a style only one man had ever used. An artist who had switched over to jewelry in a stroke of genius. He'd made only three pieces before he was murdered: a necklace and a pair of earrings. His tribe had converged to protect his legacy, and they had held on to those three items for centuries, killing anyone who tried to take them. Eventually, the tribe had dissolved, and the jewelry had been declared missing.

They were priceless—for the stones, the design and their rarity.

"Oh, God." She pressed her hand to her chest, which was too tight to breathe, the truck beginning to spin, her vision starting to darken. *This* was what Marcus had gotten them involved in?

People like Zack were just the start. And Leon . . . dear God. How much money was it really worth? Enough to make him turn on Marcus? And now *she* had it. People would be after her. Chasing her. Her shoulder throbbed. What would Leon do to Marcus to force her to give it back? He'd said Marcus needed to be alive only until she turned it back in.

If she went back, Marcus would die. And probably she would, too.

She pressed her hands to her head, trying to think, trying to focus. How did she save Marcus? Herself? Make the nightmare go away and leave them alive? She was so out of her depth. There had to be something she could do. Someone who could help.

But only Marcus would understand what they were facing. Marcus or—

She sat up, her hands clenching the steering wheel. *Marcus's son.*

From everything she'd heard about him, he would understand the severity of the situation, and he had the skills she needed. Marcus had even said the necklace had once been his special project. But he would never help his father. The hate ran so deep . . .

Marcus's son would never knowingly save his father's life, or his business, or help anyone associated with him.

But what if she asked for help but didn't tell him why, until he was too deep to get out? It was her only chance. It had to work.

Marcus's son was going to be difficult to fool, which was why he had been so good at his job.

But she had to try.

Without him . . .

She glanced at the necklace resting on the seat beside her, and knew the red stone wasn't a ruby. It was the lifeblood of everyone who had ever touched it.

And hers would be next, unless she could convince the one man in the world who wouldn't help her, to do exactly that.

And the moment she made contact with him, his life would be on the docket as well.

She hesitated at the thought. How could she endanger someone else?

But she knew she had to.

Somewhere out there, Marcus was being held by the men who had killed Roseann. She had to do something. From all she'd heard, Marcus's son could take care of himself.

But could he take care of her? And more importantly, would he?

She knew he'd try to say no, but she wasn't going to let him. He was her only option. Even a bad option was better than no option.

Car headlights flashed behind her, and she tensed. She held her breath as the car slowly passed her, but it was a light blue Mini, not the kind of car Leon and the others were driving. A respite, but she knew they were tracking her, and they wouldn't be far behind.

Now at least she had a plan. Maybe a bad one, but it was still a plan, and she was still alive. Not the best odds, but she'd survived on long odds before.

She'd had practice, and this time, the life of someone she loved was at stake.

This time, she wasn't going to fail to keep that person alive.

This time, she was going to win.

This one's for you, Mama.

She hit the gas hard and the truck leapt out into the night.

Less than thirty-six hours after the water rescue, Luke stepped out of his plane with a new, much more grue-some cargo. He ground his jaw as he opened the rear door of his plane for the paramedics.

"Out of the way!" The young medic shoved Luke aside, and Luke jammed his hands in his pockets as he watched the procedure. Nearly midnight, it was pitch black outside, and the only light came from the medics' hats and the dim interior light in his plane.

They were going through the motions, but Luke knew the female climber in the back of his plane would never climb again. She'd never do a damn thing again. The same storm that had nearly taken out his scientists had trapped another set of his clients on the moun-tain.

Because he'd gone to get the scientists first, he'd missed the window to get on the mountain, and he'd had to wait for the storm to clear before he'd been able to get up there. A deliberate, intelligent choice. The climbers were experienced enough to survive a storm.

But not a broken leg and a lost climber.

And now she was dead.

"Hey." Cort clapped a hand on Luke's shoulder. "Get a beer with me."

"Fuck that." Luke couldn't take his eyes off the ac-tion in his plane. Off the climbers huddled around the woman's body. The grim silence.

"Hey!" Cort punched him in the arm. "Cut the crap. I need a beer and you're buying."

Luke scowled at Cort. "I—"

Cort shook his head once. "Gotta let it go, buddy. It's the nature of the job." He jerked his head toward the bar just across the street. "You're nothing but a stranger sticking his nose into their business. They want space to deal. Give it to them."

Luke let out his breath, then turned and silently followed his partner across the new snowfall dusting the ground. He zipped up his jacket, hunching his shoulders against the bitterness of the night. Fall was coming hard and fast to Alaska, and the nights were getting cold. Cold and darkness had come home, and they fit his mood tonight. He kicked at a tree branch that had been ripped apart by the storm, but said nothing as they walked into the dimly lit building.

He dropped to his seat and let his head rest against the wall as he surveyed the patrons at Rick's Tavern. Their favorite place was the Shed, a tavern in Twin Forks. But that was forty-five minutes away, and after a night in hell, sometimes the proximity of a beer was more important than the atmosphere.

Like tonight.

Cort dropped a couple of mugs of brew on the table, then took over the bench across from Luke. He also looked a little haggard. Cort raised his mug.

Without a word, Luke lifted his and they clanked their mugs together.

No words needed to be spoken.

They both had felt Death's rancid breath on the backs of their necks out there tonight. The storm had still been raging up on the mountain, barely abating enough to land. And then taking bodies back . . . four total. It had taken two trips for each of them, carting the frozen dead back to the airport, along with the shocked survivors and their gear.

On the last trip Luke had lost his focus for a split second and nearly let a gust of wind take him into the side of a mountain. It was the closest he'd come to biting it in a long time, pretty much since the first time he'd soloed and crashed.

His knee still ached from that mistake eight years ago, and he was glad. That ache kept him sharp, always a reminder of the costs of fucking up in the air.

He took a drag of the beer. "Still tastes like shit," he commented. The beer was the one thing he hadn't been able to adjust to since moving to Alaska. He missed the sheer artistry of the local brews in Boston.

Cort snorted. "You need to stop pining for beer that costs a hundred bucks a bottle. You're in Alaska now, you pampered ass."

Luke wouldn't trade his new life for the kind of beer he used to drink. Freedom was worth any cost. "I'm not pining. I'm just trying to get you backwoods cretins a little more sophisticated."

Cort grinned. "No chance. We're a bunch of ruffians." He checked his watch, and Luke knew he was thinking about getting home to his new wife, Kaylie, who was six months pregnant with their first child.

Luke shifted, uncomfortable with the new relationship. Kaylie's link with Cort put her too close to Luke's circle. She could be caught in the freefall if all hell broke loose for him, and he didn't like that.

Roots were starting to form in Alaska, and people could get hurt. It might be time to move on.

But fuck. He didn't want to ditch this life, dead climbers notwithstanding. He liked it here. Liked the people, enjoyed the life, appreciated the fact that no one gave a shit who his daddy was or where he'd come from. All they cared about was whether he could be counted on in a crisis, and he'd made good on that promise repeatedly.

A simple life. Good values.

He wanted to stay.

But not at the risk to anyone, and with Kaylie pregnant, the noose was tightening.

Luke hunched forward in his seat and wrapped his hands around the mug. "Go home to Kaylie," he muttered. "Get the hell out of here."

"I will." Cort leaned back in his seat, his body relaxed. "In a minute."

The face of the dead gal from the last flight flashed into Luke's mind. Her hair had been dark brown. Ponytail. Skin so pale. Reminded him of his mother. Of that god-awful day he would never forget—

He swore and tossed back the rest of the beer. Jesus.

"If you think about it, it's incredible that this is the first body you've had to retrieve since you started flying," Cort said. "Not sure how you managed to avoid it until now."

Luke knew how. He'd been freaking insane in his efforts to keep his people safe, and it had been by sheer luck that Cort had been the one to get the call each time it had been to bring back the dead.

Until now.

Cort leaned forward, his face intense. "First time I brought a body back I was eleven. The guy looked like a monster, frozen into a block of ice. Freaked the hell out of me. Had nightmares for weeks."

Luke had seen his first body when he was eight. And it had been his mother. And yeah, he'd had the nightmares, too. Still did sometimes. "Tough thing for a kid."

Cort snorted. "Hell, yeah. My dad was so embarrassed his kid was so soft, he chained me to a beehive for a month to toughen me up."

Luke laughed then. "Well, that explains your ugly mug."

Cort grinned. "Bees cured me of all corpse-related issues. It's a little late in the season for bees, but I'm sure we could drum up something for you."

"Screw that." Luke leaned back in his seat. "I'm fine. A corpse is nothing new to me."

Cort raised his brows, clearly sensing there was more than Luke was saying. "Yeah?"

"Yeah." Luke turned his attention away from his friend. He didn't want to talk about it. Didn't feel like opening doors with Cort that had stayed firmly closed during their long friendship. They'd been partners for eight years, but he'd hired Cort on several prior occasions when he'd come to Alaska to do research.

Luke shifted in his chair as he surveyed the bar. The jukebox was blaring. A few pilots were hanging around. Some locals. Place was gloomy as hell.

It had never bothered him before. But right now, it was jagging him big time.

"I'm going outside." He shoved his chair back to stand up, and then the front door opened. In walked a woman of the ilk he hadn't seen in eight years, since he left Boston. Her dark hair cascaded down her back. Even in the dim light of the bar it was glistening. Looked as soft as the fur on a Husky pup.

It reminded him of the kind of hair women shelled out a thousand bucks a week to maintain. The gal strode up to the bartender and began hammering him with questions. She was gesturing furiously, her hands flying around like she was agitated beyond hell.

The bartender nodded in Luke's direction, and she turned and looked directly at Luke.

He immediately sat up, his body responding when he felt the heat of her inspection. Her eyes were black as the sky during a stormy night, but they were alive and dangerous. Sensuous and passionate. He knew instantly that this was a woman who ran hot, who didn't hold back from whatever was in her heart. Sort of reminded him of how he used to be, before he'd realized living that way made too many people die.

Her jaw was out, and she looked fiercely determined. Yet there was a weariness to her posture, and dark circles under her eyes, visible even in the dim light. She rubbed her shoulder and winced, her body jerking with pain.

Made him want to get up and haul ass over there and offer her help.

Her eyes widened at his expression, and a tinge of red flushed her cheeks. The she plunked herself wearily down on a barstool and gave him her back.

Just as well. Luke still had issues when it came to women in need. Big fucking issues. The kind of issues that haunted his dreams and brought him screaming to consciousness, his body drenched in sweat.

His skin began to feel hot, and it wasn't just from the strip of smooth skin peeking out between the bottom of her sweater and the waistband of her very low-cut jeans . . . He peered closer and caught a glimpse of a bit of lacy black thong above her jeans.

He'd seen that action on plenty of women, but on this one . . . shit. All his blood was heading south at full speed. Despite her attire, there was a level of innocent sensuality.

He inspected her more closely, needing to assimilate

as much information about her as possible, to explain his reaction to her. Her shoulder blades were strong, and her back narrowed into a trim waist and toned hips. The woman took care of herself. Yoga? Most of those wealthy women seemed to have so much time on their hands, they did nothing but spend hours in the gym to try to attract the powerful, rich men on whom they had set their sights.

Was that her? It didn't feel right. He narrowed his eyes, quickly tabulating all the data so he could make an accurate assessment. It was difficult to tell from this distance, but the sweater appeared to be cashmere. High quality, given its lines. He'd guess upwards of a thousand bucks for it. And her jeans . . . he recognized the designer brand on that fine ass of hers. His gaze dropped to her boots . . . heels were low and practical, but the leather was clearly soft and supple, and the seams had that extra bit of style he recognized from his own mother's closet. In fact, she seemed to be wearing exactly the kind of outfit all his dad's women used to wear, once he finished dressing them up like the Barbie dolls they were willing to be for a chance at his money and his power.

From the brief glance he'd had at had her face, however, this woman was beautiful in a natural way. She didn't need all the glam to look good, but she clearly did it anyway. She was refined, she was as far from Alaska and carnage as a woman got, and she was exactly what he wanted to bury himself in right now.

She turned toward him suddenly, as if sensing his continued perusal. When she saw him watching her, she sat up straighter, and he saw in her something he hadn't expected. The woman was a survivor. Not a weak female. She was strong, and *that* put him over the top.

Weak, scared, defenseless women scared the shit out of him. Survivors? Hot. The cashmere? An escape from the Alaskan hell he'd been crawling in the last two days.

Her gaze dropped to his mouth, but then she quickly averted her gaze, shutting him out.

"Too late, my dear," he whispered under his breath. "Too damn late."

He shoved back his chair and stood.

"You heading out?" Then Cort followed Luke's gaze, and he grinned. "She's a little too refined for these parts, isn't she?"

"Damn straight she is." And then Luke headed right for her.

CHAPTER FIVE

Isabella hadn't been prepared for Luke to look so much like his father. Or for him to be so handsome.

Luke had the same dark hair as his father and the same radiant blue eyes, but Luke's were compelling and warm, so unlike Marcus's icy gaze. Luke radiated energy and power. His presence was so strong, she'd felt him even after she'd stopped looking at him, until she'd been unable to resist the lure and she'd looked over at him again . . . only to find him still watching her.

Not just watching. Studying. Dissecting. Like he was picking apart every cell of her body and categorizing it in some system in his mind. He made her feel naked . . . and not in a good way. She felt exposed, as if he were trying to ferret out all the ugly things in her past so he could judge her by them.

She forced herself to take a deep breath and stared down at the glass of water the bartender had set in front of her. There was no way Luke could learn anything about her, no matter how long he stared at her. Even Marcus didn't know all her secrets, and he'd tried to uncover them. But Luke . . . the way he'd studied her made her realize he was exactly as the rumors had claimed: the relentless scientist born to unravel mysteries, to derive answers from the smallest clues, which was why he'd been so great at finding antiquities for Marcus before he'd left.

She'd never gotten a straight answer on why Luke had left, other than that Luke hated his father.

Which was why she was prepared to make Luke an offer he couldn't refuse. But after seeing him in person . . . she had a bad feeling she was out of her league.

A man moved in beside her, and Isabella jerked her gaze up to see Luke settle himself at the next seat.

Heat shot through her body in response, but he didn't even acknowledge her. He just propped his forearm on the bar, ordered a beer, and waited.

The woman smelled like lavender, like a field of spring flowers. Like the scent of spring—alive, fresh and vibrant.

Luke closed his eyes and breathed her in, allowing her fragrance to sift through his body, easing his tension. It was the scent of woman, of refinement, of understated sensuality lurking beneath the surface.

She adjusted her position on her seat beside him, and her scent shifted. Still flowers, but he caught the faintest hint of perspiration, of the unmitigated scent of her body beneath the delicate fragrance. It told him that it had been a while since she'd gotten dressed. Maybe she'd tossed on some perfume before coming in here, but she'd been going hard for a while.

And he liked that. He liked that there was more to her than this incredible aroma that made him want to bury his face in her neck and simply inhale. More than the cashmere and designer jeans.

She cleared her throat, and still he didn't open his eyes.

Wasn't ready to let go yet. Wanted to see what else he could glean from her scent.

A light touch brushed over his shoulder and he froze, his body going hard at the delicate sensation.

"Excuse me. You're Luke Webber, aren't you?"

Luke's eyes snapped open at the sound of her voice. It was soft and tentative, with a musical underlay unlike anything he'd ever heard. It rolled beneath his skin like a thousand drops of morning dew glittering in the Alaskan sun.

Her accent was refined and perfect . . . utterly without inflection.

But it wasn't natural. It had been learned.

The woman hadn't always been cashmere and designer goods. She'd been rough, and she'd cleaned it up.

He turned his head slightly so he could look at her. She was white-knuckling the shoulder strap of her purse, and there were tension lines around the corners of her lips.

He nodded once. "I'm Luke."

She swallowed hard, and he watched her throat work. Long and elegant, just like the rest of her . . . Then he noticed her necklace.

It wasn't the flashy bling he'd have expected—just a well-worn black leather cord from which dangled a small turquoise pendant encased in antique silver. Both the stone and the silver had carvings on them, designs he couldn't decipher, but which appeared intentional. He'd bet his ass the carvings had significance and weren't just designs.

It looked old. Lots of scratches on the surface.

The piece didn't match her outfit at all, but she was wearing it anyway, fashion be damned. It wasn't particularly valuable from a monetary perspective, which meant she was probably wearing it for sentimental reasons. It was significant to her. A woman who held on to her roots. He didn't like that. The last thing he could afford was to widen the net of people connected to him. He would have to be careful with her. Keep her at a distance.

Because he was keeping her. At least for the night.

Tonight he needed to forget, needed to wipe death from his mind.

She put her hand over the pendant, obscuring his view. "My name is Isabella Kopas."

"Isabella Kopas." He rolled the name over his tongue, enjoying the sound of it. Exotic, exquisitely feminine, but the consonants gave it a harder edge, as he suspected the woman before him carried. "Where are you from?"

She gave him a brilliant smile that went straight to his core. "I need your help."

He allowed her evasion of his question to stand. The fact that she'd avoiding answering it told him much, and he'd get the info later without her realizing she was even coughing it up. "You need a flight somewhere?" Her skin was dark, suggesting maybe a Greek or Italian heritage. Beautiful, if you liked that kind of look.

And he did.

Yeah, he'd take her on as a client. Fly her to the backwoods? In the line of duty, he'd be willing to make the sacrifice. A slow grin spread across his face, and her cheeks flushed and she looked down at her hands for a moment.

He waited for her to regain her composure, enjoying the effect he had on her.

She recovered almost immediately, and her jaw jutted out when she raised her gaze to his. "I need your help for more than flying."

"More than flying." Luke narrowed his eyes and studied her more closely. "Explain."

She hesitated, then pulled a handbag onto her lap. She winced at the movement and rubbed her shoulder again.

She was holding her body stiffly enough to make him think it was a new injury, and it hurt like hell. What had happened?

She unzipped the purse, drawing his attention back to it. The handbag was big enough to fit a couple of cats and maybe a horse or two, but he recognized the designer name on the blue striped flap. She had more labels on her than he'd seen cumulatively in the eight years he'd been living in Alaska.

He hadn't seen designer duds like that since he'd been spending time around his father . . .

Oh, *shit*. He sat up suddenly, tension skyrocketing through him. Was that the rough edge of a Boston accent hiding beneath her cultured voice? A tendency to add *r*'s in the wrong places and drop them in others? He leaned forward, studying her more closely. No longer the leisurely perusal of a man who was enjoying absorbing a beautiful woman, but the measured analysis of a potential threat.

Isabella slipped her hand inside the handbag, removed a black leather case about the size of a legal envelope and handed it to him. "I'll pay you."

"Pay me?" His fingers brushed against hers as he took it from her, and she froze for a split second, then jerked her hand back and buried it her lap.

He let her take her hand back, but he was surprised at how cold her fingers had been. Icy cold. Fear? Terror? Exhaustion? He inspected her face as he unzipped the bag. The bags under her eyes suggested exhaustion, but when she glanced over her shoulder for the third time since she'd sat down, he realized it was something more.

Fear.

Of what?

He carefully scanned the room. He knew everyone in the bar, and no one was paying attention to her, other than curiosity about a stranger. There were no threats here for her, at least not at the moment. But he still did two extra surveys, just to make sure he hadn't missed anyone. "Whoever you're looking for isn't here. You're safe."

Her eyes widened. "How do you know?"

"I know."

She closed her eyes for a brief moment, but that little gesture told him exactly how scared she was, and that his comment had eased her panic for just a minute.

The bartender let out a whistle, and when Luke looked at him, he nodded to the case Luke had just unzipped.

Luke looked down, and his gut hardened when he saw the wad of bills in the folder. He thumbed through them. All hundreds. It had to be upwards of fifty grand in there. Maybe more. *Jesus*. That was the kind of money people died for, and he knew that from first-hand experience.

Shit, this thing tasted sour as hell of all a sudden, and he felt his skin crawl.

This was the way his father operated.

Swearing, he took another careful survey around the room, suddenly itchy. But Marcus wasn't there. None of his men.

Hell, he was getting paranoid. He needed to get out of there. He tossed the case back at her, and she barely caught it. "No thanks."

"But—"

He leaned forward. "Listen—" He caught a sudden whiff of her incredible delicate floral scent. Regret that he'd have to turn her down flashed through him, but he quickly ditched it. He'd learned his lessons long ago, and self-preservation was as natural as remembering not to put his back toward the door in a public place. "I'm not interested in getting involved in anything where that kind of money is floating around. Go somewhere else."

"But I need you!"

"Why?"

She blinked and stared at him, and he felt her withdrawal.

He wrapped his fingers around her wrist and pulled her close. "Why me?"

She tried to wrench her arm out of his grasp, but he didn't release her.

He kept his voice a low whisper, and let a thread of threat tinge it. "What are you bringing to my doorstep, Isabella Kopas?"

"Let go!" There was panic in her voice now, and he instantly relinquished her wrist.

She cradled her arm against her chest, tucking it against her as if it were an injured wing. "Someone is trying to kill me."

He closed his eyes against the sudden hit of raw fury. *Not again.* "For that money," he gritted out, "you can hire an expert." He opened his eyes. "And yet, you sit here with me." He clenched his fist against the urge to grab her again. *"Why me?"*

She licked her lips. "Because I need your expertise. I don't know my way around Alaska and—"

"Bullshit. Tell me what's really going on. Three seconds or I'm gone." Luke inspected the occupants of the bar again. He was being careful. He was on edge, in a way he hadn't been in a long time. He met Cort's gaze, and his partner sat up straighter. Cort raised a brow at him, and Luke gave him a single shake of the head. No action to take. Not yet. He returned his attention to Isabella. "Talk."

She cleared her throat and visibly summoned her strength. Her shoulders went back and she met his gaze without flinching. "Your father is in trouble."

Luke went still. Surely she couldn't know who he really was. His skin went ice cold and a steel cage settled around his chest. "My father," he repeated. "You mean"—he thought fast to make up a name—"Mike Webber?"

She frowned. "No, Marcus Fie."

Luke felt as if he'd just been sucker punched in the kidney. Jesus. How had he been found? His mind started racing, carefully drilling over every move he'd made in the last eight years. No mistakes. He knew he'd covered his trail impeccably. What the fuck was going on? "I'm sorry. You must be mistaken. My father is Mike Webber. Good luck with whoever you're trying to find. Have a nice day." He stood and headed for the door without another word. Had to get outside. Had to clear his head.

How in the *hell* had he been found? Who the fuck was this woman, and how in the world had she tracked Adam Fie here? And who else had she led to him?

He shoved the door open and stepped outside. It was in the twenties now, and the air bit at him. It felt good to be smacked in the face by the cold. To clear his head. A car roared by on the highway, and his senses jerked into high alert.

His mind was racing with an intensity it hadn't been forced into for eight years, as Luke rapidly dissected the scenery. No car out of place, except one white rental at the end of the lot that was probably Isabella's.

As far as he could see, it was empty.

Had she come alone?

"Hey!" The door slammed open and Isabella followed him outside. "I know you're Adam Fie—"

"No," he snarled. The sound of his former name was like an ice pick being slammed right through his temple. How had she found him? Why? He turned on her, and glared her into silence. "Adam Fie?" he repeated, allowing himself to inject fury into his tone.

He was humming with tension he hadn't felt in years. He didn't need this back in his life again. The brand on his wrist began to burn. "I remember that son of a bitch."

Isabella got a skeptical look on her face. "What are you talking about?"

Luke nodded. "Adam came through here eight years ago. Worked on a couple planes for us. Stole some money and then disappeared. If you find him, I'd love to have a few moments alone with him to get my money back."

Isabella's brows knitted. "Adam wouldn't steal."

"No?" The woman was a fool. That was all Adam Fie had done. Besides knock off anyone who got in his way. And the rest of it . . . Shit. He wasn't going there. Another car roared past on the highway—a new pickup, and it didn't slow as it raced by. Alaska plates. He'd forgotten what it was like to hear every sound, to notice every detail of his surroundings. He didn't like it. "Why do you want Adam?"

She eyed him. "You look exactly like Marcus, you know."

"Marcus?" Luke spat the name. It tasted like poison on his tongue. He caught Isabella's wrist and pulled her toward him. Shit, her wrist was small. Her whole body was petite. She barely came up to his chin, and he was pretty sure he could span her waist with his hands.

He had a sudden urge to pull up that cashmere sweater of hers and test his theory.

Isabella bumped into him, and her breast brushed against his upper arm. Her eyes widened, and she immediately pulled back. "Don't grab me." She tried to pull away, but he tightened his grip.

"Did you come alone?" He had to know. Had to get answers. Find out how bad the crack in his new life was.

She nodded. "Of course."

"Who knows you're here? Who knows you're trying to find Adam?"

She frowned. "No one." She looked over her shoulder suddenly, and he realized she was checking out how far she was from the front door.

No one had been afraid of him in eight years. Out here, he was Luke Webber, affable guy, kickass pilot. Not someone people feared. He'd worked hard not to be that man anymore, and it bit deeply to see a woman recoil from him.

But for right now, he was okay with that. Right now, he needed answers.

If she were telling the truth and no one knew she was here, that was good. Very good. It meant she was the only chink in his shield. He squeezed her wrist, and she snapped her gaze back toward him. "You should be afraid of being alone with me," he said quietly. "I'm very, very bad news to anyone who walks in my shadow. Alaska fucks with people." But he knew the last part was a lie. Alaska had kept him sane. It was his old life that had made him so dangerous.

Her face paled. "Let me go." She tugged again, and still he didn't release her.

He wasn't finished. "What made you think Adam was still in this area? Tell me what brought you here in search of him."

She yanked her hand again, and this time he allowed her to slip free. "Why do you care?"

Shit. He had two choices. Admit he was Adam and drill her for information, or continue trying to keep his cover. Once he admitted it to her, he'd have to bury himself again, or kill her.

He didn't do the latter anymore, and he wasn't ready to abandon Luke Webber and his life in Alaska.

But he would watch her. He would track her down and learn every secret she had until he knew what was going on.

"Why do you want to know?" she asked again. There was no mistaking the challenge in her voice.

He liked her attitude. He was impressed she'd recovered from her initial bout of fear and was pushing back. He admired the fire in her weary eyes and the way that cashmere sweater curved over that body of hers. A tragedy that she'd come here looking for Adam. He'd have liked a night in bed with her. But not now. Now it was about survival. So he forced himself to shrug. "Just wanted to know if I can find the bastard myself."

She cocked her head. "You look exactly like the pictures of Adam."

Of course he did. "Adam and I look so similar, he was able to filch my wallet, walk into my bank and clean out my account."

She stared at him, her eyes narrowing. He could see the wheels turning in her head as she tried to decide whether or not to believe him. It all depended on how much information she had. He wanted to know what she knew.

But now wasn't the time.

Now he needed to disappear and assess from the shadows. He would let her go, but he would track her. Find out what she knew. He caught her upper arm. "Isa—"

"Ow!" She yelped and flinched, and he immediately released her.

"Injury?" It had been more than a simple injury. His touch had been light and her reaction had been intense. "What happened to your shoulder?"

She blinked back sudden tears and cradled her arm to her chest, as if trying to take the weight off her shoulder. "I'm fine." Her voice was laced with pain.

A total lie. He wanted to rip that sweater right off and see what she was hiding. He didn't like the way she was hunched over, or the paleness of her face. There were beads of perspiration on her forehead, despite the steadily dropping temperature. Something was definitely wrong with her.

But she was the enemy. She was trying to bring Adam Fie back to life. If he didn't shake her, she would have to die.

And that wasn't his style anymore. "Good luck finding Adam," he said, not bothering to keep the edge out of his voice. "But be ready if you do. He's a bastard."

Isabella frowned at him. "Luke, I still need your help. Please—"

"No." He realized she didn't buy his denial. She still thought he was Adam.

And that was very, very bad for her.

Slowly, he leaned forward into her space. She straightened her shoulders as he closed the distance between them until there was less than an inch between their faces. She didn't back up, and he was impressed with her backbone. Not too many people stood their ground when he got in their space. Under any other circumstances, he'd be all over the package she offered: courage, attitude and sensuality? Oh, yeah.

But today it was a whole different ball game. Today, it was about trying to keep her alive. "Isabella Kopas, let me offer you some advice."

She lifted her chin. "I don't take advice."

"Well, you should in this case." He brushed his knuckles over her jaw and he felt a smug sense of satisfaction at her quick intake of breath. "Forget about Adam Fie, and forget about Luke Webber. Death follows both of us, and you *will* get sucked in. Run while you can, sweet girl."

She snorted. "I'm not sweet, and I'm not a girl."

He let his mouth hover over hers. Felt her breath on his lips. "No, you're not. You're a sensual, gorgeous, strong woman, and you have an attitude that will get you killed. And seduced, if you're not careful." He cupped the back of her neck and grinned when she stiffened, but she didn't pull away. He lowered his head and kissed her, a hard, deep kiss that gave him the taste of something so incredible that every fiber of his body sprang into alertness.

CHAPTER SIX

After an initial moment of shock, Isabella began to kiss him back, a wet, hot temptation that made his fingers curl into the back of her neck. He kneaded the muscle there, felt the tension knots in her neck fighting him. He growled deep in his throat, wrapped his arm around her waist and hauled her against him.

Their bodies hit with a thump, and she yelped with pain.

"Shit." He released her instantly and she stumbled back, gripping her shoulder. Her face was even paler, and she started to sway.

Luke caught her good arm and steadied her. She looked up at him, pain, fear and vulnerability etched in the deep lines around her eyes. Desperation pinched her full lips.

It was then he knew Isabella Kopas was in real trouble. And the kind of trouble she brought was related to Marcus Fie.

Memory flashed in his head, of a woman's body sprawled on the ground. Covered in blood. First one face, and then it shifted to another. Two women. Both his. Both dead because of him.

And Isabella would be number three.

He released her and stepped back. "Get out of

Alaska, Isabella. Get out and forget about Adam Fie and Luke Webber. If you don't, I will come find you and make you wish you had. Run while you can."

He had to leave before he crossed that line with her. His instincts were screaming that he shouldn't allow someone who could tag him to walk away.

But the alternative was untenable.

He couldn't let another female die because of him. Not another.

He leveled a hard look at her. "Do you understand me? Forget you were here."

She stared at him, and then her hand went to the turquoise pendent resting between her breasts. "I understand," she said quietly. "I understand secrets."

And he saw in her eyes that she meant it. Isabella might not know him, but she knew about survival. He saw it in the pain in her beautiful eyes, in the way she held her necklace. It made him want to ask questions. Find out what she had suffered. Take away her past the way he'd ripped himself from his.

Not an option, but he sensed he could trust her with the secret he hadn't acknowledged, with the question hanging in the air between them. "Then you can go."

He turned his back on her and stepped off the porch. He didn't look back. No way could he afford to see that haunted look in her eyes, or the knowledge on her face that he had once been Adam Fie. She knew who he was.

How the hell had she found him? And why?

Answers he would figure out on his own. A leak he would repair without her. Getting her involved was too dangerous for both of them.

The door shut behind him, and he knew Isabella

had gone back inside. She wasn't going to chase him down.

He took a deep breath as he strode across the parking lot toward the planes. He'd done it. He'd faced down the anger and violence of Adam Fie, and he'd won. Isabella was walking away alive, and there was no fresh blood on his hands. But he could feel his edginess and a lifetime of instincts warning him not to leave her behind, despite his trust in her.

Adam Fie would never have trusted anyone. He suspected the worst and acted first.

Eight years in Alaska with good, honest people had taught Luke that some people were worth trusting, even with his own life. Cort had shown him that, and it was a lesson that had been extremely difficult for Luke to learn. But he'd also figured out it felt damn good not to watch his back all the time, and he'd be damned if he'd let a visit from his past take that away from him.

Adam Fie was telling him not to trust Isabella and to let her go. Luke Webber was saying the opposite.

But Luke was the one he believed nowadays, not some violent, narcissistic, paranoid automaton of Marcus Fie. But he still had to get on his plane and put some space between himself and Isabella, before she changed her mind, or before he did.

He reached the road and paused to let an oncoming car pass. He shifted his weight impatiently, antsy to get across the street and onto his plane.

Shit. He couldn't stop thinking about how scared she'd looked. The desperation he'd sensed in her. Her shoulder injury. "*Someone is trying to kill me,*" she'd said.

And she'd believed he could help her. Why no one

else? Because it had something to do with Marcus Fie. That was the only possibility. Which meant if she thought her life was in danger, she was right.

People died around Marcus Fie.

Luke ground his jaw, rocking restlessly on the balls of his feet while he waited for the car to pass so he could cross the street. This wasn't his battle anymore, not his world. That life had killed two people he'd loved dearly. It had been his fault, as much as if he'd been holding the weapon that had snuffed the life from their bodies. He wasn't going there again.

Couldn't go there again.

He'd made his break, and Isabella, by showing up here, could have easily just ripped apart his fragile peace by alerting his dad's enemies as to where he was.

Jesus, he needed to get away from this. Needed to get to work figuring out what was going on. Figure out his safety zone. Whether his sanctuary had indeed been violated and what mistake he'd made.

Luke scowled at the approaching car, which had suddenly slowed significantly. What the hell was it doing? He wanted it to pass and get the hell out of his way so he could take off.

Screw that. The car was crawling now, and he wasn't waiting for it to go by.

Luke sprinted across the street, making it easily ahead of the car. The headlights were bright, and he shielded his eyes to inspect the vehicle as he reached the other side and began to jog toward his plane.

From this angle, he could see there were three cars in a row, not the one he'd initially seen. The other two were tucked up behind the first one, as if they were drafting off of it.

He slowed down, frowning. That formation was unusual, and looked as if they were trying to protect the occupant of the middle car . . .

He stopped dead at the thought. It was extremely unusual for there to be three cars in a row on this road at night, let alone humped up as if they were about to get it on.

His eyes narrowed as his mind clicked in and he began to sift through the details. Driving so slowly . . . as if they were searching for something.

Or someone.

Adam?

But the moment he had that thought, he recalled that Isabella had said no one else knew about him. Only she did.

Which meant they were after her.

Luke swore under his breath and eased into the shadows of a pickup truck so he could watch what was going on. He kept his attention riveted on the oncoming cars, viscerally aware of Isabella inside that bar. Alone. Her white rental car was parked at the end of the lot near Luke, glaringly obvious in its nature.

The oncoming cars slowed, and the first car turned into the lot, followed closely by the other two. *Shit.* The cars were all black, all expensive. The kind of cars people like Marcus Fie drove.

Luke shifted restlessly. He couldn't afford to be seen. One look at him and they'd know who he was, no matter how many times he changed his name or buried the paper trails linking them.

And once he was exposed, Cort would be in danger. As would his pregnant wife, Kaylie.

He couldn't do that to them. Not again. No one else was going to die because of his heritage. No one he cared about.

He owed it to Cort and Kaylie to slide back into the darkness and disappear forever.

One car headed around behind the building to cruise the back lot. One pulled into a parking space and its headlights turned off. The third began to drive very slowly along the cars toward the rental car.

Checking license plates.

Shit. He couldn't leave Isabella in there. He took a step toward the bar, then thought of Cort and his pregnant wife. They hadn't asked to be put at risk. Isabella had. She'd chosen that life, and the payback was a bitch.

Cort and Kaylie and their baby were the innocents. Not Isabella.

"Don't risk them," Luke muttered to himself. He couldn't afford to get involved—no matter how great she smelled, no matter how much he wanted to protect her. Too much at risk. Despite his best efforts to stay unconnected while in Alaska, he realized he'd failed on some levels. His choices were no longer just about him.

The third car paused behind Isabella's, and then Luke checked out the car that had parked next to the front door of the bar. The doors opened and men got out from each side. They were dressed in black, nearly blending into the night. They began to head up the steps into the bar.

Luke whipped out his phone and punched in Cort's number. His friend answered on the first ring. "You gone for the night?" Cort asked.

"Guys in black coming in. Spread the word that they're bad news and make sure no one gives them anything. Get a warning to the girl, but don't make contact yourself. Then get the hell out of there before anyone approaches you. You don't know me. No one does. I'm a ghost."

"On it." Cort disconnected without a question.

Luke knew the questions from his partner would come later, but for now those men would get nothing but cold, silent stares when they went inside. One thing Alaskans were great at was loyalty to their own and distrust of outsiders.

Luke could vanish, and there would be no record of him inside that bar.

As for Isabella . . . he swore and forced himself to turn and walk toward his plane.

Helping her would trade her life for Cort and Kaylie's.

A trade-off he couldn't stomach.

Isabella Kopas was on her own.

Isabella propped her elbows on the bar and dropped her forehead to her palms. "Okay, Isabella, *think*."

She'd totally screwed up with Luke. What had happened to her grand plan not to tell him about his dad until he was on the plane with her back to Boston? She'd been so rattled by his appearance and by her reaction when he'd touched her. And then, when he'd rejected her so quickly, she'd been desperate to hang on to him and she'd blurted out the truth.

The intensity of his reaction to his father had stunned her. Yes, she'd been expecting resistance, but the pain in his eyes . . . after seeing that, she'd had to let him go. She understood that kind of anguish. Those kinds of secrets. But she hadn't wanted to walk away, and not just because she wanted his help. He was so compelling she'd wanted to stay, to talk to him, to have him hold on to her again.

She rubbed her hand over the wrist he'd been gripping so tightly. When he'd grabbed her . . . her first instinct had been to pull back, but after he'd released her, she'd wanted to beg him to hold on again, like he was an anchor.

The bartender slapped his palm on the bar. "Your friends are coming in the front door."

"My friends?" Isabella whirled around and met the steely gaze of a man she'd never seen before. He was wearing a dark suit, and he was flanked by two others just like him.

He smiled.

Isabella was too stunned to move for a split second. How could they possibly have tracked her here this fast? What kind of network was involved?

"Back door is behind the bar," the bartender said, as he wiped a cloth casually over the counter near her.

She shot a frantic look at the red exit sign and knew she'd never make it. God, why hadn't she anticipated this? *Shit, shit, shit!*

The man took a step toward her, and she bolted for the rear exit.

"Hey!" the man shouted, and she heard him pounding across the floor. A hand grabbed the back of her sweater, and then suddenly he pitched forward into her. She stumbled and went down as he crashed heavily beside her.

She scrambled to her feet as the other two went flying into a nearby table. She shot a frantic glance at two weathered Alaskans sitting casually at a table beside the bar. They both had their feet stretched out in front of them, in the aisle.

One of them tipped his red-and-black checked hat at her.

"Thanks!" She spun around and ran for the door as the men started to climb to their feet.

She heard a gruff voice behind her snarl something about not allowing women to be threatened in their bar, and then she slammed her palms into the exit door and sprinted outside.

The frigid air sucked the breath from her chest, and she coughed as she ran past a Dumpster toward the side of the building. If she could just get to her car, she had a chance. She was almost to the corner of the bar and—

A man stepped in front of her, his face obscured by shadows. He had broad shoulders and an arrogant swagger to his stance. "Isabella."

Isabella skidded to a stop at the deep male voice, her heart leaping with joy. "Luke? You came back?"

Then he took a step out of the shadows, and she realized it wasn't Luke at all.

It was the man who'd shot Roseann.

Nate raised his gun and pointed it at her. Isabella froze, unable to think of anything but Roseann's body splayed on the floor, and his utter lack of hesitation to shoot her friend. And the gun he had aimed right at her heart. "Nate—"

He suddenly raised his hands and dropped the gun. "Fuck."

Luke's grim face appeared over Nate's shoulder. He moved slightly, revealing a shotgun he had lodged in the back of Nate's neck.

Isabella's heart leapt. "Lu—"

He shook his head once and sliced a hand through the air in front of his face to tell her to be silent.

Isabella clamped her lips shut.

Silently, Luke grasped Nate's shoulder and used the gun and his hand to turn the man into the wall, so his face was buried against the side of the building. In that position, Nate couldn't see either of them.

Luke jerked his head toward something behind Isabella.

She turned and saw acres and acres of dark, endless woods. The forest was pitch black, miles and miles of untamed wilderness, in a night that was dipping quickly to well below freezing. Was he kidding? "But—"

He shook his head once and held up three fingers, then dropped one.

The countdown.

Three seconds to run for her life.

She turned and ran.

CHAPTER SEVEN

Luke waited until he could no longer hear her crashing through the brush. Until Isabella Kopas had been utterly and completely swallowed up in the Alaskan outback.

A black car circled behind the bar, and its headlights flashed near Luke.

He pressed the gun harder into the back of his captive's neck, certain the Dumpster would keep them shielded from view. But he could feel the tension building in Nate's body, and Luke knew his prisoner would not stay submissive for long. And if Nate had known who was holding him pinned . . . he wouldn't have played possum for even a second.

Jesus. Nate holding a gun on a woman. What had he become? The man had once been Luke's best friend. Before all hell had broken loose.

No time for regrets. Luke had to vacate. Nate would recognize him if he so much as coughed, let alone showed his face.

Luke swore under his breath, quickly scanning his surroundings for an option. He had to get out without being seen. Without crossing the line that separated him from his birthright.

The easiest choice was to knock Nate out.

His muscles flexed, itching to do it. He was still enraged by the look of stark terror and utter capitulation on Isabella's face when Nate had stepped out of the darkness.

Luke's blood might have run black, and there might have been bloodstains on his hands, but there would never be any new ones. And he knew all too well that he couldn't afford to cross the line into violence, not even slightly.

Because he was, in the worst way possible, his father's son all the way to his core, as evidenced by the pulsing desire within him to make the man before him pay.

Luke suddenly realized his finger was closing down on the trigger of the shotgun, and he instantly released it. *Shit.*

The black car disappeared back around to the front, and he knew he was out of time. The guys inside would get free, the car would come back, his prisoner would snap at any second.

With a muttered curse, Luke looked around again and figured out his best option. He pulled Nate off the wall and shoved him toward the Dumpster. The stench was rotting and putrid, and Nate balked.

Luke pressed the gun toward Nate's neck. A door slammed and Luke jerked his head around as he heard voices on the back porch.

Time was up.

Luke grabbed Nate by the collar of his shirt and threw him into the Dumpster. He slammed the lid shut and slid the lock.

Nate started yelling instantly, and Luke slipped out of sight as Nate's comrades came running.

Luke glanced at the woods, but he couldn't risk drawing their attention to where Isabel had gone.

So he went the other way.

A branch snapped back and slashed across Isabella's cheek. She gasped at the pain and pressed her palm to her burning skin.

Her shoulder was aching, and her legs were shaking.

She was so cold.

But she was also sweating. She had a bad feeling her shoulder had gotten infected and she was running a fever from it. But she couldn't stop running. Not yet. She had to keep going. If she stopped, she was so afraid she would never start again.

How long had she been out there?

She stumbled over a rock and fell, her hands barely catching her. She dropped her head, succumbing to exhaustion for just a minute. Just to rest for a second. She was just so tired.

Wearily, she sat down and leaned back against a tree trunk. The ground was frigid, sucking the heat of her body through her jeans. The bark was rough, and her sweater snagged on it. She shivered and hugged herself, trying to hold in her body heat. Her stomach was trembling now, and there was a layer of perspiration on her forehead.

She was definitely getting an infection. She needed to get out of the woods. Find a doctor. Get help.

But which way was out?

She let her head sag back against the trunk and closed her eyes to listen. No sounds of cars whizzing by, to indicate she was near a road. But also, no footsteps of an approaching enemy.

Just the wind grazing gently through the treetops. The creaks of branches. The scuttle of little feet on the ground. Nature. Alaska. She could smell wet dirt, and dampness in the air, as if a storm were coming, or had just swept through the area. Or both. She'd never smelled nature like this before. Never smelled anything so fresh and clean. She could almost feel all the grime slipping off her soul . . .

Something tickled her cheeks, and she slapped at her face.

Wearily, she opened her eyes.

A thick black sludge of night. No lights. No people. No homes.

Just utter isolation.

Solitude. Fear. Exposure.

Exactly like the first night she'd gone back to the apartment she'd shared with her mother after her mother had died. She'd huddled in the corner of the floor in the darkness, so terrified, so alone—

Panic threatened to overwhelm her, and Isabella shuddered and hugged her knees to her chest. *No. I will not think about that again.* "On the plus side," she said aloud, her voice startling in the silence. "I'm probably pretty safe out here from the bad guys. So, that's a bonus. And it's always good to break in new clothes." She forced herself to smile. "Adventure is always a good thing."

How many times had she gone through this exercise in her life? Silly little things to take the edge off enough that she could function. "And Nate didn't shoot me right away, so there's something else that's going well."

His hesitation had told her he wouldn't shoot her until he had the necklace and everything she knew about it. She had it hidden in her pants, but how long would that work? She should stash it for later retrieval. She sighed and leaned her head back against the towering pines. What if she concealed it up there? Marked the tree somehow? If she could make it up there—

Isabella stood and slung her bag across her shoulders.

She grabbed the bottom branch, then gasped when pain shot through her injured shoulder. Her head spun, and she let go of the branch, staggering under the agony. She knelt in the damp pine needles, clutching her arm while she fought to stay conscious under the onslaught of pain.

Her head spun and she let herself collapse to the ground. She would give the pain a moment to subside.

Then she would get up and soldier onward. It was pretty obvious she couldn't afford to stop again.

But as she let the cold forest floor seep into her body, she had a bad feeling she wouldn't be able to start again. That she'd reached her limit.

"No!" She braced herself on the ground and shoved herself to her knees. "You will not give up."

She grabbed a branch and pulled herself to her feet, gritting her teeth against the agony.

And then she began to walk again.

She didn't even know what direction she was going. She just went.

Luke moved silently through the forest, staying just out of sight and sound of Isabella as he followed her progress.

He'd slipped past her stalkers and headed into the woods after her. Not to make contact. Just to make sure she was all right.

He'd picked up her trail easily enough, and he'd caught up after about thirty minutes. He was keeping vigil to see if the others were following her, but as far as he could tell, they hadn't ventured into the woods.

Isabella had evaded them, and he'd been surprised by how far she'd made it by the time he caught up.

He was equally surprised by how long she'd continued to press on, even when she began stumbling from exhaustion.

She was a survivor.

A woman who wouldn't sit down and let the bad guys take her, unlike—

No.

He wasn't going there. He wasn't revisiting memories.

Isabella let out a squawk of pain, and Luke jerked his attention back to her. She was on her knees again. Her long hair was tangled, her clothes muddy.

He swore and forced himself not to go to her, but each time she stumbled, it was getting more difficult. "Come on," he whispered. "You can do it."

There was only another mile until she'd hit a road. If she could make it there—

"Get up, you lazy dog," Isabella muttered. "This is the perfect way to burn off all the junk food you've been eating the last three days. Feel the burn, dammit!"

Luke grinned as she surged to her feet again. "Atta girl," he said quietly. "You can do this."

But as he watched, she began to sway.

Dammit.

With a feeling of certain impending doom that he was going to damn them both, as well as Cort and Kaylie, Luke acknowledged that without him, she was done.

And that was something he couldn't live with.

No other woman could die because of Marcus, no matter what the circumstances. "Damn you, Marcus."

Isabella staggered and her knees began to buckle, and all hesitation fled.

Luke was by her side before she hit the dirt.

CHAPTER EIGHT

Luke caught Isabella just as she started to fall. Her body was lean and curvy as he scooped her up.

She tensed instantly and leapt out of his arms. Her eyes were wide as she stumbled backward to get away from him. "No!"

He held up his hands. "It's Luke. I'm not going to hurt you."

She stared at him, her black eyes unreadable in the darkness. "Luke?" she repeated. Her voice sounded foggy with confusion and exhaustion. "What are you doing here?"

"I don't know." He walked over to her. "You okay?"

She nodded. "I'm fine. I needed the exercise."

Luke frowned and pulled out the penlight he kept stashed in his pocket whenever he was flying. It was tough as hell to fix an engine in the dark without a light. He flashed it over her face and narrowed his eyes at her ashen skin tone. "Let me see your shoulder."

She pulled back farther. "My shoulder?"

"I can tell it's hurt." He gestured impatiently, trying to keep it professional. Not so easy when she was calling upon every protective instinct in his body. "Let me see."

She hesitated, and for a moment he thought she

would resist. Then she grabbed the cuff of her sweater and pulled her arm out of the sleeve.

Luke averted the flashlight as Isabella pulled her sweater half off to reveal her shoulder. But even with the light redirected, he was viscerally aware of her bare midriff, of the shadows of her bra across her breasts.

"Ready." Her voice was throaty and trembling with nervousness.

Instead of inspecting her shoulder, Luke gently cupped her chin, his fingers gliding over the softness of her skin. "Hey," he said quietly. "I'm not going to hurt you. Relax."

She stared at him, and after a moment, she took a shuddering breath and nodded. "Okay."

He smiled and thumbed the scratch on her cheek. "Good girl."

She pulled her chin out of his grasp. "Just look at my shoulder."

Luke raised his brows at her resistance, then grinned. Yeah, the woman had pluck. Damn if he didn't like pluck.

Isabella closed her eyes as Luke released her chin at her command. The moment he stopped touching her, she was consumed with raw regret at the loss of physical contact. Yet at the same time, she shuddered with intense relief.

How long had it been since a man had touched her in such gentleness? It felt so good, so amazing. To feel the heat of his fingers on her skin.

But at the same time . . . it terrified her. After falling so hard for Daniel, she didn't want to put herself out there again. She couldn't do it. Not for any man.

And Luke was all male. Elemental, raw and rugged.

Everything she responded to . . . which was why he terrified her. Her need for Luke was so much more intense than what she'd felt for Daniel, and even the little of herself she'd offered to Daniel had burned her so badly. She'd been unable to see what was really going on because she'd been so desperate for what he'd offered her. All he'd wanted was to get his hand in Marcus's till, and she'd been so needy to belong to someone, to have a home, that she'd refused to see the truth until it had almost been too late.

And that was nothing compared to the intensity of her need for Luke. For his touch, for his kiss, for his arms around her, for him to protect her . . .

But she couldn't trust her reactions anymore. For God's sake, she'd even been wrong about Zack. His invite to Marcus's birthday had turned into a near abduction. No more trusting men, especially not in Marcus's world. They all wanted something from her, and she was going to make sure she controlled the situation. Luke had so much baggage, so much pain and so much hatred for Marcus that he was the last one she could afford to fall for.

"I'm going to move your sweater up so I can see your shoulder," Luke said.

"Okay." She tensed when his fingers brushed her arm as he lifted her sweater aside. God, it felt good to be touched. She wanted to lean into him and just breathe in the feeling of his skin against hers.

Light flashed as he turned his beam on her arm.

For a moment, he said nothing.

She twisted around to try to see her arm, but her sweater was in the way. "Is it infected?"

"Someone shot you." It wasn't a question. It was

a statement. His voice had gone hard. Low. "Jesus, Isabella."

She shuddered at the violence in his voice, an icy chill that sounded exactly like Marcus at his worst. "I know, but how does it look?"

Luke flashed his light to the side, so both their faces were lit up. He looked grim. "You need antibiotics."

She sighed. "I thought so." Not good. So not good. "Do you know anywhere I can get them?"

Instead of answering, Luke laid his hand across her forehead. His hand was so cool against the raging heat burning her up, and this time, she couldn't stop herself from leaning into his touch. It just felt too good.

"Fever." His voice was grim.

"Felt like it," she whispered, resting her head against his palm. She was too exhausted to fight her need to lean on him. "I'll pay you to take me to a doctor who won't report my visit to anyone."

"No, thanks."

He wouldn't even help her get to a doctor?

He began to pull her sweater back down.

Tears of exhaustion filled her eyes, and she pulled out of his grasp. "I can get dressed myself." She tried to work her arm into the sleeve. She didn't want him touching her anymore, not now that she knew he wouldn't help her even get to a doctor. God, she was so exhausted . . . No. She could handle this. She would find a way to do it on her own.

She struggled to get her arm in, but moving it was too painful. She sucked in her breath at a stab of pain, and he silently caught her forearm and helped guide it into her sweater. His touch was gentle but firm, not giving her the chance to fight it.

Not that she could.

She needed his help, and she had to be smart enough to take advantage of what was offered, even while making sure not to count on it. He'd already said he wasn't going to help her. He was leaving. Period.

At least he was honest about it. That was a point for him over Daniel and Zack.

"Can you walk?" he asked.

She nodded. To her surprise, as she began to walk, he fell in beside her. He said nothing, and the tension built. Why was he staying with her?

She stumbled, and he caught her arm and righted her almost before she'd lost her balance. "Thanks."

He gave her a grim smile, but said nothing.

She resumed walking and he again stayed beside her. He caught her again when she tripped. After the third time she stumbled, he cupped her elbow and didn't let go. His grip was strong, and he somehow absorbed her instability each time her legs wobbled. She felt as if she were being supported by a steel beam that would never falter.

She'd never felt protected like that before. It felt as though even a tornado wouldn't be able to move a hair on her head because Luke would block the wind for her. How did he make her feel like that? Especially when he wouldn't commit to helping her?

He was so tough, he was exactly what she needed right now. Not just because he was Marcus's son and because of his background and expertise, but because he was so solid. A rock.

"Luke?" God, her head hurt. She was cold. Hot. Sweaty. Trembling. *Focus, Isabella*.

"Yeah." His grip tightened on her arm, and she realized she had just stumbled again.

"I would make it worth your while to help me." She tripped again, and this time she would have gone down if Luke hadn't caught her.

Without a word, he picked her up and turned her so she was tucked against his chest, front to front. Too intimate, and she started to pull away.

"Stop fighting." His grip tightened behind her back. "Put your arms around my neck and your legs around my waist. It's easier to carry you this way. Unless you think you can walk another mile." His voice was calm and businesslike with none of the intentional seduction Daniel always had used on her.

His professional attitude eased some of her tension, and she realized he was right. She couldn't walk anymore, and he clearly wasn't trying to cop a feel. She would take it. Cautiously, she slipped her arms around his neck and locked her feet together behind his back, still holding herself stiffly so her breasts didn't touch his chest. "Where are we going?"

"I haven't decided yet." Luke anchored his hands beneath her bottom and began to stride out through the forest. His grip was secure and his step was steady and direct. Despite his claim, she sensed he knew exactly where he was going and what he was planning.

It felt good to be taken care of.

Until he ditched her. Unless she could convince him to take her money, there was nothing keeping him around to assist her. "Luke," she said. "I—"

"I'm not taking money."

"But—"

He squeezed her to silence her. "I'm not getting involved in anything relating to Marcus Fie." His voice was cold and hard. "I'm going to get you safely out of Alaska, and that's where it ends. I don't want money."

It was getting difficult to hold herself away from him, and she cautiously let herself relax against his chest. The heat from his body warmed her, and she closed her eyes. "I appreciate that, but getting me out of Alaska won't make me safe."

He said nothing, but his grip tightened.

"Your dad—"

"He's not my father."

She nestled her face into the curve of his neck. The gentle sway as he walked was soothing, and she could almost imagine she was somewhere safe, in the arms of someone who actually loved her, who would never leave. "Fine," she mumbled. "Marcus, then. He's—"

"He's irrelevant." Luke shifted his grip on her, tucking her even more tightly against him. Creating a cocoon of warmth and safety. She hadn't felt safe since she'd left Marcus's party three days ago. Hadn't relaxed. Had barely slept.

But in Luke's arms . . . he was keeping an eye out for her. She could rest, for just a few minutes. She should rest. Take advantage of the moment.

"Why?" she mumbled, too exhausted to keep her head up any longer.

He moved his head, and his cheek brushed her hair. "Why what?"

"If you hate Marcus so much, why are you helping me?"

It had been so long since Luke had held a woman.

And it felt so damn good.

"Luke?" Isabella's breath teased his neck. It was warm and gentle, a seductive tease across his skin. "Why are you helping me right now?"

Luke ground his jaw at the question. A part of him didn't want to tell her about how truly bad Marcus was. He could already tell she held an affection for the bastard, and on some level, he felt like a jerk stripping her of that belief. Isabella Kopas was clearly tough and a survivor, but at the same time, the way she was huddled against him made her seem so vulnerable. He wanted to protect her, not shred her world with a truth he sensed would rock her. He could feel the heat from the fever burning up her skin, and her body was shaking against his. And a bullet wound . . . Jesus.

The moment he'd seen her injury and realized what it was, he'd known he was in. Regardless of whether Isabella had invited this fate by aligning herself with Marcus, he was simply incapable of walking away from a woman who was endangered by Marcus.

"Why do you hate him?" Her question was muffled against his neck. "He's a good man."

Luke closed his eyes for a second at her tone. He could hear the genuineness of her statement. She really did believe in Marcus.

And that delusion would kill her, as the bullet wound showed.

The truth might hurt her now, but if it saved her life, if he could save *one* life with what he had gone through . . . it wouldn't atone for those who had died—nothing would—but it might take one bit of the edge off the pain. He decided to be honest . . . to a degree. There was no point in lying about who he was anymore. Isabella knew Marcus personally, which meant she'd known he was Marcus's son the moment she'd laid eyes upon him. If the truth could save her life, he needed to do it. "He killed my mother."

Isabella stiffened against him and she lifted her head to look at him. "What are you talking about? I thought she died on vacation."

"Yeah. Vacation." Suddenly, he was back there again. Eight years old, stashed on some Caribbean island with his mom. And then the men had come. With guns. His mother dead. Sprawled across the floor.

"Luke? You're hurting me."

Luke immediately loosened his grip, startled to discover he'd been crushing Isabella against him. A bead of sweat trickled off his brow, and he shook his head to flick it off. He stopped walking and pressed his face into her hair, breathing in her scent. The hint of lavender, the perspiration, the musty scent of real woman. He narrowed his mind until he was entirely focused on the scent spreading through his body. He drilled his attention down like he did when he was engaged in an experiment, or flying in bad weather. Utter focus.

Isabella squirmed in his arms, and Luke lifted his head from her neck. "You okay?" he asked.

"You're wigging me out."

He grinned, hoisted her higher on his hips and resumed his trek toward the road. "Psychotic Alaskan redneck?"

"Something like that." But she sighed and put her head back on his shoulder. It was actually more like she let her head flop back down because she couldn't hold it up anymore. "Why are you helping me get out of Alaska? And for free?"

Her repetition of the question triggered something in Luke, and he frowned as it registered. It wasn't a casual question. Isabella needed to know why he was helping her. Why was it so important to her?

"Luke?"

"I won't allow another woman die at the hands of Marcus Fie," he snarled. His mother first. Then Anna.

Anna had been what changed it all for him. Anna had been the point of no return. Anna had been a tragedy that still made his very soul turn over at night when he tried to sleep. Which was why he avoided sleep as much as possible.

Isabella tensed against him. "You sounded like Marcus when you said that," she said. "The Marcus that scares me."

Luke stopped in his tracks, stunned at her words. "I did?"

She lifted her head to look at him. There was fear in her eyes. "Does that side rule you, or can you control it? I can't live with it."

His fingers dug into her hips. "I am not Marcus," he snapped. "I would never hurt you, or anyone."

She stared at him, searching his face for answers. He tensed at her hesitation, and he replayed his response in his mind.

And even when she shrugged and put her head back on his shoulder without answering him, he wasn't satisfied.

He knew she was right. He had, for a split second, once again become the man Marcus had spent a lifetime trying to turn him into. Cold, ruthless, willing to kill.

A man he had become for one night eight years ago, and the blood was still caked on his hands.

Luke had walked away from that life, from that destiny, from that side of himself eight years ago, when he'd moved to Alaska.

And in one night, Isabella had taken him back to that person, to the edge of that path that led to hell. To the side of himself that was his truth. A truth he despised. A truth he would not allow.

Even if it meant leaving Isabella to the vultures trying to kill her?

He swore as he looked down at the injured woman clinging to him. After Anna, after his mother, after that night eight years ago, he *had* to protect Isabella.

But as God was his witness, she was *not* going to bring his old life back to him.

CHAPTER NINE

It took almost three hours for Luke to circle back through the woods to the airport. Isabella had long since fallen asleep in his arms, her body slumped against his as he worked his way unerringly through the woods. She was trembling from the cold, and he'd long ago ditched his sweater and wrapped it around her. His adrenaline was so high he barely felt the cold wind whipping through the trees.

Like most bush pilots, Luke flew on instinct more than on instruments, a talent that allowed him to cover dense forest on foot without a compass and never make a misstep. He'd decided that heading toward the road with no transportation was asinine, so he'd decided he needed to get back to his plane to get out.

But he had to do it without being seen.

Luke crouched at the edge of the woods, surveying the airfield. He'd crossed the street a couple miles up from the airport, and worked his way back down carefully.

And now, he'd been watching the airfield and his plane for almost twenty minutes, and he'd seen no movement. No action.

The black cars were still in the parking lot at the bar, and he knew those guys wouldn't let up until their big boss called it. They'd turn every stone, trying to figure out where the hell their prey had disappeared. He itched to find out who they were, to learn whom they were working for, to take them out one by one, Alaskan style . . .

But this wasn't his game anymore.

He would get Isabella to safety, and that was it. Periphery only. He was a ghost.

Isabella shifted against him and let out a low moan. She was shivering violently, and he knew he couldn't wait much longer. He had to move, or she would suffer the price.

Luke eased to his feet and moved out into the open, keeping to the shadows of the other planes.

He was glad Cort's plane was gone. He hoped his friend had gotten out without any backlash connecting him to Isabella or himself. The first inkling Luke got that Cort or Kaylie had been noticed, and Luke was going to take off for parts unknown. He'd leave a clear trail to get the bastards out of Alaska, then disappear forever.

Just as he'd left behind the identity of Adam Fie, he would do it again with Luke Webber.

But the thought churned through him, and anger rose fast. He didn't want to lose Luke Webber. He liked his life, and he wanted to keep it.

But not at the risk of people he cared about.

Never again.

He would disappear when it was time, and he'd pray he hadn't risked it by not leaving immediately, by hoping he could pull it off.

He heard raised voices in the hangar, rough voices with Boston accents. *Shit.*

Isabella groaned, and he put his hand over her mouth. "Shh, baby."

Her eyes flickered open, a weary slit in the heavy eyelids.

He gave her a reassuring smile.

Her eyes closed again, and he pulled her more closely against him as he listened to the conversation.

"The girl had to have come through here," a man said. "We've checked all the roads. I want a list of all flights that have gone out."

Shit. If they got Cort's name—

"Nope." Luke recognized the voice of Les Fitch, who was the main man at this airfield. "We don't keep track of that info out here. Just make sure no one crashes and that's it."

Luke grinned, knowing Les spoke only a half-truth. He didn't write down the info, because he kept it all in his head. He could still call up details from twenty years ago. The man was a freak of nature, a vintage Alaskan who lived by his instincts and God-given talents instead of technology or anything too shiny and new.

He always kept a loaded shotgun behind his desk, and he enjoyed pulling it out whenever anyone pissed him off.

Les would hold his own with those bastards and give up nothing. And it was clear from the questions that the men hadn't tagged Luke or Cort, but were merely chasing their tails in the wind.

For now, he and Cort were safe. If he could get Isabella out of Alaska without further contact, he just might pull this shit off. Keep her safe and still be a ghost.

Luke eased past the hangar, resisting the urge to peer inside and get an ID on his pursuers. Distance was the only safe approach, especially with Isabella in his arms.

He moved silently across the tarmac and wrenched open the door to his plane. He climbed into the plane and grimaced at the scent that still lingered from transporting the bodies.

Isabella mumbled something as he set her in the co-pilot seat.

"Hang on there, Isabella. We're going for a ride." He quickly strapped her in and grabbed a blanket from the back to tuck around her. She was still trembling violently, and he had a feeling it was as much from the fever as from the cold.

Luke didn't dare take time to administer meds to bring down the fever. He brushed his hand over her cheeks. "You're going to be okay," he ordered quietly.

She didn't respond, and something turned over in his gut. The way she lay there, just like Anna. Lifeless, dying, because of him—

"No," he snarled. Isabella wasn't dying and no more bullets would rip into that fragile body of hers. He was getting her out of this.

This circle of death that followed him ended now.

It ended with Isabella.

Luke grabbed his harness and jammed the buckles in, his mind already furiously turning over options. Evaluating the risks of each choice. Figuring out his plan, the plan that would end this shit *now*. But as fast as his mind worked, he realized almost instantly that to close the deal, he needed more information from Isabella.

He looked over at the woman who was so pale and still next to him, already sensing it would not be easy to pry information from her. He would have to convince her.

A slow smile spread over his face at the thought of how he could try to persuade her. Not that he'd take advantage, but the bush pilot in him had long ago learned to cross certain ethical lines when lives were at stake. Isabella's life was at risk, and he'd do what it took to save her.

She seemed so small and vulnerable, huddled in the seat. He was unable to stop himself from resting his palm against her cheek. She mumbled in her sleep and pressed her face into his hand.

Luke froze at the intimate movement, at the gesture of trust, of her seeking comfort from him. God, how long had it been since anyone had reached out for him like that? So gently, such innocence, such need. Slowly he leaned forward and pressed his lips to her forehead.

For a long moment, he didn't move. He just closed his eyes and basked in the taste of her skin. A little salty, a sweetness that made him want to drop his head and kiss her for real. To feel her tongue against his. To taste—

He heard a shout, and he instantly pulled back. Jesus. How could he have forgotten where he was?

He started the plane, and the engine roared to life. One of Isabella's pursuers appeared in the doorway of the hangar and gestured at the plane.

Luke ignored him and began to taxi toward the runway. He called Les to get clearance to take off. As he did it, he squeezed Isabella's hand. Her skin was on fire, and her hands were sweaty. "It'll just be a few," he told her. "I've got you. Just sleep. It's good for you."

"You're good," Les affirmed.

Luke heard shouted questions over the mike, and just before Les signed off, Luke heard him mention dead climbers. Luke realized the out-of-towners were about to get a gruesome story about life as an Alaskan bush pilot.

Knowing Les, he'd probably warn them that Luke had been tossing back a few at the bar and that they ought to stay out of the way. Drunk bush pilots were not to be trifled with.

Luke almost chuckled as he positioned his plane at the start of the runway. The poor bastards would have their hands full, trying to get Alaskans to help them. He liked that about Alaska, liked that people protected their own.

Yeah, this was his world and these were his people, and he was going to keep them safe.

He jammed the plane into gear and took off down the tarmac.

But just as the wheels left the earth, he looked over at the office again. The three men in black had come outside and were watching him take off.

And he knew the game wasn't over.

"You bring food?"

Two hours after leaving behind Isabella's pursuers, Luke shut off his plane's engine and grinned as a huge lumberjack in filthy jeans, paint-splattered boots and a ten-pound beard scowled at him from the edge of the woods. Eight huskies flanked him, barking furiously at the plane. A rifle was slung over his shoulder, and three small animal carcasses hung from his massive hand. Doc Eddie was Alaskan all the way up his family tree, and he was a part of this territory, more so than anyone Luke had ever met. At seventy-three, Doc Eddie still competed in the Iditarod every winter, a dogsled race that was two weeks of brutality, frigid temperatures and risk.

Doc Eddie distrusted anyone who didn't have at least four generations of Alaska in them, and he'd hated Luke on sight.

But when Luke had plucked Doc's entire team from a raging river that had swept them off their feet, he'd become the man's friend for life. Doc's first and only Lower 48 comrade, a fact Luke was not supposed to share.

Doc had a reputation to uphold.

"It's business," Luke said.

"Business?" Doc Eddie surveyed Luke. "You finally want me to remove that brand on your wrist? It makes you look like a piece of cattle."

Luke shook his head. He wanted that brand. It kept him focused on moving forward. "I have a girl who needs you. Bullet wound."

"Hell." Doc Eddie strode forward, his jovial tone gone. "You shoot her?" There was no mistaking the hopefulness in Doc's tone. He still thought Luke was a little soft for an Alaskan.

But Doc didn't know about Luke's past.

"Nope." Luke ducked back into the plane and un-buckled Isabella. She was still asleep . . . at least he hoped it was simply sleep. Not unconsciousness. He'd slipped her some aspirin for the fever and managed to rouse her an hour ago, but nothing since.

He scooped her up in his arms, frowning at how light she was. Asleep, small, injured . . . she was vulnerable. Protectiveness surged inside him and he swore at the thought.

He had no responsibility to this woman. Whatever fate befell her was her doing, not his. He'd help if he could, but his duty ended there.

But as he climbed out of the plane with her cradled

to his chest, he had a bad, bad feeling he wasn't going to find it all that easy to walk away from her.

Doc frowned as Luke climbed down. "She's Lower 48."

"Looks that way."

Doc set his hands on his hips, making no move to look at Isabella's injuries. "I don't treat outsiders."

"I know." Luke shifted her weight, holding her tighter against his chest. She was still shaking, and her skin was on fire. "But she's being stalked by some Lower 48 bad guys who are using muscle, guns and money to manipulate the locals into betraying her and anyone associated with her."

Doc's gaze met Luke's. "You think if you took her to another doctor, he might ante up for them?"

"I do."

"Stakes that high?"

"Seem to be."

"Well, damn." Doc Eddie rubbed his jaw. "I do like to fuck with outsiders." He broke into a wide grin. "What the hell. Bring her inside. Let's see what's doing."

Luke grinned as he followed Doc across the clearing toward his hunting cabin. Doc had a house in town, which was where his main practice was located, but he had never hung out a shingle. He took clients on word of mouth only, and he frequently exercised his right to turn down work. He'd gone to medical school to provide care to his peeps, and he'd never wavered from that purpose. He made enough money to run his practice and race his dogs, and he never worked a minute more than he had to . . . unless one of his mates needed help, and then he was available for as long as it took, no matter the time of day or day of the week.

Twice he'd dropped out of the Iditarod with less

than a day to go because someone from town had been in desperate need of his services. But if an outsider needed help? He'd step over the bleeding body on the way to getting a beer.

Luke had been taking a risk that Doc would help Isabella, but he knew Doc was the only one he could trust to keep Isabella and his connection to her a secret, especially in the face of the leverage he knew Marcus could exert on them.

And he'd apparently made the right call.

Luke vaulted up the steps, careful not to trip on the dogs bounding around him. One of them leapt up to lick his face, and Luke grinned as the pink tongue slathered across his cheek. Reminded him of the puppy he'd had growing up . . .

Then his smile faded as he recalled the fate of that dog and why he'd never gotten another one.

No animal should be used as leverage to get a seven-year-old boy to cough up where his daddy was on a Sunday morning.

"Put her on my table."

It took Luke's eyes a minute to adjust to the dim light inside the cabin, which was lit only by the sun. Dark wood, unfinished, a one-bedroom cabin. A bed, a kitchenette, an easy chair, a fireplace and a large wooden table that Luke suspected doubled as food prep and stitching up hunting accidents.

Doc tossed a thick black blanket over the table. He whipped it under Isabella a split second before Luke set her down, in a synchronized move Luke was sure had been practiced many times. "Bullet wound in her left shoulder," Luke said. "I think it's infected—"

Doc pulled out a knife and began cutting through the sweater. "Have you gotten naked with this girl?"

Luke pulled himself up. Had he been that transparent in his desire of her? "No, I—"

"Then get out. I'll call you when I'm done." Doc pointed his knife at door. "Out."

Luke hesitated, not wanting to leave Isabella unattended. It was a nonsensical instinct, given that they were isolated in the woods, untraceable by the men stalking her, and his trust of Doc was so complete he'd tell the old man about his past if there was ever a reason to.

"Go."

Isabella looked so fragile, sprawled across the table. She was pale, shivering, and he knew his hesitation could cost her dearly. He brushed his fingertips across her ashen cheek, then turned and forced himself to leave.

He stepped onto the porch and looked at the woods surrounding him. For the first time in years, he didn't see the beauty, the freedom. He didn't hear the sounds of the forest. He didn't appreciate the squirrel racing across the clearing and the joy of the dogs as they tore after it. He didn't feel the lightness in his heart as he basked in the honor, ingenuity and humanity of the life he'd chosen.

Instead, he saw shadows. He saw places for the threats to hide. He surveyed treetops for the glint of a gun barrel. He listened for sounds that didn't resonate with nature. Darkness and tension invaded his body, making his muscles tense and his skin itch.

Just as he'd done when he first moved here.

When he'd still been Adam Fie in his heart.

CHAPTER TEN

Isabella woke up to a dull ache in her shoulder, the itch of a scratchy wool blanket against her skin and the feel of a hard bed beneath her. No pillow. *Mama?* She bolted upright, her heart leaping with joy, then blinked in surprise.

She wasn't back in the one-room apartment they called home.

No mom.

No ratty clothes hanging on a rope to dry.

She wasn't sleeping on the floor, curled under the blanket that was almost too short for her nowadays.

No, the past was still gone. Her mother still dead.

The present . . . she was in a one-room home again. A cabin this time. Windows on all sides gave her a view of a setting sun turning trees a beautiful shade of orange. She was surrounded by forest. There were no sounds of traffic or voices. Just the wind rustling leaves.

She wasn't in the city.

She was deep in the Alaskan woods.

But where? And how did she get here? Had she been found?

Frantically, she scanned the room, searching for any sign of Nate. Rough wood furniture was sparsely placed in the rustic room. An old stained carpet. A smallish wooden bed with a few faded blankets and several mis-shapen pillows. But on one wall was a gleaming white cabinet with a glass front. Inside were extensive medical supplies. Syringes, bottles of medication, bandages, surgical blades that made her shudder.

A doctor's office? But who had brought her here? Who was waiting for her? Nate?

Her heart pounding with fear, Isabella swung her feet over the edge of the table and sat up. She waited for the hit of dizziness, but it didn't come. The fever was gone.

She braced herself to push off the table. Her shoulder ached at the pressure, and a fuzzy image flashed through her mind. Of Luke picking her up. Carrying her. Giving her aspirin. His lips brushing over her forehead. His deep voice, telling her it was going to be all right.

Luke had found her. Not Nate.

She shuddered and dropped her face to her hands as tears suddenly burned in her eyes. *He'd helped her.* She hadn't paid him, hadn't offered him anything in return, and yet he'd come back and helped her anyway.

He'd saved her.

Her throat became thick, and she swallowed hard. "It doesn't mean anything," she said aloud. "He already said he won't help you. Take it as a gift and don't count on anything more. You don't need him anyway. You're strong."

Strength flowed back into her, and she felt a hard protection build around her heart again, cutting off the vulnerability. She pressed her hand to her necklace, and she heard her mother's voice in her mind. The soft, gentle tones she had reserved only for her daughter. *"You can do anything you want, Isa. Always know that. You don't need anyone. You are enough."*

"I am enough," she whispered. "Thank you, Mama."

She squeezed the pendant one more time and began to assess her situation. She pulled the blanket off her shoulder and inspected her injury. A clean white bandage neatly covered her wound, and the angry red streaks no longer emanated from it. It still hurt, but the pain was less. She wasn't trembling anymore.

Luke had taken her to a doctor, just as she'd asked. He'd scooped her out of the woods and brought her here. Tears threatened again, and she quickly blinked them back. Dammit! What was wrong with her? Was she really so starved for attention that she'd get all weepy over a trip to the doctor? Luke had already said he wouldn't help her. His attitude toward his father was clear, and every second spent sitting around was another second that Marcus was suffering at the hands of Leon.

If Luke wouldn't help her save Marcus, she had no time for him. Besides, he was everything she didn't want. He was her worst nightmare. A man who had eschewed family, money and his own father in return for this barren existence.

She looked around the cabin. God, she couldn't live like this again. It was too hard. Too brutal. And this was a doctor's cabin, for heaven's sake! What kind of life would a bush pilot have? She couldn't go back to a life of deprivation.

Her stomach clenched, and she slid off the table, suddenly desperate to get out. To get away from this world of financial hardship, of not enough food or furniture, of a wood stove in the corner because there was no heat . . .

Her sweater was tossed over the back of a faded armchair, and she hurried over to retrieve it. She still had her bra on, and her jeans—

Oh, God. The necklace. She ran her hand over her crotch and sighed with relief when she felt the familiar bulge. She'd sewn it into the low-slung crotch of her new jeans so it wouldn't be found in a quick search.

She didn't want to think about what Nate would have to do to find it.

She picked up her sweater, then sighed when she saw it had apparently been cut off her. Obviously a male doctor. A woman would have appreciated the sweater and taken the time to remove it intact. She folded the sweater and set it back on the chair. No matter how many clothes Marcus had made sure she owned, she had never gotten used to that kind of money, to the luxury of the material against her skin, and she still treasured it.

She reluctantly picked up the crusty sweatshirt that had been laid next to it. How many times had she worn clothes like that to school? Pulled out of a Dumpster. Washed repeatedly to try to get the stains out.

The money had all been spent on making her mom look good. On the short skirts. The makeup. The wigs.

Isabella ground her teeth, yanked the oversize sweatshirt over her head, and headed for the door.

To Luke.

She would try one last time to pay him to help her, and if he refused, she was done. She was out of there. She knew it would be futile, knew his hatred for Marcus ran too deep, but there was no harm in trying, right? The fact that he'd taken her to the doctor had touched her, had given her hope that maybe he would change his mind. If he said no, then she would move on. She would figure out something else, because there had to be someone else, somewhere else she could turn.

She always found a way, and with Marcus's life at stake, she would not stop until she succeeded.

Or until Leon and Nate killed her.

She banished the thought from her head as quickly as it came, but she couldn't fight off the pall that sank over her, like a gossamer veil of danger and death.

She pressed her lips together. She would keep moving. Ditch Luke and his hatred of Marcus. Find another option. But even as she thought about it, her mind came up blank.

Her lack of ideas was a temporary condition.

All she needed was to get away from Luke and her mind would clear. But when she shoved open the door and saw what was outside, she realized her plans meant nothing.

They were surrounded by woods in all directions. The only vehicle in sight was Luke's plane, sitting silently by the woods.

She was trapped—entirely at the mercy of a man who believed his father should rot in hell.

"Luke!" If she'd had any idea how to fly a plane, Isabella would have marched over to the decrepit-looking aircraft and flown herself out of there.

But she didn't, which meant she had to find Luke and get what she wanted from him.

Unfortunately, she had a feeling a man like Luke didn't do anything he didn't want to do.

No matter what.

"Luke!" She shouted his name again, getting antsy to find him. To take action.

"Southwest at ninety degrees." Luke's deep voice drifted out of the trees. It rolled through her like the rumble of a distant thunderstorm: a dark threat laced with the kind of energy that made the world tremble in response, a promise of a bright flash of lightning to thrust electricity right into the depths of her soul.

A loud crack followed his reply, and she jumped.

She realized almost immediately it wasn't a gunshot, but it took her heart a good minute before it agreed with her.

"Like I know where southwest at ninety degrees is," she muttered, as she tried to pinpoint the direction of another loud thwack. "Right or left?" she yelled back.

She heard what she thought was an amused laugh, and she bristled at it. Just because she wasn't a master scientist with more sense about nature than about the importance of family didn't mean he had the right to judge her. She had heard enough about him to know he was brilliant, but clearly anyone who could make the choices he'd made couldn't have all the marbles in his drawer, right?

"Go right," he called back.

"Right," she muttered as she stalked across the clearing. "Would it have been so difficult to just say that the first time?" She almost laughed at her comment as soon as she heard it. Feeling out of her element always made her cranky, and trampling across an Alaskan clearing with no sense of direction wasn't exactly her area of expertise.

She liked being in control of her surroundings and knowing exactly what was going on, and out here . . . she had nothing.

Which was why she had to get back.

A loud whack sounded again, and Isabella adjusted her path slightly to the left. "What are you doing?"

But as she emerged from the woods, she didn't need an answer.

It was obvious.

And from the way her body was burning in response, it was equally obvious she was in trouble.

Deep, deep trouble.

Luke grinned when Isabella's mouth gaped at her first sight of him. Her gaze swept over him, and his body hardened at the raw attraction so obvious on her face.

She was a different woman from the one he'd already met, and he liked what he saw. No longer pale and wan, Isabella's cheeks were now flushed with energy. She held herself erect, her shoulders pushed back. She looked strong and determined, not a pale wavering flower.

He'd been protective of her when she was hurt. He'd wanted to hold her and keep her safe. And he'd resented the hell out of it. Weak, vulnerable women were his worst nightmare. Literally.

But now?

With her luscious dark hair billowing about her shoulders in the breeze, that crappy old sweatshirt flapping around her thighs, the way she'd spread her feet and set her hands on her hips, and that fire in her eyes . . .

He wanted her.

Naked.

Under him.

Sharing that fire with him.

Luke ditched the axe he'd been using to cut the wood they'd need for tonight, grabbed his T-shirt off the ground and wiped the sweat off his brow as he headed toward her.

He had only one thought in mind right now.

Isabella's eyes widened as he approached. "On, no, don't—"

"Afraid of me?"

She stiffened and halted her retreat. Her chin went up. "Never."

"Good." If she'd yes, he'd have stopped right there. Instant turnoff.

But she hadn't. She'd said no, and he could tell she'd meant it. And *that* was the turn-on. Luke stopped himself mere inches from her. He let himself lean over her, forcing her to look up to meet his gaze. For a moment, tension hovered between them.

No words.

Just an invisible cord twisting tighter and tighter.

Isabella Kopas had come from his past. She knew who his father was. She knew at least something about the man he'd been.

And yet she wasn't afraid of him.

He let his lips brush over her forehead, and she closed her eyes. Not speaking. Not pulling away. Just a long, deep, utterly female sigh that made his cock even harder.

The hell he'd brought with him was already a part of her life.

He couldn't put her in more danger than she was in already. He couldn't risk her life any more than it was already risked.

For the first time in his life, he'd met a female he couldn't drag down into his hell.

She was already there.

He couldn't hurt her.

A lifetime of responsibility fell from his shoulders, and he made a guttural noise he didn't even recognize.

And then he claimed her.

CHAPTER ELEVEN

She was lost.

The moment Luke's mouth descended on hers, Isabella was lost to the heat, the fire, the all-consuming intensity of his kiss. Daniel had kissed her. Zack had tried. And there had been others. Countless others, including those who had thought that because of her mama's profession, the daughter was fair game.

She'd learned to resist. To shut herself down.

She was an expert at keeping an iron grip on her emotions. She'd learned not give herself away when lips came together.

But all that was gone. *Gone*.

Swept away by the most intense sensations she'd ever felt, by the sensual caress of Luke's warm mouth on hers, by the prickle of his whiskers against her face, by the unbelievable feeling of his lips parting hers, of his tongue—

She tensed as his tongue brushed against hers, and then she shivered. With need, with passion, with sensations more intense than anything she'd ever felt in her life. It was an invasion, but at the same time, it was the most tender, most intimate caress, and she was falling into the kiss.

Tentatively, she splayed her palms against his chest,

and his muscles bunched under her hands. He made a low noise in his throat, snaked his arm around her waist and pulled her in.

She could feel his strength binding her, trapping her against him, and it felt good. Safe. Like he was strong enough to protect her. His body was so hard and so powerful, an unshakable force nothing would dislodge.

Heat began to pulse in her belly. She wrapped her arms around him and inched even closer. His kiss shifted then, from a passionate temptation to a carnal assault. Deeper, harder. His hands roamed over her back, across her hips, down her bottom.

"Isabella," he whispered as he broke the kiss.

Goose bumps popped up as he feathered kisses down her neck. Like a butterfly dancing across her skin, the lightest touch—

His mouth caught on the cord of her necklace, and she felt it tug. She had a sudden image of the night she'd pulled it off her mother and put it around her own neck for the last time, because her mother would never wear it again.

And all the feelings of fear and isolation and loneliness came flooding back, along with the realization that Luke represented everything she was so terrified of.

He cupped her face and lowered his head to kiss her again, and she shoved against his chest. "Stop!"

Luke froze. "What's wrong?"

"I can't." She tried to twist out of his grip, dismayed to find her heart was still racing and that she wanted desperately to fall back into that kiss and his arms.

Luke tightened his grasp, pulling her back against him.

She went still, but her body was trembling, with

need and with fear. "You won't help me," she whispered. "I can't trust you not to leave me. Let me go."

He raised his brows. "I am helping you. I brought you here."

"Marcus—"

"No." He released her then, and she knew he was so strong that she was utterly at his mercy. Trapped, until he decided to let her go. He was a man in every sense of the word. He was power and strength, everything that Marcus strived to be.

The difference was that Marcus used expensive suits, a gun, bodyguards and cash to create his aura of strength.

Luke? He was wearing nothing but jeans and boots, a layer of perspiration across his bare chest. He eschewed money and power . . . and yet it was a part of his persona far more than it ever had been with Marcus.

Luke was Marcus's son in every sense of the word.

Except the one that mattered: loyalty.

Luke had walked away from family and a father who loved him, and that told her all she needed to know about him.

He swept his axe off the ground and slammed it through a piece of wood. The defined muscles on his back were easily visible through his taut skin. "I need answers from you."

Isabella hugged her body, trying to protect herself from a spike of lust. "What kind of answers?"

"Who shot you?"

Isabella frowned. "If you aren't going to help me, then why do you care?"

Luke slammed the axe down again, then turned toward her. "I'm going to get you to safety, but to do that,

I need more information. And you're going to give it to me."

She stiffened. "Don't order me around."

"Dammit, Isabella, you want my help or not?"

"Yes!"

"Then answer the questions." Luke yanked the axe free and tossed the piece of wood into a huge leather satchel. "Who shot you?"

Isabella sank down on a tree stump and pulled her knees up as she watched him load the wood. His muscles flexed each time he grabbed a log. She didn't miss the rifle leaning up against a tree, mere feet from his leg. Within easy reach, should he need it. "Leon."

The muscles in Luke's back went rigid, and he turned to look at her, log suspended in midair. "Leon Pareil?"

She nodded.

"On purpose?"

"Yes."

Luke swore under his breath and straightened up. The log still in his hand, Luke took a long, careful survey of the woods around them. He paused, and his eyes narrowed as he stared into the woods behind her. His head cocked ever so slightly, and she knew he was listening intently.

He didn't move for a long moment, and Isabella's heart began to race again. "Luke?" Her voice came out a whisper.

"Leon and I used to work together." His voice was barely audible across the clearing.

"So?"

Luke picked up his rifle. "So, Leon is the one man who is better than I am."

Isabella swallowed. "Better at what?"

"All of it." Luke didn't take his eyes off the woods, but he snapped his fingers at her and held out his hand. "Come on."

He was so tense Isabella didn't hesitate. She leapt to her feet and grabbed his hand. "All of what?"

"Antiquities." He began to lead her across the clearing, the axe and the wood abandoned. "Tracking. Predicting the enemy's next move." He stepped over a branch and gestured for her to do the same. "Assimilating the small details to figure out the big picture."

Isabella looked over her shoulder at the woods. The shadows were too dark, too dangerous.

Luke tightened his grip and tugged her along. "He knows me." His jaw was tight, the tendons in his neck strained. "If Leon realizes he's dealing with me, he'll know what I'm going to do before I do it." Luke sounded grim. "And Leon owes me. He's been waiting eight years for payback." He looked down at her. "Leon and I are the same, with two differences."

"Which are?" God, he was scaring her. She knew Leon was tough, but she hadn't realized how tough.

"He's better than I am, and he won't hesitate to kill." Luke stopped suddenly and aimed his gun at a tree.

Isabella went still beside him and held her breath.

A mouse scuttled out from behind the tree and ran across the leaves.

Isabella stared at Luke. "You heard a mouse? That's impressive."

He set the rifle back on his shoulder and resumed progress back toward the cabin. "Leon can hear a ghost. When we get back to the cabin, you're going to tell me what in the bloody hell you did to bring him down on you."

She frowned. "I didn't do anything. It was Marcus."

"Marcus," Luke repeated. "Son of a bitch." He scowled at her as he hustled up the path toward the cabin. "Marcus unleashed Leon on you, and you want to save the scum?"

"It wasn't like that—"

"Wasn't it?" Luke shoved open the door to the cabin. He strode inside and began slamming shutters over the windows, dropping the bar over each one. Making the cabin darker and darker. He was also eliminating any exit. "What are you doing?"

"Doc has to lock up against anyone wanting to steal his meds. Shutters on the outside to keep the storms from breaking his windows. Shutters on the inside to keep intruders out." He shut the last one, and the cabin was pitch black.

Isabella edged toward the open front door, feeling trapped. "Can we leave?"

"Not yet." Luke walked to the door. "I need more info before I can figure out our next steps. Now that I know Leon's involved . . ." He swore under his breath. "This changes everything, my dear."

The endearment might have meant nothing to him, but the words made a warm sensation run down Isabella's spine. No one ever called her that. Not since her mom.

"I'm going to get the wood. We're going to crash here tonight and then head out in the morning. And you're going to tell me everything in that pretty little head of yours."

She stiffened. "I have a PhD."

A grin spread over Luke's face. "Well, damn, woman. I was already planning to take you to bed tonight. Now? Don't plan on getting any sleep at all."

Then he shut the door and was gone.

* * *

Luke's cell phone rang the minute he stepped out of the cabin, interrupting his thoughts before he had a chance to digest Isabella's announcement. It was Cort. "What's up?"

"The whole territory appears to be crawling with more suits," Cort said. "They're hunting Isabella."

Luke's hand went to his rifle. "How many?"

"Not sure. I'm just hearing rumors. They're talking to everyone, including pilots."

Luke scanned the sky. Blue sky. No clouds. Perfect for flying.

"They're figuring Isabella got away on a plane, and they're following up."

His hand tensed on the gun. "They finger you yet?"

"Nope. Les isn't talking. My plane was gone by the time they got over there. But it won't take much asking for them to learn that you and I both brought back bodies earlier in the day."

Luke felt the noose tightening around his neck. "Go back to the office and destroy everything that has my picture on it. There shouldn't be much." He'd been vigilant about keeping his mug out of print when he first arrived, but he'd gotten lax lately.

The name Luke Webber would mean nothing to them, but his picture would.

Especially if Leon saw it. "Has there been a guy with red hair involved? Six five, heavyset, scar on his right cheek?"

"Not that I've seen, but I'm staying low."

"Can you take off for a few days?"

Cort paused. "To where?"

"Seattle." That was where Kaylie was from. Not that far from Alaska, but, he hoped, far enough.

Silence. "Why?"

Luke loaded up chopped wood, his senses on hyper-alert for every sound. "You know how I told you when we first became partners that I left behind a pile of shit and changed my name."

"Yeah." Cort's voice was cautious, well aware Luke had never opened that door.

"It might be coming for me, and I don't want it to hit Kaylie."

Luke sensed Cort's instant tension. "They wouldn't touch her."

"They would. And you. And your baby." Luke dropped the load of wood outside the door of the cabin. "Anything to get to me."

"You been marked yet?"

"Don't think so."

"Then we're not leaving yet. I've got your back."

"Fuck that, Cort. Don't be a hero."

"I'm not. I'm a friend."

"Shit, no." Luke wiped a bead of sweat off his fore-head. "Not a friend. Too risky—"

"Too damn bad. You're Alaskan now, buddy. Friends are like pit bulls. Damn near impossible to shake off your leg."

Luke chuckled despite his tension. "You're an ass."

"Appreciate the compliment. I'll be in touch." Cort hung up before Luke could argue any more.

Luke swore under his breath as he scanned the sky again. Isabella's stalkers were talking to pilots? The fastest way to search was by plane, and if they knew Isabella had been shot, Doc Eddie was well known.

And Luke's plane was in full view.

Luke broke into a jog, heading for his plane. He swung up inside and started the engine immediately.

The door to the cabin swung open, and Isabella came out onto the porch. Luke expected her to start waving frantically, to tell him to wait for her, but she didn't.

She simply stood there, grim resignation on her face.

He realized she'd expected him to abandon her. In the middle of the woods with no way out.

Anger surged in him as he backed the plane into the woods. Was that what she'd learned from Marcus? That he'd leave her stranded? It pissed him the hell off.

He watched the wings carefully as he edged the plane as far under the pine needle cover as he could. The right one brushed against a tree, and he finally stopped.

He got out and surveyed his position. The gleaming metal of the plane was fully under the tree line. A casual flyby wouldn't see it.

Hidden, but he wasn't positioned for a quick get away, and that didn't sit well with him. Didn't like it at all.

Hiding didn't sit well with him either, actually.

But openly engaging with this enemy had killed the woman he had loved eight years ago, and he was smart enough to know when to check his ego at the door.

This was one of those times.

Luke slammed the door shut and headed toward the cabin. Isabella was still standing on the step, frowning now. She was rubbing her turquoise pendant, and she looked confused. Suspicious.

Luke scowled as he walked across the clearing. He'd forgotten what it was like to be around cynical people. After all his time in Alaska, he'd gotten used to being around folks who had one another's backs, even if they hated each other. You knew you could count on people when the shit hit, because they would need to count on you someday.

He didn't like Isabella's attitude.

It reminded him too much of his old life, of how he'd been raised. Never trust. Never feel secure. Always check a gift for razor blades.

Isabella's attitude reminded him of his mother, and the pain she had lived with every day until she had been snuffed out.

He liked it better when he didn't remember.

Luke vaulted up the steps and grabbed Isabella by the shoulders before she could pull away. "You need to know something," he said. She was so fragile beneath his touch, and he found his grip softening to a caress. His anger faded, replaced by a need to reassure, to give her security. "I'm not going to leave until you're safe," he said quietly. "It's the way I am. So get used to it."

Her eyes widened. "But I'm not paying you anything."

"I'm not doing it for the money." He couldn't hide his disgust and the flicker of sympathy for the hardness of the lessons she had learned. Lessons he'd grown up with as well. He remembered when he had been like her. It was a crappy way to be. He slid his hands down and rubbed her upper arms. "This is a different world. Money means nothing out here. It's a different set of values."

She shook her head, her gaze searching his. He saw the desperation there, the resistance, the refusal to believe. "No one stays just to stay. Not even Marcus."

Luke sighed. "Of course not Marcus. He's—"

There was a sudden hum in the distance, and Luke looked up. "Searchers."

"What—"

He shoved Isabella back inside and shut the door. It was impossible to see inside the shuttered interior.

The sound of the plane grew louder. "Luke?" Isabella's voice was tense, laden with fear.

He latched his hand around her wrist and tugged her to him. She didn't resist. He slung one arm around her neck and kept his rifle free.

"Did they find us?"

"I think they're guessing." The engine grew louder, and Luke had to fight the urge to go outside and watch the sky. If they were low enough, they'd see him standing out there. Right now, the cabin was boarded up and the plane hidden. To the casual observer, it would look as though no one had been there for a while. "Do they know you're hurt?"

Isabella's body was warm against his. He could feel her heart hammering against his chest. "I don't know," she whispered.

"They're guessing then." The roar of the plane was almost deafening, and Luke figured they were flying barely above the tree line right over the clearing.

Close enough to see into the shadows and catch sight of his plane? Yeah, maybe.

He tightened his grip on his gun and forced himself to wait it out.

The plane passed by, and he felt Isabella shudder. "They're gone."

"Not necessarily." Luke leaned his head back against the door and closed his eyes so he could focus on the sound of the plane. He could tell from the engine that it wasn't one he and Cort owned. Someone else then. Hired pilot or an innocent simply passing by?

Doc had taken off earlier in his own bush plane to

head back into town. Luke knew Doc wouldn't spill. But that was before he had known Leon was involved.

Fuck. If Doc got hurt—

"They're coming back!" Isabella moved closer against him.

"Figured they would." The question was: were they going to land?

CHAPTER TWELVE

Isabella held her breath as the engine grew louder. It sounded like it was right over her head, and she closed her eyes as paralyzing fear began to slide down her spine. All she could think about was Roseann.

They were trapped in this cabin. If that plane landed, she and Luke would never make it to his plane in time. Marcus had taught her never to be trapped. To always have an exit. And they were trapped! "Luke—"

He put his hand over her mouth and pulled her close.

She tensed, ready to fight, but then she realized his grip was loose and soft. Reassuring. He wasn't trying to confine her at all. Slowly, she relaxed against him and closed her eyes. "If they land, we have no way out."

"Trust me," he whispered. "This is my territory here."

Trust. God, how many times had her mother told her not to trust? And Marcus? Marcus had been burned by trusting the wrong person. Betrayed by Leon and Nate, his own people. She pulled free as the roar grew deafening. "Let's go to the plane so we're ready to fly out if they land."

He shook his head. "They can't see my plane from

the angle they're flying in at." He caught her arm and pulled her against him. His body was hard and muscular against hers, and she couldn't stop herself from leaning into him.

In the dark, it was less personal. In the dark, it felt safe. It was easier not to think about the fact that it was Luke's body she was wedged up against, who had kissed her so thoroughly earlier. In the dark, she needed to feel the reassurance of his touch.

"If they'd seen the plane on their first pass, they'd have come back at a different angle for a better view. But they're checking the other places now. They didn't see it." He squeezed her arm. "I think we're clear."

The roar of the plane was deafening now, and she wanted to plug her ears. It felt like it was going to land right on top of the cabin and drop through the roof. "But they might land! We need to go!" She felt for the door, needing to get out. To escape.

"Hey!" Luke grabbed her around the waist, spun her around and pinned her to the wall with his body.

"No! Let me go! We have to—"

He caught her face in his hands and kissed her.

Not a gentle kiss.

An assault.

Deep, wet, fierce, dominating. She responded instantly, unable to resist the taste of his mouth, her body needing to melt into his immense strength. Just the feel of his body against hers, of his mouth, of his hands anchoring her hips, made her feel safe, protected. Not trapped.

Tentatively she wrapped her hand around his neck and pulled him closer. Needing more contact. More of his strength.

"Isa." He whispered her name, then deepened the

kiss. His hands went to her bottom, and he pressed her belly against his pelvis and the hardness of his erection.

Excitement flared low in her body, and she wiggled closer. She felt desirable, sexy and protected. His words echoed in her mind. *"I'm not going to leave until you're safe. It's the way I am. Get used to it."*

Her throat tightened, just as it had when he'd uttered those words before, but this time, she couldn't muster the will to argue. To tell herself no one ever meant that. That the only person she could count on was herself. With Luke's arms around her, his mouth so hot against hers, the strength of his shoulders burning beneath her hands, she wanted to believe him. She wanted to trust him. She wanted to live in a world she could trust without fear or reservation.

But she couldn't afford to forget the lessons that had enabled her to survive, that had given her the tools and strength to prevail over the life for which she had been destined.

Luke made her want to forget, and God help her, that would be the biggest mistake of her life.

Forgetting would kill her.

He slid his hand over her ribs and cupped her breast. Heat shot through her body, ripples of fire exploded in her belly—

"No!" She jerked back, and her head banged into the wall of the cabin.

"Hey, it's okay." Luke caught her and pressed his lips to the back of her head where she'd hit it.

She tried to shove him off her. "How can you kiss me when they could be landing right now?"

"They left. Listen."

Isabella realized the sound of the plane was growing

faint in the distance. "How do you know they won't come back?"

Luke trailed his hand through her hair. "Alaska is huge, and there's no way they can afford to land everywhere. They're doing drive-bys and if anything alerts them, they'll check it out. Nothing here clued them in. They're going on."

Isabella closed her eyes. A respite. "You're sure?"

"For now."

She opened them again, straining to see him in the dark. "They'll be back?"

"Eventually. If Leon is involved, he'll figure it out." Luke squeezed her arm. "But by then, we'll be gone."

"Gone," she echoed. "To where?" Boston? To find Marcus and save him?

"That, my dear, depends on you." Luke moved away from her, and she lost contact with him.

"Me?" In the darkness, without Luke touching her, Isabella felt vulnerable. Isolated. Alone. She didn't like it.

She should be fine with it. She was used to it. Alone was power. But being held by Luke had given her a sense of safety and warmth she simply couldn't generate on her own. He had shown her what she'd been missing.

She heard Luke strike a match, and light flared, illuminating his face with a golden glow. He lit a kerosene lamp, and the small cabin filled with flickering light. "Doc saves his generator for severe patient situations."

He set the lamp on the table and held out his hand. "Come."

Isabella couldn't resist the urge to move from the darkness into the light, so she walked over to him and let him take her hand. He settled her at the table, then took a seat next to her. "It's time to talk," he said. "Tell me everything."

Isabella hesitated, knowing full well that his definition of everything might not be the same as hers. "Everything about the night I got shot?"

He raised a brow. "We'll start there."

"Okay." Isabella cleared her throat, trying to get comfortable. She wasn't used to asking for help, to sharing family secrets with a stranger, but Luke wasn't a stranger, and if there was any way she could get him to help her rescue Marcus, she had to do it.

She had to tell the story in a way that convinced him of the good in his father.

But as she looked into his grim face, she knew the odds were low.

And she also knew Luke was her only chance.

Failure wasn't an option.

Luke braced his palms on the windowsill. He'd opened the shutters back up and was scanning the nighttime forest as he listened to Isabella talk about the life he had left. His skin felt tight, and his scalp was itching from all the memories her stories were bringing back. His fingers ached from digging into the wood. Bitterness was like a lead weight in his gut.

"So, then . . ." Her voice broke. "He shot Roseann."

Luke's jaw tightened. "Your pregnant friend." The voice didn't sound like his. It was flat. Emotionless. Hard. He hated this side of him. Despised the man he used to be. "Nate shot her." Nate. The man who he'd trusted with his life so many times. Son of a bitch.

"Yes. I don't know . . . I don't know if he killed her. I just ran, and I should have stayed and—"

"No way." Luke whirled around to look at Isabella.

She sat on the lone bed, her knees pulled to her chest, tears reflecting on her cheeks. "You'd be dead if you stayed. That wouldn't have helped her."

"She was my friend," she said fiercely. "She and Marcus are all I have, and I ran away."

"Hell, Isabella." Luke stalked across the room and leaned on the bed. "You're a survivor, and you did what was necessary to get out alive. Ditch the guilt. Get on living. You can't save anyone but yourself."

She stared up at him. "I'm not like you, Luke. I can't walk away from my own family just because—"

"He's not your family," Luke interrupted. He couldn't stand to see Isabella's loyalty to Marcus.

Isabella lifted her chin. "He's all I have."

Luke frowned at her response, and his heart softened for her. "Where are your parents?" he asked quietly.

She began to pick at the hem of her sweatshirt. "My mom died when I was seventeen. I don't know who my dad is." Her voice took on a defiant edge. "And neither did my mom."

There was a challenge in her eyes, daring him to question her mother's morals. He liked that loyalty. He appreciated that she had the courage to stand up for those she loved, no matter what society might say. It reminded him of what he liked about Alaska. Loyalty that went to the depth of the human soul instead of to money and power. He brushed his finger over her pendant. "This was hers?"

Isabella set her hand over it. "Yes."

"I like it."

A little furrow of confusion formed between her eyebrows. "You do?"

"I do."

"But it's ugly. Not fashionable."

He shrugged. "I like it."

A tiny smile tugged at the corner of her mouth. "Thank you."

"You're welcome." Luke had a sudden urge to kiss that little smile. God, he wanted her. The sight of her on that bed . . . too much.

He dropped to the blanket beside her and lay down on his back. He clasped his hands behind his head and stretched his legs out so his hip was touching hers.

Isabella tensed. "What are you doing?"

"Digesting." Their dinner had been meager and cold, because Luke had decided not to risk a fire. The wood for the stove sat untouched outside for the same reason. The temperature in the cabin was dropping fast, and he knew it was going to be a cold night. But he'd heard planes passing in the distance several more times, and it wasn't a risk he wanted to take.

"Can you digest somewhere else?"

He didn't bother to answer. The lack of furniture in the cabin spoke for itself. There was nowhere to sit except the bed.

Besides, he liked where he was too damn much. Isabella's hip was still against his, and each time she moved, the bed shook. Yeah, he liked being here.

He closed his eyes and quieted his mind, putting himself in strategy mode. He needed to assimilate now. Fill in the missing pieces. "If Leon is involved, he must be running the show. He's been chafing under Marcus's rule for a long time, and I doubt he'll want to work for someone new. He'll be leading the pack if he can."

Isabella sighed, clearly giving up on getting him out of the narrow bed. "What about Zack? And the other man Marcus was meeting with? Simon?"

"Zack Savat." Luke rolled the name Isabella had given him over in his mind. It sounded familiar. He was sure he'd heard it before. Somewhere in his past . . . but fuck . . . he didn't want to open those doors again.

He would let it sit for now.

It was enough to know Leon was involved. And that he'd gotten Nate on his side. Shit. *Nate.* "Nate used to be my best friend," he said quietly.

Isabella shifted beside him. "Really?" Her sudden tension was evident. "Are you still friends?"

"Haven't spoken since I left." He and Nate had been tight. The same. Luke had left. Nate had stayed. And now Nate was shooting pregnant women.

Would that have been Luke's path if he'd stayed? He had a bad feeling about that answer. And what would happen to his path if he opened those doors again?

He opened his eyes, not wanting to go down that road. Isabella's dark hair was hanging in tangled curls over her shoulders, and her face was pale. There were circles beneath her eyes, and she was slumped over in exhaustion. Unable to resist, he took a lock of hair and rubbed it between his thumb and forefinger.

Isabella said nothing, and she didn't pull away.

"I know Nate," he said. "I can predict him. He's smart, but I'm smarter."

She nodded. "Good."

Her hair was so soft. He fisted his hand in it and tugged.

Isabella didn't move toward him. "So, what do we do?"

"I'm still deciding." He pulled again. "Come here."

"No!"

"Touching you helps me think." He wasn't lying.

The demons from his past were circling him now, edging at his concentration. Listening to Isabella talk about that night was like a sucker punch in the kidney about the life he'd left, about the man he had left behind . . . only he knew he hadn't really left him behind.

The man Luke didn't want to be was a part of his soul all the way to his core.

A dark side. A side that killed.

A side that needed to be soothed by the feeling of Isabella against his skin. "You're tired. You need to sleep. I'll watch out for you."

Her relieved expression told him he'd hit a chord. Without another word, she snuggled up against him, almost as if she needed the contact as much as he did.

He wrapped his arm around her shoulders and pulled her tightly against his side. She tucked her head on the front of his shoulder, not fighting the intimacy.

Luke closed his eyes again, and the noise in his mind subsided. He breathed in her scent, let it drift through him, easing his tension in the same way it had when he'd met her in the bar. Neurons began to come to life in his mind, the ones that were fire and energy. He could almost hear the crackles of electricity as he began to think again, to problem solve in a way he hadn't had to do since he'd quit being a scientist and walked away from his old life. Flying was about instinct, not an analytical breakdown of the situation. Today, his life was about being calm and relaxed, not the hypervigilance that went along with knowing those you dined with could pull a gun on you tomorrow.

On some level it felt good to have his brain alive again. He hadn't realized he'd missed it.

There was something bothering him about Isabella's story. "I don't believe they're after you simply because you saw them take down Roseann. Too many resources are being spent to find you."

Isabella was quiet for a moment. "I think they want to use me for leverage against Marcus."

Luke felt blindsided. That was what had happened to Anna—only Luke had been the one they'd been trying to manipulate. Jesus. Not again.

Isabella lifted her head to look at him. "What's wrong?"

He shook his head. He needed to focus. Bring it home. "What does Leon want from Marcus?"

He'd thought Marcus had learned his lesson about letting anyone get close enough to be used for leverage. How could he have let Isabella get that close? Stupid bastard. He had to have known it would endanger Isabella to let her become important to him, yet the selfish son of a bitch had done it anyway.

"They want a necklace," Isabella said.

Of course. It was always about the antiquities. The money. "What necklace?"

She hesitated a fraction of a second, so briefly he wouldn't have noticed if he hadn't been paying such close attention. "I don't know the details about it. It came in that afternoon, and I hadn't had time to research it."

Sudden certainty made Luke tense. "You have it."

Isabella's face became wary. "No, I don't. I—"

"Son of a bitch, Isabella." He was standing now. "Do you have a death wish? Leon is ready to kill for this thing and you took it?" Shit! No wonder they were pressing so ruthlessly for her. "That's why you kept saying that getting out of Alaska wouldn't make you safe. You know they'll hunt you down until they get what they want and you're dead."

"I didn't *take* it," she retorted. "Marcus made me wear it for his birthday party, and when I ran, I still had it on. They all know I was wearing it. It's the only thing keeping Marcus alive. It's my leverage."

"It's suicide." He held out his hand. This changed everything. "Let me see it."

Isabella began to unzip her jeans. "I hid it in here." She began to tug her jeans over her hips, and he couldn't drag his gaze off her flat belly, the curve of her hips, the black lace of her underwear . . .

His cock hardened instantly.

"Turn around," she demanded.

"No."

She scowled at him. "Luke!"

He turned.

It was the longest three minutes of his life before she tapped him on the shoulder.

Her pants were back up, but she hadn't buttoned them yet. Disappointment hit him like a chainsaw in the gut, and he realized he was sunk. All he could think about was burying himself—

"Here." She set a warm piece of metal in his hand. "I wasn't lying when I said I didn't know what it was. I haven't had time to research it." But something in her eyes said she knew more than she was letting on.

Luke dragged his gaze off her to look down at the necklace. It took a moment to register, and then he recognized it. "Bloody hell."

They were in deep shit.

That necklace meant it wasn't just about Isabella.

It was also about him.

CHAPTER THIRTEEN

Isabella hadn't even gotten her jeans buttoned before Luke grabbed her hand. "Let's go."

"Where?"

"We're getting rid of this."

"What? No!" She stopped. "It's our only way to get Marcus free."

Luke spun on her, his jaw twitching. "I searched for this necklace for seven years. It's part of a collection."

Excitement pulsed through Isabella. It was just as Marcus had said. "You've heard about this necklace?"

"Yeah. That's why we're getting out of here." He yanked open the front door. "Into the plane. Now."

"Okay." Isabella followed his lead and they ran across the moonlit meadow toward his plane. She was so excited. She'd known Luke would be able to help her.

They were strapped in and taxiing within minutes.

"The entire set dates back only about three hundred years," Luke said as he circled the clearing. "It's a necklace and matching earrings." He slanted a look at her, as if assessing how much of this she already knew. "The key is the stones. They were part of a collection that belonged to a Ciradian tribe, who believed they had mystical powers to provide safety and love and wealth."

"Ciradian?" Isabella gripped her seat as the plane bumped over the clearing as it picked up speed. She had been so right that Luke would know enough to help her. As much as she knew, he clearly knew a whole lot more. "They were known for violence?"

The plane caught loft. "Yep. They believed their role was to protect the earth at all costs." He rubbed his jaw. "They were scientists way ahead of their time. I couldn't believe they were able to—"

"The necklace, Luke." She grinned at his distraction into the scientific realm. No wonder he was interested in this area, and it was clear why Marcus had put Luke on the trail of this particular artifact.

"So, yeah, they put the stones of protection into the set of jewelry, and the elders of the tribe wore them. To the Ciradians, the jewelry was about protection, but others were simply interested in the monetary value of the jewels. The tribe protected those jewels at all costs, and they became increasingly violent in the face of so many treasure seekers."

"Like Marcus."

He glanced over at her. "Like Marcus."

"How much is the necklace worth? Or the set together?"

Luke whistled softly. "The set's enough to make Leon decide it's worth it to turn on Marcus." He nodded at her injured shoulder. "Enough that it's worth a few lives."

Isabella hugged herself. "So do you think Leon has the earrings? Is that why he's acting now?" She shook her head. "No, I would have known if the earrings had been found. I would have heard about it."

Luke was silent.

She raised her brows at his sudden reticence. "Luke? Do you know something about the earrings?"

"I do."

"What?"

"I found them."

She shot a sharp look at Luke. "You did? When?"

"Eight years ago." His jaw was hard.

"Oh my God. So now the whole set has been recovered." Isabella hugged herself. No wonder Leon was after her. "Does Marcus still have the earrings? Or did he already sell them?" Surely he hadn't kept them all this time. "And who did he sell them to? Do you remember?"

Luke's jaw flexed. "Marcus doesn't have them. He didn't sell them."

"He didn't?" Isabella frowned. "So where are they?"

"He has no clue. They disappeared." Luke banked the plane and the half-moon was on Isabella's side now.

Isabella rubbed her shoulder, which was starting to ache again. "Did you actually retrieve them? Or just locate them?"

"I got them."

Isabella heard an edge to his voice that made her wary. "You stole them? At gunpoint?"

"Yep. Nate and I did it together." There was resignation in his voice. Bitterness. "Scared the shit out of the three children. Nothing like having two gunslingers invade dinnertime to fuck up a kid."

Isabella studied the necklace still clenched in Luke's hand, a sinking feeling in her stomach. "Did Marcus know you stole it?"

Luke raised his eyebrows in surprise. "Of course he did. It's his business model."

Isabella leaned her head back against the seat. She

had had suspicions over the years about how some of those items had been retrieved. Not the ones he sold in his store, but the ones dealt out of his storeroom in his basement. The ones that never made it into the public eye. Deep down, she'd known. But it still made her heart ache. "I'm sure he didn't want to endanger the children, though." Not the children.

Luke said nothing.

Isabella looked over at him. "Luke?"

"Don't ask me for answers you aren't ready to hear. I won't lie for him."

A deep ache gripped Isabella's chest. "I know he's not perfect," she said. "But I love him as if he were my own father."

Again, he said nothing, but his mouth was tight. She knew he was thinking only about how much he hated the very man she loved.

How could they resolve this? How could they work together on this? Luke wanted Marcus dead. She wanted Marcus safe. There was no common ground. Right now, the only thing they agreed on was keeping her alive, and she still didn't understand why Luke cared.

Or maybe he didn't.

Maybe he was simply using her to get back at Marcus . . .

Betrayal thudded in her stomach and she closed her eyes in dismay. *Please, not again.* "Where are we going?" she whispered.

"We're putting it back."

Her heart congealed with dread. *No, Isa, don't lose faith. You have to believe.* "Back? What do you mean?"

"One of the elders for that tribe lives in Northern Alaska. We're giving it to him."

Isabella sat up. "We can't! That necklace is my only leverage to bargain for Marcus's safety! And they won't stop coming after me—"

Luke's expression was unyielding. "We'll make sure Leon understands that it's gone, and then you'll disappear. I've done it once, and I'll show you how."

"But Marcus—"

"Will die, if he's not already dead." His voice was flat. "I know."

"No!" She yanked the necklace out of his hand. "I won't do it!"

His grip tightened on the controls. "You don't get it, do you, Isabella?" His voice was soft. Quiet. Lethal.

"Get what?"

"It doesn't matter what you want." His voice was hard and unyielding, as was the tense set to his shoulders. "I'm going to save your life, and you have no say in it."

"But—"

"Your choice was made the day you walked into my life and handed your life over to me."

"I didn't hand my life over to you! I asked you to help me save your father!"

"No. You asked for my help, and you said someone was trying to kill you." His jaw was hard. "They will kill you, Isabella. You brought these bastards down on you, and down on me, and it ends now." He gave her a hard look of barely contained fury. "You brought this shit into my world, and now we play by my rules. The necklace gets lost and then you disappear. End of story."

Luke's shoulders were set, his muscles rigid, his tone brutal and hard. He was a man who was going to get exactly what he wanted, and he didn't care one bit what mattered to her. As she clutched the necklace, a feeling of doom settled over her. After a lifetime of struggling for control over her life, of fighting for what she wanted, Luke was stripping it all away. Her father, her home, the only security she'd ever had . . . he was ripping it from her grasp. "You're a jerk—"

"And you're mine."

The tin shack was exactly the same as it had been when Luke had come eight years ago, seeking absolution he hadn't gotten.

The building was tilted to the side, rust crawling up one wall. A stovepipe stuck out of the roof, emanating a thin spiral of gray smoke. But the house was flanked with the most amazing fauna he had ever seen.

Luke had spent hours that day with the man who called himself only Ren. He had been blown away by Ren's knowledge about the earth and plants, and he'd picked Ren's brains for every shred of information.

At the end of his visit, Luke the scientist had been humbled and awed by the wizened, bent man. Luke had also sensed the remnants of violence in Ren's past, an echo of Luke's own soul, and he suspected Ren had felt the commonalities between them.

Which was why Ren had told him never to return, and why Luke had listened.

Until now. When Luke had realized what artifact Isabella had brought with her, it had changed everything. Because now, if anyone found out he was involved, the hunt for him would be ruthless and relentless, because he was the one who had made those earrings disappear. Now that they had the necklace, it tripled the value of those earrings, and if anyone realized where Luke was, they'd hunt him and do anything it took to get him to reveal where those earrings were today.

It would no longer be just about Isabella. It would be about him, and Cort and Kaylie and everyone else he cared about would pay the price. Getting Isabella out of Alaska had been urgent before, but now, it was at crisis level.

He still couldn't believe that necklace had been found. Of all the damn items that could have been involved, it was his Achilles heel. Which was why he was returning the necklace to Ren. If he could get the necklace to disappear, the earrings would lose value again, and there was a chance Leon and Marcus would let Isa walk away before all hell broke loose.

It was his best opportunity for heading this thing off before people started dying, and he was banking on the fact that Ren wouldn't follow through on his promise to kill Luke for returning. Luke had stolen his family's heritage, and for that, he could never be forgiven.

Luke understood. He didn't forgive himself for his past either.

But if he could save Isabella . . . maybe some of the blackness on his soul could be expunged. Not that she was making it easy on him. The woman still believed she could save Marcus, and that his soul was worth the risk of hers.

To say she hadn't wanted to return the item to Ren was an understatement. Unfortunately for Isabella, she'd been trapped in a plane and had had nowhere to go. She had argued fiercely with him for the first two hours of the plane ride, but he hadn't engaged.

Didn't know how, really. She unsettled him. Took him out of his zone. Mostly because she called to him in a way he hadn't experienced before. Her courage, her loneliness, her loyalty to her mother . . . inside the veneer that had been tainted by Marcus's world was a woman with a heart that loved, that could break, that deserved to live.

And he was going to make sure that happened, even if it made her hate him forever.

He hadn't listened to his instincts before, and two women he loved had died.

Isabella wasn't going to follow that path.

She'd eventually given up arguing, but the hostility was palpable, and he knew she was going to make a break for it at the first opportunity.

She was silently assessing the tin shack as he shut down the propellers. He didn't kill the engine, just in case they needed to bolt quickly. He had full faith Ren would be on Leon's radar sooner rather than later.

And as for Isabella . . . She was eyeing the rusted Land Rover parked haphazardly next to the shack. He held out his hand for the necklace. "Hand it over."

"No way."

"I'll get it myself if you want me to." The thought of digging into her jeans sent a flash of sudden heat through him.

Isabella's cheeks flushed. "You wouldn't dare."

He didn't waste time with an answer. He just grabbed her around the back of her neck and hauled her toward him. Her eyes widened, and she started to protest, but he slammed his mouth down over hers before she could get a word out.

She tasted like the hot sun on an Alaska day, like the damp moisture in the summer air after a storm. She tasted of freedom, of courage, of survival. Things that reached into his core and hit hard. Despite the fact that Isabella Kopas embodied his worst nightmares, she was also his chance to escape from that life.

After a moment of hesitation, she kissed him back. Tentatively. But it was enough, and with a low growl, he pinned her to the seat and deepened the kiss. He loomed over her, needing to take her. He wanted to possess her, to lose himself in her, and he pushed relentlessly, unwilling to pull away when he felt her responding. Despite all the shit between them, she wanted him as much as he wanted her, and it felt damn good. *She wanted him.*

He ran his hands over her body. The curve of her hips, her narrow waist . . . satisfaction rippled through him when her stomach trembled beneath his palm. She tightened her grip and pulled him closer. Her kiss turned frantic, answering everything he gave her.

Luke grabbed her hips to haul her onto his lap, and he felt the bulge of the necklace in her pocket.

They both froze, and Isabella pulled back. "I need it," she said, an edge to her voice. "Kissing me won't change my mind."

For a moment, he was tempted to give her exactly what she wanted. To be the man she wanted him to be. To stand by her side and help her get everything she desired.

But he knew she was living in a fantasy world, and if he gave in now, he'd be standing over her grave within days.

He couldn't do that to her. Wouldn't allow it to happen again. "I can't." He slid his fingers into her pocket.

She clamped her fingers around his wrist. "Don't."

He pulled the necklace free and twisted his hand

easily out of her grasp. Her fingers slid away, and there was a look of such fury and betrayal on her face he felt it stab him. "I'm doing this for you," he snapped, his voice harsher than he'd intended.

"No. You're doing it because you're a bastard."

"Not going to argue that one." He dropped the necklace into his pocket. "I'll be ready."

Confusion flickered across her face. "Ready for what?"

He nodded at the truck parked outside the plane. "For you to run."

Her mouth opened, then shut again.

No denial.

The battle lines had been drawn.

CHAPTER FOURTEEN

Isabella ignored Luke's offer to help her as she climbed down from the plane. How could she have let him kiss her? She'd wanted to believe he was kissing her because he wanted to, but it had only been a ploy to get the necklace.

He was there to strip away everything she cared about. So why did she keep responding to him? Dear God, she'd lost her only chance to get Marcus free, all because something about Luke touched her heart in a way no one else ever had.

She knew why he affected her so intensely. She'd seen the pain on Luke's face, the flashes of loneliness in his eyes, and she knew he understood what it felt like to be truly alone. He was a man whose soul wanted company as much as hers did. Something about the way he kissed her and held her made her feel cherished . . .

Not that it mattered. Luke might understand her in a way no one else did, but how dare he try to take her choices away? How dare he try to tell her who was worth fighting for? And if he didn't love his father because Marcus had made some bad choices, what would he think of Isabella and the choice she'd made the night her mother had died?

Her stomach congealed. She hadn't thought of that.

Of course Luke wouldn't be able to accept what she'd done that night. If he couldn't forgive his father, there was no chance he'd have empathy for her. Dear God, she had to stop herself now. No more kissing, no more letting him under her skin. God, how she missed her mother and the unconditional love they had shared. Why could no one else love her that way? Was it too much to ask for—

A faint melody drifted across the wind and Isabella spun around. "What's that?" It sounded like a wooden flute, much like the one her mother used to play every night when Isabella went to sleep.

She had entertained Isabella with it before she headed out for a night of work. Isabella would spend the night home by herself, lying awake all night, wondering if her mama would come home this time, or whether she would get one bruise too many and not get up.

Isabella had sat up and played that flute for her mother every night, all night, using the music to call her mama home.

And now . . . her heart racing, she frantically spun around, trying to pinpoint the music. "Where is that coming from?"

Luke pointed to a cluster of trees off to the right of the shack. "But I don't think we should interrupt—"

Isabella was already running, desperate to find the source of the haunting melody. She slowed as she hit the woods, dodging low branches and fallen logs. The music seemed to drift in and out of the trees, ebbing and flowing, shifting directions. "Where is it?"

Luke set his hand on her shoulder and turned her to the right. "This way."

She followed his lead. "How do you know?"

He shrugged. "I can just tell."

No wonder he'd been so good at working for Marcus and doing his scientific studies. The man missed nothing. Why would he give all that up to fly around Alaska? What could Marcus possibly have done to warrant it?

"Whoa." Luke stopped her suddenly, and she looked up to find the barrel of a shotgun one inch from her nose.

The music was gone, and staring at her with an utterly impassive expression was a man with dark, roughened skin and black eyes. The wrinkles on his face were crevasses of shadow and evasiveness, and his gray braids were like leathery whips hanging past his hips.

"Ren." Luke set his hand on her shoulder and ever so slowly began to pull her behind him. "She's innocent."

The man's eyes bored into her as if he could see the secrets of her soul. She had the uncomfortable feeling that he was actually uncovering all of them. Every last one.

One minute both hands were on the barrel of his gun, and the next moment a small wooden object was whipping through the air right at her head. She hadn't even seen his hand move.

Luke snatched it out of the air before she had time to react, and the tip of it brushed against her nose as he swept it away. He held up a wooden flute similar to the one her mother had had.

Her mother's had had deep etchings of flowers, and the only paint left on it had been occasional hints of blue and white on the blossoms.

This one was a lighter shade of brown, and the paintings were vibrant and alive. No flowers. Crimson splotches the color of blood. Vines twisting around the wood, as though imprisoning it. Little flecks of silver that reminded her of daggers.

She shuddered. No, it wasn't like her mother's at all.

For a brief second, she'd felt like she was home again. But it was a lie. There was no home for her anymore. Maybe she was a fool for continuing to look for it. Maybe she should just give up having a place and a family. Go it alone, like Luke had. Stop striving for the kind of love her mother had taught her to believe in.

But as she looked at Luke's icy features, her heart sank. *I don't want to be like him.*

The man Luke had called Ren nodded at the flute. "Play it."

She tensed, not certain she could deal with the memories. But as she reached for it, Luke put the flute to his own lips and began to play.

The melody was haunting and eerie. Chills ran down her spine, and she wanted to hug herself. It wasn't anything like what she'd heard before. This was violent, dangerous and penetrating. Hearing the flute had, for a moment, transported her back to her childhood . . . but this spooky tune was what she should have played while waiting for her mother to come back from a night of selling her body to the highest bidder.

Luke finished and handed the flute back. "I haven't forgotten what you taught me." His voice was quiet. Respectful. Cautious.

Ren took the flute and shoved it into the deep pocket in the front of his cargo pants. He gestured with the barrel of the rifle.

Luke took Isabella's hand and guided her through the woods. Ren fell in behind them, keeping the gun pinned to her back. She started to look over her shoulder, and Luke squeezed her hand once. "No," he whispered. "That will insult him. You need to show you give yourself over to his safekeeping."

"But I don't!"

Luke squeezed her hand. "Then trust yourself to me. Pick one or the other, but don't doubt him."

Isabella swallowed, remembering what Luke had told her about the tribe Ren was from. Violent. Deadly. And she had stolen the object they killed to protect. What were she and Luke doing here?

They reached a small stream, and Luke sat down on a small patch of dried grass. He gestured for her to do the same, and she carefully lowered herself to her knees, positioned to bolt if she got the chance.

This felt wrong. So wrong.

Luke's jaw was tense and his eyes alert, carefully studying everything around them, and she realized he sensed the danger as well. Was it the overly silent woods? The rigidity of Ren's stance? She didn't know, but she felt exposed and endangered sitting out on the grass mat.

Ren sat across from them, his gun still pinned on Isabella.

For a long moment, no one said anything, and Isabella couldn't take her gaze off the black cavern of the gun aimed right at her heart.

The silence drew on and on, and she sensed Luke growing restless.

Finally, Luke said, "You're stalling."

Ren said nothing.

Luke swore suddenly. "Son of a bitch. You're holding us for someone."

Ren nodded once.

Luke inched closer to Isabella, thinking of his gun stashed back in his plane. Bloody fool he'd been to leave it behind. "The girl, or me?"

"Both."

"Both." Luke repeated the words, the grimness of his tone indicating that he'd just learned something monumental that was bad news for them.

But what?

Luke leaned forward, unwilling to leap to judgment until he had all the facts. "Do they want you to hold the man who is with Isabella, or me specifically?"

Ren met his gaze. "They said Luke Webber would be coming."

Shit. How had they known he was with Isabella? The only ones who knew were Cort and Doc, neither of whom would talk. Yeah, he'd figured Leon would tag Ren, but this was faster than he'd imagined. They'd gotten to Ren first. And how did they know about him? And did they know Luke Webber was also Adam Fie, or not? "Who came to see you?"

"A man. Red hair."

Red hair. *Leon.* Shit. He was in Alaska? The hair on the back of Luke's neck stood up. "Why are you dealing with them?" It wasn't Ren's style to do anything for a man like Leon.

Ren's expression was unreadable. "I'm waiting."

"For what?"

"Grandpapa!" There was a rustle in the woods behind Luke, and he spun around to see a teenage boy racing toward them. He had short black hair, and wore jeans and hiking books. His coloring was dark like

Ren's and he had the same mouth. He had the skinny, gangly body of a boy growing into manhood, but not quite there.

"Dillon!" Ren leapt to his feet and embraced the boy as he flung himself at his grandfather.

The hug lasted less than a second, and Ren broke away. He aimed the gun at the woods, surveying them carefully. His gun was no longer pointed at Isabella. His face was urgent, his body tense. "Get up. Let's go. Hurry."

Ren's hostility was gone, and Luke jumped to his feet as Ren tossed a rifle at him. "What's going on?"

"This way." Ren broke into an effortless sprint. His grandson was in the lead, and they were hauling ass.

Luke caught their urgency and grabbed Isabella's hand, sending her first. She didn't hesitate, running hard after Ren and his grandson. He appreciated that she didn't waste time asking questions. She was ready to move, and he suspected that was a damn good thing

"What's going on?" she asked.

"They said you were coming." Ren slowed down to lope beside Luke, not even winded. "Took my grandson. Trade, you for them."

Luke swore. A child. Used as a pawn. Just as he had been.

Isabella followed his gaze, and her face paled. "He's just a boy."

Her horror was obvious, and she wasn't faking her shock. How had she possibly maintained her sense of innocence being a part of Marcus's world for so long? Dangerous naïveté or a survival mechanism? A tool she'd used to find peace in a world she was forced to live in?

Something tweaked inside him, and he tightened his grip on her hand. He had a sudden desire to protect Isabella from the hard truth about Marcus, about that life. Which was stupid. He should be forcing the truth into her mind. It was the only hope she had to survive, but at the same time, he didn't want to tarnish the innocence and hope within her. Her steadfast belief in the goodness of those she loved was exactly what he appreciated about Alaska. Isabella wasn't only of his past. She fit into both his worlds.

"I knew Dillon would get free," Ren said. "But I had to wait."

Luke kept a tight grip on Isabella's hand. "I understand." Apology implied and accepted.

"They were watching for your plane." The path turned and Dillon took a hard right into the woods off the trail. "You'll have less than five minutes."

Almost on cue, Luke heard the distant hum of another plane approaching. Son of a bitch. They would never outrun a plane on foot.

They were sunk.

CHAPTER FIFTEEN

Smart bastards, not to leave their plane on the ground where he could see it. He'd done a flyby first to make sure there was no one there.

"They're coming!" Isabella tripped.

Luke caught her before she fell. *Shit*. He had to get her out of there.

"They told me you have the necklace," Ren said.

Luke urged Isabella to go faster. "I do. I brought it for you."

"No." Ren held up his hand. "I don't want it. It brings death. I don't want to bring that onto my grandson. He's the last of the tribe, and I don't want him killed by a past that is about death. I have new ways and I want him to as well. The cycle of death must end."

Luke swore. "It's yours." He needed to ditch it. "Take the damn thing."

"No." Ren shook his head. "I don't accept it."

"Don't make him," Isabella panted. "We need it."

They headed down a steep hill, and Luke had to slow to let Isabella keep up. "For God's sake, Isabella! Don't you get it? The only answer is to get out. Ditch the necklace and leave."

"Like you did?" she snapped. "Abandoned your family? What did that get you? Loneliness? A changed name? No past, no present, no future? Is that a life?"

"Yeah, it is, as a matter of fact. A damned good one." But even as he spoke the words, he knew they weren't entirely true. He wasn't home. He didn't have roots. Didn't allow them. And he'd been feeling more and more like he wanted to put some down. Not in Boston. In Alaska. He wanted to be here. Isabella was making him want things he'd never let himself contemplate.

And he couldn't have them. It would endanger anyone around him.

Because he hadn't left behind Adam Fie. He never would. It pissed him off.

"This way," Ren said. There was a small boat tied to the river's bank. It had a motor in it, old and decrepit. "In."

Luke lifted Isabella into the boat, and was surprised to feel her muscles trembling beneath his hands. Shit. She was barely recovered from her infection and bullet wound. This was too much for her. He swept her up in his arms, sat down and anchored her in his lap, enfolding his arms around her to support her.

"Let me go." She started to struggle.

He tightened his grip on her. "You need to rest. Let me help."

She shot a wary look at him, and he recognized that expression in her eyes. The same one he'd seen before. The lack of trust, the inability to lean on someone, the refusal to let down her own guard and count on anyone but herself.

She might have on rose-colored glasses about Marcus, but life had taught her the same lessons Luke had learned.

In Isabella's expression, there was only loneliness. Desperation. The hard realization that the only one she could count on was herself.

He hugged her tightly and pressed his lips to her hair. "Just rest on me for now," he whispered. "Take advantage of the moment. You can go on your own later."

"Just for now," she repeated softly. The words seemed to relax her. Tension seeped from her body, and she slumped into him as she allowed the exhaustion consume her. He sensed the moment she stopped fighting, the instant she turned her safety and well-being over to him.

It should have made him tense to have a woman counting on him to keep her safe from Marcus. It should have stressed him. He didn't want to be responsible for a woman, especially one threatened by his father. Not again.

But with Isabella leaning on him, it just felt right.

He pressed his lips to her hair again and rested his chin on her shoulder as Ren launched them into the river. The frigid water lapped at the metal hull, and Luke eyed the sludge at the bottom of the boat. Slow leak? "Rest while you can," he said quietly to her. "We'll be on the run again soon."

She snuggled deeper against him, and he wrapped his arms around her, trying to imbue her trembling body with his heat. "Thank you," she whispered.

He rubbed his cheek against her hair. "For what?"

She leaned into his touch, making him smile. "For the break."

He nodded. He knew what she was talking about. A respite to let down her guard. To rest so she could go back to battle. Isabella was a survivor, and he knew she was replenishing her tanks. She wasn't giving up, she wasn't abdicating her mission to take care of herself, and she wasn't giving up her own strength. She was using his strength to bolster her own. She was smart, tough and beautiful.

He grinned. Also stubborn as hell, but it kept life interesting. He nuzzled his face in her hair as he watched the sky. He could hear the plane getting closer, but he couldn't see it. It sounded like it was approaching from the other direction, so, with luck, the aircraft would land at the campsite and the occupants wouldn't see them on the river. But he knew they were short on time. "Tell me everything, Ren."

Ren nodded as his grandson steered them down the river. "A week ago, they came to me and said you might be coming. I was supposed to alert them if you did, and I refused." Ren gave Luke a solemn look. "You stole from me, but you came to me for forgiveness. I saw you had changed your path, much as I was doing for myself. These men are the past you were trying to escape, and I wanted you to have the chance to let it go."

Luke cleared his throat, aware Isabella was listening to Ren's analysis of him. "So, yeah, then what happened?"

"They left, but I knew they would be back."

An inconsistency suddenly clicked in Luke's mind. "Wait a sec. When did you say this was?"

"Eight days ago."

He lightly squeezed Isabella's waist. "Isabella? When did you leave Marcus's?"

Her forehead was furrowed, and he knew she was making the same connection he was. "Three days ago. The necklace arrived that day and Marcus had me wear it that night for his party." She sat up slowly, and he supported her as she did so. "So how did they know you were going to be coming here that far ahead?"

Luke ground his jaw, not liking the thought that had jumped into his head. That it had been arranged. That this whole thing had been manipulated to draw him out. If that were the case . . . if he'd been exposed . . . if this was all about him . . . if Isabella had been used as a pawn to draw him out . . . "Shit." If that was the case, had Isabella been an innocent tool, or had she known what she was doing the whole time?

He eased her back from him so he could watch her face more intently, so he could scrutinize her. "How did you find out where I was?"

She was concentrating, and he could see the wheels in her mind turning as she tried to sort it out. "Marcus asked me to find you two weeks ago. He told me not to tell anyone or to even use my computer."

Luke checked the sky, but the oncoming plane hadn't come into view yet. He could hear it though, getting louder. "And did he mention I knew about the necklace?"

"Yes." She shifted on his lap. "The night of the party." She was quiet and thoughtful, putting together the pieces. "He asked me if I'd found you, and I said I had."

Luke swore. "You were sent after me. It was a setup."

She tensed and pulled back so she could see his face. "You think it was all a setup from the start? They wanted me to find you?"

"Yeah."

"But why?"

"Because they think I have the earrings."

She stared at him. "Do you?"

He went rigid at the question. Jesus. Had Isabella been in on it the whole time? Was she part of the plot? It all made so much sense. Once Marcus had realized he was on to the necklace, he'd probably realized he wanted them back, but he would have known Luke wouldn't cough up the earrings to him. So he'd sent Isabella to work her way under his skin.

She was already shaking her head. "No, no, it couldn't be about the earrings. If so, Marcus would have had to fake the kidnapping by Leon, so I would think I had to get your help to save him."

Luke tensed. There was no way he'd believe Isabella didn't think Marcus would set up a fake kidnapping. She might believe in Marcus, but she wasn't that naive.

But she wasn't finished. "I admit, he might set up a fake kidnapping, but he wouldn't have had Roseann shot. There's just no way." She looked up at Luke, and there was anguish in her expression. "Would he, Luke? Would he have a pregnant woman murdered in cold blood just to get me to run to you? I would have done it anyway. She didn't have to be shot." Her hand went to her heart. "Oh God, Roseann," she whispered, and then her voice broke.

And Luke knew in that moment that he believed in her. She hadn't come here to expose him. She was doing the best she could to survive. Whatever her role in this was, she was still an innocent.

He knew it in the core of his soul.

So he took her into his arms and held her close. He pressed his lips to her hair. "No, babe, I don't believe Marcus would kill a pregnant woman if he didn't need to." And as he said those words, he realized he believed them. Marcus was a lot of things, but he didn't kill for the sake of it. Marcus was a better man than that. Maybe he'd set up the kidnapping, but Nate and/or Leon had taken it further on their own.

"Thank you." Isabella raised her face so she could see him. Tears were glistening in her eyes, but they hadn't fallen. "Thank you for saying that."

"I believe it." He bent his head and kissed her softly.

She snuggled deeper against him and kissed him back. It was a gentle kiss, unlike anything he'd ever experienced. It wasn't a kiss of hot passion. It was a kiss of tenderness.

And it felt damn good.

Ren cleared his throat, and Luke broke the kiss. God, it felt good to trust her. He hadn't believed in anyone for a long time. He smiled at her and ran his fingers through her hair. "So, somehow Leon knew you'd be heading here before you even did. Did anyone besides you know where to find me?"

"No. Marcus didn't even want to know."

Luke had to give Marcus a nod on that one. If Marcus had known, then it was something people could try to leverage out of him. But he was a bastard for storing that information in Isabella and endangering her. "So Leon might have accessed your computer trail, somehow."

"He didn't even ask me. If he wanted to know, wouldn't that have been his first choice?"

Luke couldn't help the shudder that went through him at that suggestion, at what a man like Leon would be willing to do to an innocent like Isabella to get what he wanted. He tightened his grip on her, crushing her against his chest, trying to wipe away the images and memories in his mind. The blood, the carnage, the glazed visage of death . . . "Fuck." He pressed his face into her hair, and she wrapped her arms around him, as if she sensed his need.

She held him like no one had held him in years. And it felt incredible.

Which was why it was so fucking dangerous for them both.

With a grim smile, he pulled back. Now was not the time. It would never be the time. Not as long as Adam Fie still ran in his blood. Which meant never. Some ghosts couldn't be outrun.

But he'd become damned good at managing them.

"He didn't ask you because he didn't want you to know what he was planning. If you knew, then I would figure it out. The only way for it to work was if you were in the dark."

She leaned her head wearily against his chest, and he held her tight. "So why wouldn't he come after you directly then?"

"If he'd asked me for those earrings, he wouldn't have gotten them. But they probably figured I wouldn't turn you away." And they'd been right. "So, they set you on a path where I was your only option, and then figured that if you showed up with the necklace, I'd go see Ren, which I did." Luke eyed Ren's gun. It was resting on his lap, but it was still pointed at Luke. By accident or intention? "When did they take your grandson?"

"They came back about four hours ago," Ren said. "Took Dillon and said he would be returned when I handed you two over."

Luke rubbed his face in Isabella's hair. "Both of us? Did they say I would be with Isabella?"

Ren nodded. "They wanted both of you."

Did they want Luke Webber? Or was the hunt for Adam Fie? Had they made the connection yet between his two identities? He had to know the level of exposure. "Did they mention Adam Fie?"

Ren shook his head as the small craft bumped over the rough water. "No. Luke Webber."

It told Luke nothing. They could have kept his other identity under wraps. "I'm sorry Dillon was put in danger." And he was. One visit eight years ago had brought this death threat to Ren and his grandson. Yeah, it was possible that Leon had found Ren on his own, but Luke doubted it. Luke had identified Ren while he was still working for Marcus, so Leon had probably just acted on old files and assumed Luke would make contact again.

Which, of course, he had.

Luke realized he'd been fooling himself, thinking he could hide out in Alaska and not endanger those he came into contact with. He thought of Cort and Kaylie, and he knew his time in Alaska was up.

And for the first time since he'd walked out of his life eight years ago, he felt a heaviness in his chest that actually hurt.

Ren gave him a grim look. "You're different from them, Luke Webber. You have a rare quality. But by coming here today, you brought death back into my life and threatened my grandson. Inside you festers the same poison that drives those men."

Luke had no rebuttal. He knew he was poison, and he could already feel it boiling to the surface after so many years of being held in abeyance.

"For the good in your heart, I gave you a head start from your demons. For the second, I have to let you burn in your own fires." Ren nodded at the river. "God-speed on your journey."

Luke didn't have to look at the water to know it would be a death sentence for Isabella. He could probably survive it. Not Isabella, in her weakened state. "I accept responsibility. And I will do my best to fix it."

Ren shook his head. "I don't need your help. I can take care of my own. Our paths split now and will never cross again. Leave us."

Isabella stiffened against him, and a plane came into view over the treetops. It was heading straight toward the river. "Take us to shore." It was a long shot, but if he could make it back to his plane—

"No. You get out now." Ren raised his gun and cocked the trigger. "Now."

Luke could tell from Ren's expression that he was prepared to kill. Adam Fie would have accepted those stakes and upped the ante. Despite Ren's claim that the poison still ran in Luke's blood, and despite the urge to rip that gun out of Ren's hands and take over the boat, Luke forced himself to sit still. He could not open that door to Adam Fie. It was too dangerous. "The girl will die if we jump."

The plane was overhead now, and Isabella gaped up at it. It was flying low, maybe ten feet above their heads. Close enough for his face to be seen, but Luke didn't look up. As long as there was a chance he was still only Luke Webber to their pursuers, he wasn't giving them game.

Keeping his face hidden in Isabella's hair, he cradled her against his chest and moved so he was sitting on the side of the boat. "Wrap your legs and arms around me." He wasn't going to force Ren to kill a friend.

Besides, getting a bullet in the chest wasn't exactly conducive to saving Isabella from the bad guys, was it? Luke always prided himself on keeping the ultimate goal in mind. Such as staying alive.

A swim in a subarctic steam was crappy, but it was better odds than being shot in the chest at point-blank range, which he knew Ren would do without hesitation.

"Come on, Isabella. We're going for a swim."

"Dear God, I hope you know what you're doing." She plastered herself against his front and he wrapped his arms around her.

The plane was past them now, and he knew the pilot would have to circle back around to see the boat again. For the next forty-five seconds, they were invisible to their pursuers.

Now was the moment.

"Hang tight." He met the older man's gaze, and without breaking eye contact, Luke tipped himself and Isabella backward into the river that would kill them within minutes.

CHAPTER SIXTEEN

The shock of the cold water ripped the breath right out of her. Her muscles went rigid. She couldn't breathe. She was so cold. Frozen.

Dying.

Luke kicked them to the surface and she gasped as her head burst above the surface.

"Take a breath," he ordered. "We're going back under."

Isabella didn't take time to argue. She sucked in what she could, and then Luke pulled them back below the surface. Her arms were so numb she couldn't even tell whether she was still holding on to him. Her arms were like noodles, her legs useless.

But Luke's grip on her was like a vise, his body a shield from the buffeting waters that felt like daggers ripping through her skin. Her lungs were starting to burn. She needed to breathe again.

Luke shoved them upward, and her head burst out of the water. She gasped, sucking in air. God. So cold. Had to get out.

"I know, babe. I know. One more time."

Luke started to drag them down again, and this time she fought it. She was terrified she wouldn't come up again.

"Isa." Luke's voice was a reassuring sound in her ear. "You have to trust me right now."

With her life? "I can't," she gasped.

"You have no choice." His ruthless, determined arrogance drilled through her panic.

She realized he wouldn't let them die. Not her. Not him. Not yet. *I trust you.*

She nodded and stopped fighting. She put herself in his hands and prayed she was right.

He didn't reply. Just kept his gaze on hers as he pulled them below the surface again.

Isabella sucked in a breath and let him take them down into the icy depths for a third time.

Luke knew he had less than a minute to get Isabella out of the water. Her lips were blue, her eyes were sunken, and she was shaking violently against him.

Fifty seconds.

The time clicked off in his mind as he kicked them fiercely through the water, toward the one oasis he'd been able to locate on their first surfacing. The plane had been roaring overhead, but it had been flying low, upstream away from him, as if they hadn't seen them go over into the river.

Forty seconds.

He swam harder, toward the small fishing boat that had been drifting not too far from them. The minute he'd seen it, he'd known it was a better option than trying to reach shore. On shore, they'd be too vulnerable once that plane landed. The boat would keep them moving in the right direction, and its small cabin was large enough to hide them.

His lungs were starting to strain, and he shot them to the surface so as not to tax Isabella beyond what she could handle. He popped them up. The boat was only a few feet away. "Hey!" he shouted. "Help!"

No one appeared.

"Hey!"

He heard the plane roaring, and he looked over her shoulder. It was banking to circle back. Once they were on the approach, there was no way Luke would be able to get them in the boat without being seen, but Isabella was out of time in the water.

She was limp in his arms. Her head was on his shoulder. She was utterly still, except for the violent trembling of her body. "You're not going to die," he commanded her. "Come on!"

He broke out toward the boat and launched himself upward. He caught the rail with his hand, but the force of his descent ripped his numb grip right off it. He swore as he fell back toward the water—

A hand shot over the edge of boat and clamped around his wrist.

Luke grinned as a weathered face appeared over the edge. Black hair, dark skin, a native Alaskan all the way. A man who was probably in his forties, but carried enough sun and wind in his skin to pass for seventy. "Can we get a ride?"

The man barked over his shoulder, and another face appeared. A woman this time. Younger, with eyes of natural beauty and grace. She immediately reached out for Isabella, and Luke didn't hesitate. He didn't stop to question whether the woman had the strength to help. He simply shifted his weight and then basically threw Isabella upward toward the gal.

He stayed ready to catch her, but the woman caught Isabella under the arms and dragged her over the rim.

Luke's anchor extended his other hand, and Luke

latched on to it. Wrist to wrist, a grip tight enough to withstand the pull of the river on his body.

"On three," the man said.

Luke nodded and braced his boots on the side of the boat.

"One, two, three!"

Luke shoved himself off the boat upward toward his rescuer. His momentum gave them the leverage they needed, and together they dragged him over the rail. He landed on his face on the boat. His muscles were shaking, but he shoved himself up. The woman was bent over Isabella, already unbuttoning her wet clothes.

"The plane is after us," Luke said quickly. "We need to hide."

The man and the woman looked skyward at the plane, which was about three seconds from finishing its turn and coming into viewing range again.

The man ran to the miniscule cabin and jerked aside the curtain as Luke lunged for Isabella. He scooped her off the floor and dove into the tiny opening as the plane completed its turn. The man dropped the curtain, throwing them into near darkness, while the roar of the plane filled the air.

Luke was surprised to discover that the front of the cabin stretched below the deck, making it long enough for them to lie down. He bent his head over Isabella. "Hey, Isa." He rested his hand on her icy cheek. "Come back to me, hon."

He felt like cheering when her eyes flickered open.

"We're safe now," he said. "We need to get the wet clothes off you, okay?"

"Y-y-y-yeah." Her teeth were chattering so hard he

could hear them knocking as she stared to fumble with her sweatshirt.

The flap lifted and the woman poked her head inside. "I'm Inite," she said. "My husband is Roger. You both need to get those clothes off and get dry ones." She set a pile of thick blankets inside. "There are clothes on that shelf." She pointed to a plywood board braced above Luke's head. "Put them on. We will watch the plane. They just flew past and are turning again. We will see if they noticed you come on board."

"Th-th-thank y-y-you," whispered Isabella.

"This is Isabella, and I'm Luke." He caught Inite's hand as she started to pull back. *Thank you.*

She smiled, a large, genuine smile. "You think we would let you drown?" She was still laughing as she ducked back outside.

That was Alaska. The land he loved. Where people put survival first.

Damn it. He was finding a way to stay.

But first, they were staying alive.

Which meant the clothes were coming off. Now.

Isabella couldn't stop shaking. Her head was pounding. Her fingers throbbed with pain when she tried to grasp the hem of her drenched sweatshirt. "Luke."

"I'm on it." He pulled her upright and settled her between his thighs so she was resting against his chest.

Even through the soaked sweatshirt, she could feel the heat from his body and she tried to push herself harder against him.

Modesty and propriety didn't make either of them hesitate, and she held up her arms as he dragged the sodden material over her head. He jerked his own shirt off next, and he immediately wrapped his arms around her, pulling her back against his chest.

His arms were doubled around her. She could feel him trembling as well, and his skin was cold, but beneath his flesh was heat. Warmth she couldn't generate herself. "God, you feel good." She wanted to get closer.

"Pants. Lie down." He shifted her so she was on her back and unfastened her jeans.

The light was dim, but not so dark Luke couldn't see her. Sudden heat flushed through her as Luke worked the drenched material over her hips. She was still trembling violently, her insides shaking as if they were going to rattle right out of her belly, and yet she was aware of each inch of exposed flesh as Luke pulled off her jeans.

He looked up at her face as he pulled them over her feet, and his gaze was intense. So intense.

He didn't break their connection as he stripped out of his own jeans and underwear, and then he was crawling back over her. Naked. As she was, except for her bra and her thong underwear.

She was so cold, and suddenly she didn't care that they were almost naked. The wet material was like ice. She fumbled for the straps, but she couldn't make her hands work. "My bra. Get it off."

Luke moved fast, ditching her final garments with swift efficiency. Then he was above her again, his knees on either side of her hips as he snagged the blankets. His thighs were icy and his body trembling almost as much as hers was. He shifted his weight as he tossed the blankets over him and wrapped the worn fabric around them, tucking the edges beneath her.

And then he settled himself on her naked body so they were skin to skin from head to toe.

It was too intimate, too romantic, and it was the only thing that was going to save her life.

So she wrapped her arms around him and welcomed his weight, his heat and his body. She pulled him closer until he was blanketing her in the most sensual, erotic embrace of her life.

Except, of course, for the fact that her teeth were chattering uncontrollably and she couldn't stop shaking.

"Hey, Isa." Luke slid his arms beneath her shoulders and wrapped her up in an all-consuming embrace. She buried her face in his muscular shoulder and shuddered against him as he tangled his legs with hers. Thigh to thigh. Their calves were entwined. His feet were wrapped around hers. "You're okay. We're safe now."

But as the words left his mouth, she heard the roar of the plane again. "They know," she whispered. She started to shake again, this time from fear. "I can't go back in the water. I'll never survive it."

"I know." Luke tightened his arms around her and pulled her closer with his legs. "We're not going in again."

His skin was warm now, and she felt heat beginning to build between them. The warmth was starting to penetrate the deathly chill trying to consume her. She thought he was still trembling, but she was shaking so hard she wasn't sure whether it was him or her.

Luke pulled the blanket over their heads, enveloping them in darkness. "Listen to me, Isa." His voice was low and confident. Unworried. "If they knew we were on the boat, they'd have dropped someone on here by now. They're still trying to find us."

The air beneath the blanket began to heat up, and

Isabella took a deep breath, inhaling the warm heat. "They'll check the boat, won't they? I mean, where else could we be?"

"Hey." He rested his cheek against hers, and she snuggled closer to his heat. She craved more of his warmth. She needed him to quell the aching coldness in her body. "They'll drop someone to search the shore for us first. The odds are higher that we went to land."

His breath was hot against her neck, and her tremors were lessening. "So, you think they won't check the boat?"

Luke settled deeper onto her, and her legs slipped apart as he slid his own between them. She tucked her feet around his thighs to pull him closer, trying desperately not to think of the intimacy of their position.

It was dark under the blanket, and the rhythmic pitch of the boat kept rocking them against each other, building a tempo between them.

"They'll come back for the boat," Luke said. "If it's Leon, he'll check it out before leaving."

"So what do we do?" She wiggled her arms out from under his weight and wrapped them around his neck, hugging tightly. He felt so good she didn't want to let go. She didn't want him to move.

"We'll be gone by then. The minute they go back upstream to drop searchers, we'll jet."

She nodded, not bothering to ask where exactly they were going to go. She had a feeling Luke didn't know yet, but that he'd create the opportunity when it was time, just as he had in the river.

She shuddered as her muscles began to relax. Despite the constant hum of the airplane as it searched the river for them, she felt safe. Luke's body was heavy, and his strength was obvious. He'd kept them alive in the water, and she still remembered the sensation of him tossing her up into Inite's arms, despite his own exhaustion and depletion. He was smart and strategic, keeping them just ahead of their pursuers.

And now . . . he was bringing her back to life with the heat of his body.

In the darkness of their shelter, with the intimacy of their position . . . it felt surreal. A special world where rules didn't apply. She felt close to him. Bonded. Intimate in a way she'd never been with anyone, not in her whole life.

It was a fleeting moment. A sensation that would fade the moment they pulled back the blanket and faced the world again. She knew her sense of isolation would come back. And Luke would still refuse to help her save Marcus. He would still leave, and she knew she couldn't count on him.

Right now, though, he was staying where he was, and she knew, with absolute certainty, he would never leave her behind on this boat. And that felt good. Really, really good.

She wanted to live this moment. Make it the most she could, so she could relive it again and again, and remember what it felt like to be safe, truly safe.

So she would never forget her ultimate goal, to find a home and security. To create a life for herself in which she would feel safe, secure and loved every day, every hour, every second of her life.

He shifted his weight, lifting off of her slightly. "Am I too heavy?"

"No!" She used her legs to pull his hips back down on top of her, and he came willingly. Only this time, she felt the first hints of the hardness of his erection as he settled between her legs again.

Excitement pulsed deep inside her core, and she knew she should shift and move him to the side. But she didn't want to. She didn't want to lose this moment and the intense feeling it gave her. "Luke?"

"Yeah." He adjusted his hips and nestled himself deeper between her thighs. The tip of his penis was resting right against the crevice at the top of her inner thigh. So close. Just a shift and he'd be inside.

But he was utterly still.

She sensed he was waiting.

For what?

CHAPTER SEVENTEEN

Luke wanted to be inside her.

More than he'd ever wanted any woman in his entire life.

His quads were tense, vibrating with the effort of not making that final movement. Her body felt amazing beneath him. Her breasts were crushed against his chest. Her left foot was making small circles on the back of his calf, and he had a feeling she wasn't even aware she was doing it. Her skin smelled amazing. No more scent of lavender. She simply smelled like herself. Like damp skin, with the faintest aroma of something sweet, getting more intense as she warmed up.

She slid her fingers into his hair, and he closed his eyes at the sensation. A gentle, tentative touch exploring his head. It wasn't a caress. Not yet. It was an exploration, an instinct. He knew what she was feeling.

He needed to touch her as well.

Hell, he'd needed to touch her since the first moment he'd seen her in the bar. But now that he'd seen her courage, her vulnerabilities, she was so much more. He didn't just want to be inside her. He needed it.

"Luke?"

Something trembled inside him at the sound of her

voice. So soft, so feminine, low pitched with the back-ground music of delicate bells. "Yeah."

"Why do you hate your dad?"

Luke tensed, and he felt that all-too-familiar hard-ness boil in his chest. "I don't want to talk about it."

She moved, and he jumped at the sudden sensation of her hands on his cheeks. "Luke," she whispered, "I need to know what Marcus is really like. I need to un-derstand why I have a bullet in my shoulder and why Ren's grandson was taken."

They were the words he'd wanted to hear. The green light to set her straight, so she could take back her life. But now that he had the opportunity . . . shit. He didn't want to break through that golden bubble she'd erected around herself. Damn Marcus for being such a bastard and not being worthy of this woman's love.

She stroked his cheek lightly. "I can handle a lot, Luke. It makes me stronger to get information and to know what I'm facing."

Shit. He could have said those words himself. He was always hungry for information, and information had been his weapon his whole life. How could he turn that down?

He put his hand over hers and squeezed.

She responded in kind, and he focused on that sen-sation, the physical connection with another human being. A liberty he hadn't allowed himself in so long.

And then he thought of the story he'd never told to anyone.

The one he hadn't even allowed himself to revisit.

The past that had been off limits for so long was fi-nally about to be put back on the table.

He began to talk.

*   *   *

Luke released Isabella's hand, and she sensed he was putting distance between them.

She felt the loss of his touch, but she didn't hold on. She knew what it was like to need distance.

"I was eight years old," Luke said. "Sound asleep in my room."

He fell quiet then, and she sensed he was revisiting something. "Luke?"

He shifted his weight. "Sorry. I was remembering my room. Haven't thought about it in a long time."

Isabella ran her finger through his hair. "Lots of toys, I bet."

He snorted. "Yeah, all in the closet. Marcus had a fit if I trashed my room. Too much money spent on the decor."

Isabella's heart tightened for the boy who hadn't been allowed to be a child. She sensed there was far more weight to his childhood than messing up his room. "Your dad didn't play with you?"

Luke made another noise of disgust. "Marcus, play? He was working all the time. He'd been dirt poor his whole life, and he was working his ass off to become rich as hell. He opened his business right after I was born, and he was working 24/7 on that thing."

"What about your mom?"

"My mom." Luke's voice completely changed, and she wished she could see his face. He sounded so tender, so soft. "She was the best. She was so different from Marcus. So loving. So gentle. She didn't partake in his world, and we just did our own thing."

Isabella's throat tightened. "My mom was like that," she said. "She was my best friend."

His hand cupped her chin. "She died?"

"Yes." Tears surged, and she had to blink them back.

"But we're talking about you now, not me. Tell me about that night. What happened?"

"That night." His voice had gone flat again and she felt his body stiffen against hers. "My mom woke me up. She was still in her nightgown and I could tell she was terrified." There was no emotion in his voice, just a hard shield. "She said we had to go. I didn't have time to pack. She grabbed my hand and we ran down the hall." His voice grew distant, as if he were remembering. "I could hear an argument downstairs. Men yelling. My dad shouting. My dad never raised his voice. Ever. Scared the hell out of me to hear him yelling."

Isabella could see it in her mind. The little boy racing down the massive hall in his pajamas, clinging to his mother. God, she'd lived with that kind of fear so much. It was awful.

"We got in her car and peeled out of there. My mom's hands were shaking, and she wouldn't tell me where we were gong. She just said Marcus had gotten into trouble and we needed to go away for a while." There was an edge to his voice now, a bitterness.

She wanted to touch him so badly, to comfort him, but she didn't dare. "And then what happened?"

"We hopped a plane to the Caribbean. Camped out on some beach. Had a little bungalow."

Her heart began to race in fear of the ugly finale she sensed was coming.

"It was just before dawn that they came," Luke said. This time, there was emotion in his voice. Pain. "I was out on the beach fishing for crabs. Should've been in the cabin with my mom, but I was tired of her crying and acting so scared, so I snuck out. Ditched her. Then a black jeep drove up. There were four of them. I could see the faces of only two, but I'd seen them in my dad's office before. I wasn't supposed to talk to anyone my dad worked with. So I stayed in the water while they went into the cabin. Then I heard her scream."

Isabella set her hand on his face, and he pulled away.

"I started running for the bungalow. She was screaming again and again. Not for me. Just screaming with agony. With pain. With suffering."

Tears filled her eyes, but she said nothing, sensing he wanted no comfort or sympathy. She had to fist her hands to keep from reaching out for him.

"I got to the door and ran inside. She was on the floor, covered in gashes. So much blood. Jesus, there was so much blood." His breath was coming heavier now, and his body was slick with sweat between her thighs. "I tackled the nearest one, but he just threw me aside. I landed next to my mother. She was gasping for air at this point, and she grabbed me and she told me she loved me. That she would always love me. And then she said he hadn't meant to endanger her. That he hadn't meant to do it. That I should forgive him and let him take care of me."

"He?" The word stuck in her throat.

"Marcus." Luke spat the word. "Before I could respond, before I could even say I loved her, one of the guys yanked me away, and I realized I'd fucked up. That I'd forgotten to protect her. But it was too late. He held me. Told me to watch. Told me to take the message back to Marcus."

Isabella closed her eyes.

"And then he shot my mother in the head."

Luke hadn't felt the pain in decades.

Hadn't smelled that metallic scent of blood.

Hadn't heard the anguish in his mother's voice.

And now it was back.

All back.

As if he were eight years old again.

He dropped his head, trying to find his protections again. To shut it down before it could debilitate him. Had to—

Isabella's fingers brushed over his cheeks. The lightest touch. Barely there. So tender. So tentative. So fragile. "Luke."

He didn't move. He just lay there, concentrating on the feel of her skin against his. It felt good. So good. She was alive. She was life. She was courage. Somehow, he doubted Isabella would lie down and let someone work her over like his mother had. She would fight, and she wouldn't stop until she'd won.

Isabella was different.

She tugged lightly on his chin and he allowed her to turn his head. She kissed him, and he froze at the sudden, intimate touch. A feathering and then it was gone.

A deep need roared to life inside him. "Isa." He tunneled his fingers into her hair and tugged her face toward his. He needed to wipe away the memories with the touch of her flesh, the kiss of her lips, the courage that vibrated in her very core. He didn't give her a chance to stop him or to doubt her own response. He just lowered his head and took her the way he wanted to.

Her mouth was hot and wet, and she kissed him back greedily. No hesitation. His body lurched at her instant response, and suddenly there was nothing stopping him. His kiss deepened, and she met his assault with equal fervor and desperation.

She slipped her arms around his neck, holding so tightly he was surprised by her strength. It felt good, damn good, to have her hanging on to him, as if she were trying to get closer, to deepen the kiss. He ran his hand down her side. Her skin was so soft, her body firm and muscled, but with all the curves of a woman.

"Isa." He growled her name and yanked her closer. Kissed her hard. No more seduction. Just a raw wanting. A need. For her. Her kiss and her touch were more powerful than the memories. Her kiss was about life and Isa was about survival.

She wasn't weak and afraid like his mother had been.

Isa was a fighter. "You're so strong," he whispered, as he kissed his way down her neck. "You're so sexy. So courageous."

She tunneled her fingers in his hair. "I'm scared all the time."

"Doesn't matter." He kissed her breast, then pressed his lips to her nipple.

She made a small noise and arched her back. "Except with you," she whispered. "Sometimes you make me feel safe."

"I swear I'll keep you safe." Luke kissed his way along her ribs, across her belly. "I won't let anything happen to you." How right those words felt. The idea of being responsible for another woman had been his worst nightmare for years, and yet it felt so right to claim Isabella's safety as his own.

He needed that.

He needed to protect her.

To stop the cycle of violence with her.

She was his respite. Somehow, he knew if he could save her, the demons would be gone. "Isa." He growled her name and took her mouth in his again. His kiss was ravenous now. A ruthless assault on her, and when she responded, his whole body amped up.

He needed her. Now. He needed to sink deep inside her, to make her his, to declare he was taking responsibility for her. "Isa." He whispered her name as he kissed his way back down her body. To her belly. To the smooth lines of her skin. He stopped as he encountered bare skin where thick curls should be.

Blood surged to his cock as he kissed his way over the velvet skin. Waxing? Shit, he had no idea, but it was incredible. The feel of her bare skin against his lips. He kissed lower, found a small tuft of hair at the peak of her femininity, and then he kissed lower. Her skin was damp and warm. An incredible taste. Sweet and musky. A combination of softness and strength, just like Isabella.

"Luke." His name was a whisper on her lips.

"Isa." He moved his way back up her body and moved his hips between her legs. Positioned himself at the core of her entrance as the blanket slipped off his shoulders. He bent his head and kissed her as he began to nudge. "I need to be inside you."

She opened her eyes and met his gaze. "I need you, too. Just for now. Just for today."

Yes. Intense burning filled him and he tensed himself to plunge inside.

"Hey!" The curtain flipped up and Inite poked her head into the small area. "The plane's coming back! It looks like they're going to drop someone on the boat!"

Luke swore and rolled off Isabella as Inite dropped the curtain. "Shit. I thought we had more time." He grabbed jeans and a shirt off the shelf and tossed them at Isabella.

"The necklace. We can't forget it." She was already on her knees, yanking the black sweatshirt over her head.

Luke shoved his hand into his pants pocket and tossed her the jewels. She tucked it into her jeans while

Luke rifled through the dry clothes. By the time Luke had concluded that none of the men's clothes were big enough, Isabella was already buttoning her fly. He jammed a dry T-shirt over his head, yanked on his wet jeans and then shoved his boots onto his feet.

The plane's engine was louder now, a deafening roar. Maybe twenty feet away? "Shit! Come on!"

Isabella tugged on her boots. "Are we going over again?" Her voice was steely. Resolved. Determined. Not panicked.

"Yeah. I don't want Inite and her husband to get in trouble—"

There was a sudden thump and the boat shook.

"*Shit.*" Luke grabbed Isabella's hand and yanked her to the side, away from the curtain. "Get back."

"What? I—"

"Stay back," a male voice ordered, and Luke gritted his teeth at the familiar voice. "Head toward shore up ahead and then get out."

Nate Sampson. He'd recognize Luke in an instant.

Luke grabbed Isabella's wrist and pulled her behind him. Her skin was damp, and he could feel her pulse hammering in her wrist. "Nate doesn't know you're here," she whispered. "You can still hide from him."

There were no windows. No way out except through Nate.

A hand grabbed the curtain and yanked it back. Light flooded the cabin, exposing Isabella's terrified face.

Luke took one look at her and didn't hesitate. He ripped the curtain out of Nate's hand, shoved Isabella into the shadows and then stepped out onto the deck of the boat, right into the gun of Nate Sampson.

CHAPTER EIGHTEEN

Nate's ruddy face went blank with shock as he met the gaze of the man who had once been his best friend. *"Adam?"*

Luke lunged for the gun. Nate jerked in response and fired off a shot as Luke came at him. Luke swore as the bullet grazed his shoulder and he dove to the right to evade a second shot.

Shit. Nate's reactions had become much quicker since Luke had last known him. Eight years ago, the six-foot gap between them wouldn't have given Nate enough time to pull his shit together, and Luke had been banking on that fact.

Not anymore.

Luke jumped up and spun around. Nate had both hands on the gun, which was aimed at Luke's heart. Stalemate.

For a moment, neither man said a word, and Luke felt his shoulder burning. Nate's face was pale, and his blue eyes were still wide with surprise, but Luke could see the wheels turning in his mind as he quickly assessed the situation. As he realized the value of what he had at gunpoint. Nate's mind was sharper than it had been eight years ago, and his grip on the gun steadier.

Nate had been working on his skills.

Luke had been trying to forget his.

Nate looked the same. Shaved head trying to hide the effects of balding, narrow black eyes, a perpetual half growth on his face. His face harder now. More lined. No longer was there a quirk at the corner of his mouth ready to smile.

He wasn't wearing Marcus's standard-issue expensive coat and tie. He wore jeans and boots, and a heavy jacket. Ready for hunting a girl through Alaska.

Luke felt his upper lip curl as he stared into the face of the man who had once been his best friend. His only friend, really.

A man who had shot a pregnant woman only three days ago.

A path that would have been Luke's if he'd stayed. But he felt no sympathy for the man who'd been sucked into Marcus's hell. Just disgust. "Nate."

Nate still looked shocked. "What the fuck are you doing here, Fie?"

Luke shrugged. Didn't bother correcting Nate as to his real name. Yeah, he'd been tagged, but at the moment, Nate wasn't connecting Luke Webber and Adam Fie, and the longer he kept it that way, the safer Cort and Kaylie would be. Though he had a bad suspicion that even though Nate had been blindsided by the appearance of Adam Fie, Leon and Marcus knew exactly whom they'd been hunting. It did show that Nate was on the bottom of the food chain, though. Leon or Marcus was running the show, for sure. "I'm just passing through," Luke replied. "You?" He noted that the plane had gone up ahead and appeared to be banking for a landing just off to the right of the river.

"Looking for a girl." Nate's eyes flicked toward the canopy. "Seems like you got her first. Isa. Come out here."

Luke tensed. "I'm alone."

"Yeah? Then you won't give a shit if I shoot a couple holes in the cabin?" Nate raised the gun at the cabin.

Inite squeaked in protest, and her husband pulled her against him, his hand over her mouth. She went still against him, but Luke knew Nate wouldn't hesitate to use them for leverage if he thought it would work.

"There's no girl," Luke said quietly. He began to edge toward the side of the boat, as if he were going to try to make a break for it. If Nate believed Luke was trying to get away, he'd also believe there was no Isabella. Nate knew Adam well enough to know he'd never leave an innocent like Isabella behind to take the heat.

Nate raised the gun at Luke as he neared the edge. "You try it, and I'll cap your ass. There's no way I'm losing you."

"You'll have to shoot me, then." Luke moved closer to the side, took his gaze off Nate long enough to inspect the water, as if trying to assess the best route.

But he kept his attention on Nate, waiting for the slightest hesitation. All he needed was one small opening. Luke nudged the anchor with the toe of his boot. Small. Maybe eight pounds. He hooked his boot under it and lifted it lightly as he pretended to look over toward the shore.

He knew he could flip that anchor into his hand and have it in the air moving toward Nate in a fraction of a second. All he needed was that opportunity. He'd underestimated Nate's reaction time a moment ago.

Not again.

Luke could see Nate considering the options and debating who was worth more: Isabella or Adam.

He knew he was.

Except that Isabella still had the necklace. Fuck. He shouldn't have given it back to her.

All Luke needed was for Nate to decide to check out the cabin and then he'd have his opportunity. So he shrugged. "Check it out for yourself. See if I'm telling the truth."

Nate didn't move, and Luke could see his friend trying to work over Luke's words in his mind. He clearly knew Luke had a plan, but he couldn't decide the best angle to combat it.

Luke grinned to himself. Maybe Nate hadn't changed so much.

Nate narrowed his eyes. Then, without taking his gaze off Luke, he whipped his gun toward the cabin and began to shoot.

The first bullet tore through the wood inches from Isabella's cheek. The wood exploded and splinters flew into her face.

Isabella dropped to the floor and covered her head as another bullet hit where she'd been standing. And another. And another. Rapid fire.

Light began to pepper the small cabin.

The next shot was lower, barely skimming her head. *Shit!*

There was a sudden shout of fury. Light flooded the cabin as Luke burst through the opening and dove on top of her. He pulled her beneath him and his arms went around her head, cradling her with his body. His legs were on either side of hers, and his body was a human shield.

The gunshots stopped immediately.

"You okay?" Luke's voice was harsh. Strained. "You hit?"

Tears filled her eyes at the sensation of his body around hers. At the realization he'd charged into a battlefield just to protect her. "I'm fine," she managed.

Luke let out his breath and he dropped his head to hers.

For a moment, neither of them moved. She didn't want to move. Didn't want to dislodge him. He was so heavy, and it made her feel safe and protected. Cherished. Like she wasn't alone in her battle anymore.

"You bringing her out or should I start shooting again?" Nate's smug voice drifted through the curtain.

Luke swore, and he rolled off her. He pulled her to her feet, and blood seeped from his shoulder. "You're hurt—"

He intercepted her hand on its way to his injury. "Listen to me."

She caught the urgency in his voice. "What?"

"He's going to try to get us into the plane. Stay back and out of the way, and run if you get the chance. I need to co-opt that flight. We can't get on it. Do you understand?"

God, it felt good not to be trying to fight on her own. "What can I do?"

He gave her a grim look. "Not sure yet. Just stay alert and we'll figure it out on the fly." He narrowed her eyes. "You okay with that?"

"Absolutely." Her whole life had been an on-the-fly survival trek. She'd never had enough stability to plan ahead.

"Then let's go." He squeezed her hand. "I need to pretend I don't care about you, so don't take offense."

Pretend he didn't care? Did that mean he did?

"Three seconds," Nate warned.

Isabella tensed, remembering Roseann's body.

"Isa?"

She quickly nodded. "Okay. I won't take offense if you start saying nasty stuff about me."

He grinned. "That's my girl." He kissed her forehead, then turned and walked out. "Stay behind me," he said.

She followed Luke out into the sunlight.

Nate was waiting for them, and the sight of that gun trained on them made her stomach turn. Her legs began to tremble.

Nate smiled. "Isa. Nice to see you."

Luke moved so he was between them.

Nate had his phone to his ear. "Yeah," he said. "It's me. Guess what I found."

Luke swore and she felt him tense to go after Nate. She caught his arm as Nate closed his finger on his trigger and aimed at her heart. Not at Luke's heart. At hers. Because she was a bigger threat than Luke?

That made no sense.

But even as she stood there, she sensed Luke stand down. Still ready, but no longer about to attack. That threat had been enough.

She looked up at him as Nate spoke into the phone.

"Adam Fie." Nate sounded so smug. "In the flesh."

Luke flinched as if he'd been struck, and then a dark anger settled on him. His shoulders were rigid, and the tendons in his forearms bulged from his skin. Eyes narrowed, jaw clenched, raw anger etched on his face.

Nate smiled at them. "Yeah, I'll bring him in. Got the girl, too." He paused and then grinned at Isabella. "I'll have no trouble convincing her to tell me where the necklace is." His smile faded. "Fine. I'll let you do it."

He clicked the phone off, and grinned at Luke. "Welcome back, Fie. There's quite the party forming in your honor. You've been missed. You'll be an asset to have back on the team."

"I'm retired," Luke bit out.

"On sabbatical."

Isabella couldn't believe Nate's arrogant tone. He'd always had an edge she hadn't liked, but he was even worse now. Like he was finally the man. The power. Staring into the visage of the man she'd known for six years, whom she'd trusted, Isabella couldn't hold it in. "She was pregnant! How could you do that?"

Nate barely spared her a glance. "What are you talking about?"

"Roseann! My friend who you shot! She was pregnant!"

Nate shrugged. "She should have answered my questions then."

Luke set his hand on Isabella's arm. "Easy, hon," he said quietly.

He sounded so gentle, but when she looked up at him, he was studying Nate intensely. Watching his reaction. Learning? "You bastard," Luke said quietly. It wasn't a comment.

It was a threat.

Nate scowled at him. "Hey, fuckup, you took off. It's your fault we're in this mess, and you're just the guy we need to fix it."

Luke narrowed his eyes. "What mess?"

One bead of sweat trickled down Nate's brow. "That whole night got totally out of control. Marcus's plan went to hell—"

"Marcus's plan?" Isabella interrupted. "You guys kidnapped him!"

It was Nate's turn to flinch. "Hell, no! That was how it was supposed to look. He's fine. He's had us searching for you to make sure you're okay."

Hope welled up in Isabella's heart. "He's okay?"

Luke took her arm. "Don't trust him," he said quietly. "He shot Roseann. That's all I need to know."

A capillary twitched beneath Nate's right eye, and she heard Luke's sharp intake of breath, as if that little twitch spoke volumes.

What had Luke just learned?

That twitch had spoken volumes to Luke.

Nate was telling the truth: there was a hell of a mess going on and Nate was nervous as shit about it.

Chaos created opportunity, and Luke was the king of taking advantage of opportunity. "You didn't mean to shoot Roseann, did you?"

Nate shot Luke a look. "No."

Luke nodded, pretending to give his friend sympathy. "Sucks."

Suspicion flickered across Nate's face as the boat bumped up against the shore. "Not so bad."

Shit. He'd pushed it too hard. Difficult to think clearly with that fucking gun aimed at Isabella's heart. He was afraid to push it until he had her out of range. Too many damn memories. He was getting it right this time. No screwups.

But he also needed to know what he was up against. "Who were you talking to?" Who knew Adam Fie had been found? Jesus.

He'd been found.

Instinct told him to kick ass and bolt. To disappear again. But his tight grip on Isabella's arm was like a ce-ment block wrapped around his ankle. She had to be safe first. Had to be. Couldn't leave her behind. Had to get her safe first.

But it wasn't so easy anymore. Because Adam Fie was a wanted man, and his presence would bring all hell down on anyone associated with him.

Especially now that the necklace had been found.

With that new tidbit, Adam Fie and the information in his head were worth over five hundred million dollars.

Bloody hell.

Inite and her husband scrambled out of the boat onto the shore. Roger grabbed a long rope and backed away, still holding onto his boat. "We're here."

Nate waved his gun. "Out. Both of you."

Luke caught Isabella's arm and helped her over the edge of the craft to shore, keeping his body between her and the gun. His mind was still whirling as he strategized ways to get the gun back and get the plane. Chances were good he knew the pilot. A little help from a fellow Alaskan? Yeah, maybe.

But he couldn't afford to get anyone shot.

"If Marcus is part of this, let me talk to him," Isabella said to Nate, interrupting Luke's thoughts.

Luke took her arm. "He's playing you," he muttered.

She shot a frantic look at him, and he saw the desperation in her eyes. The need to know Marcus was okay. The need to be reassured. "Don't trust Nate," he said quietly. "He shot Roseann," he reminded her again. He'd seen the pain in her face. He knew that would register.

Her face paled. "Marcus would never have ordered that."

Maybe. At this point, Luke wasn't placing bets.

If Marcus had had any idea Adam Fie was findable, he'd have done anything to get him back.

Isabella had found Luke. She worked for Marcus.
Something was off.

He glanced over at Isabella as he guided her through the trees toward the roar of the plane up ahead. Had she been a trap sent to snare him?

She looked up at him, and he saw the worry in her eyes. The fear. Blood seeping through her shirt on her shoulder from the bullet that Doc had removed.

And he knew.

She may have been set up, but she hadn't been a trap. Not intentionally.

He trusted her.

The thought shook him. He trusted rarely, and he was a fool to trust someone who was from his old world, who thought Marcus was a god.

But he did. And once he trusted someone, she was in.

Isabella's eyebrows went up, as if she read something in his eyes. "Luke?"

He shook his head. "Be ready," he whispered.

She nodded.

Isabella was a survivor, and he liked that.

There was a roar as the plane landed up ahead, and Luke peered through the trees to inspect the plane. In his efforts to keep his face averted from the plane, he hadn't looked at it carefully. But now was the time to see if he knew who would be getting out of the pilot's seat.

It was a six-person plane. Big for the bush——
Jesus.

It was one of his planes. Did that mean——

The pilot door opened and out stepped Cort, harsh lines embedded on his face. "They have Kaylie."

CHAPTER NINETEEN

A deep, brutal fury began to rise in Luke, a violence he hadn't allowed himself to feel for eight years. His fingers flexed and his skin began to itch. How dare these bastards come into his sanctuary and prey on innocent people? "Where is she?"

"Back at my place," Cort said. "They wanted me to fly after you, and I said I was busy." He gave a grim smile. "Apparently, they'd heard I was the best and they wanted the best. Didn't appreciate my saying no."

Luke felt the world crushing down on him. This was his fault. He'd brought this to Cort and Kaylie simply by being a part of their lives. He'd kept his distance, hid his roots, and still it had come.

Son of a bitch.

Two other men got out of the plane, both of them packing handguns. Two men Luke recognized from his days working for Marcus. The taller one was Dirk, and the shorter one with the shaved head was Paul. He didn't know them well, because he'd associated primarily with Marcus, Leon and Nate, and even that had only been when he couldn't find a reason to be away on a scientific expedition.

Of course, Marcus had usually found some work for him to do that conveniently happened to be in the same place as Luke's current scientific run. He'd wondered more than once if the funding he'd received had been due to Marcus's influence and his desire to direct exactly where Luke went and what he did.

Which was why Luke had gotten out.

Now no one called the shots but him. Including now.

Luke didn't waste attention on Dirk or Paul. He kept his attention on his partner.

"Get in the plane," Nate said.

Luke didn't move. Cort didn't move. Something passed in the air between them. No words were needed. They both knew.

"You bastard," Cort snarled at Luke. "You brought this crap to Alaska. If anything happens to Kaylie, you'll fucking pay." Cort spun around and headed back to the plane without waiting for Luke's answer.

Wouldn't have been much of one. He agreed with everything Cort had said.

Paul broke off and followed Cort back to the plane, no doubt to make sure Cort didn't take off with their ride.

Luke waited until Cort was in the pilot's seat. He sensed Isabella's gaze on him, but he didn't dare look at her. He had to have faith she'd know what to do when he pulled the trigger.

Cort reached forward to adjust the controls. The moment his fingers touched the dash, Luke whirled around and slammed his fist into Nate's face.

"What the fuck?" Nate dropped his gun and stumbled back. Luke grabbed the gun and shoved Nate to the dirt. Ground his foot into the back of Nate's neck and took aim at Dirk, who raised his gun at the same instant.

Gun to gun they stood. Luke had been toting around rifles and shotguns for the last eight years, but he hadn't held a handgun since he'd left Boston. The small weapon felt light. Foreign, but natural at the same time. Too fucking natural in his hand.

He wanted a rifle.

"Drop it, Fie," Dirk said. His voice was calm, entirely focused.

He, too, had refined his skills since Luke had left.

"No, you drop it, you son of a bitch." Cort stepped out of the plane. He had a shotgun trained on Dirk, and Paul was sprawled across the ground, blood seeping out of a gash in his head. Per their unspoken agreement, Cort had taken out Paul at the same moment Luke had taken on his two assailants.

Two against three had not been a fair fight for the bad guys. Cort nodded at Luke, who returned the gesture.

The hostility had been for show, but Luke knew there had been some truth to it. Cort was desperate to save the woman he loved. He would never blame Luke directly, but they both knew it was his demons that had caught her in their ricochet.

Dirk took his gun off Luke and aimed it at Isabella. His finger tightened on the trigger.

Cort swore, and Luke tensed. "Don't you dare," he said quietly. "I will blow your head off without a thought if you so much as breathe on her."

The words were supposed to be empty, but they felt so right. So perfect. So true. A thread of violence working its way through his body.

Fuck. Those thoughts weren't supposed to feel right anymore.

Pull your shit together.

Isabella started to look frantically around her, and Luke knew she was searching for an out. For a safety route. For anything to get out of the line of fire.

Luke was stunned by her ability to continue to think with a gun aimed at her heart. Anna and his mother had frozen in the face of death. Let it take them. They hadn't been able to fight. But Isabella was struggling for survival even as he watched. Despite the bullet wound in her shoulder and the gun aimed at her heart, she was still thinking, still reacting, still fighting. She was soft inside, both afraid and loving, but she also had a core of steel.

She was different. Different from his past.

She looked at Luke and moved her chin to the right. There was a large boulder by her right leg. If she could drop behind it, it would protect her.

He raised his brow and nodded, unable to stop the slow grin at her creativity.

It would do.

"Drop the gun, or she dies." Isabella's assailant had a smug smile on his face. His finger moved slightly and Luke knew he was a hair from firing that gun.

Luke's finger twitched on his trigger.

No.

He wouldn't allow them to force him to be that man again. He would not shoot to kill again.

"Luke?" Cort's voice was low. A question hung in the air.

He knew Cort would shoot Dirk. He wouldn't hesitate to save Kaylie. Or Isabella, for that matter.

Screw that. Luke couldn't let Cort suffer that black mark on his soul. He knew the price.

Nate squirmed beneath Luke's boot. "Drop the gun, Fie. You're done."

Dark anger exploded inside Luke. "Fuck that." He was doing it on his own terms, and he was doing it *now*.

He lowered the gun. Dirk grinned and relaxed his grip on his own weapon. The moment Dirk let down his guard, Luke charged. His target's eyes widened, and then he raised the gun to fire it. Too late.

Luke slammed into Dirk's side just as the gun went off. Luke shoved Dirk's arm away from Isabella as she dove behind the rock. The explosion rang in Luke's ears as they went down, and he cracked a blow on the bastard's throat.

Dirk sucked in his breath and clutched his throat, writhing on the ground. Luke grabbed his gun and dropped to one knee. He had a gun in each hand, one aimed at Dirk and one at Nate's heart.

Nate was already on his knees, blood streaming from his face. "You stupid bastard. It didn't have to be this way."

"Down on your stomach." Adrenaline was pulsing through Luke, and his hand was vibrating with the urge to shoot. "Now."

Nate dropped facedown to the dirt, and Luke let out a breath. All three men were down, but alive. He'd beaten them at their own game without crossing the line of his past. He hadn't killed them. He had won. He almost felt like grinning as he looked over at the rock Isabella had dived behind. "Isa. You all right?"

She crawled out from behind the rock. Intense relief settled over him at the sight of her face. "Yes, I'm fine."

He grinned then. "You did good." He wouldn't have been able to risk tackling the gunslinger if he hadn't been fully confident Isabella would follow through and get under cover. She could handle her own.

"Thanks." Her hands started to tremble.

"Hey." He held his left arm steady, keeping his gun aimed on Nate. Dirk was still trying to breathe and wouldn't cause any trouble for a few minutes. "Come here."

Isabella stumbled to her feet, her hand pressed to her injured shoulder. "I think I ripped the stitches."

He caught her as she fell into him, and he held her against him. She was trembling, and he knew the shock of the situation was hitting her. He kissed her hair. "You were great. We'll get your arm fixed."

She nodded and buried her face in his shoulder.

Luke kissed her hair, and saw Nate lift his head and look at them. Take in their intimacy.

A lead weight hit Luke in the gut.

After eight years of not getting close enough to anyone to endanger them, he'd broken his rule, and he'd been caught. Isabella could now be used against him, and Nate knew it.

Luke ground his jaw against the sudden onslaught of memories. This wasn't Anna again. This was different. Isabella was strong.

But as strong as she was, she was no match for a gun.

What the fuck had he done? Shit! Eight years of strategy all blown in a single afternoon. He released his grip on her, tried to put distance between them. "Isabella. Go to the plane. Get on board with Cort. I'll follow you in a second."

She nodded toward Nate. "What about him?"

"I'll handle it. Go." He pushed her to her feet. He

needed her off him so he had space to think and strategize. Yeah, he'd managed not to kill them and it had worked, but how long could he keep it up? How long could he keep himself and Isabella alive without playing their games? How did he get them off their tails? He—

"Oh, no! Cort!"

He spun around at Isabella's frantic shout. She was running toward the plane.

Luke glanced at the aircraft, and something in his heart went utterly still.

Cort was facedown on the ground, blood pooling beneath his chest.

The errant shot that had been for Isabella. The one he'd deflected when he'd chosen to tackle Dirk instead of shooting him.

The bullet had hit Cort.

Luke sat by the hospital bed. The monitors were beeping. The machines were pumping.

Cort wasn't breathing on his own.

Kaylie was holding Cort's hand to her heart, and tears were rolling silently down her cheeks.

It had been easy enough to pry Kaylie free from Nate's cronies. He'd made a call to Richie, his new state trooper pal, and Rich had taken care of business without too much trouble, as they'd left only two men behind to guard her. The rest had come with Cort to hunt Luke.

When the staties had rescued Kaylie, she'd been unharmed. Scared but fine.

Until they'd told her about Cort.

Luke wrapped his arm around Kaylie's shoulder and kissed her head. Words were inadequate. "My fault."

She shrugged off his grip. "Just try to reach my brother again. I need him here."

Luke ground his jaw at her rejection. Of course she'd be pissed at him. He deserved it. "I'll keep calling." Unfortunately, her brother, Mason, had gone MIA in the spring and Kaylie had been unable to reach him for months. Luke wasn't holding out hope for a miracle right now. "What else can I do?"

Kaylie's red-rimmed eyes were full of accusation. "I think you need to disappear," she said quietly. "Take your life away from here. For good."

Luke clenched his jaw and nodded once. "I agree." He looked over at Cort. "Tell Cort I'll leave the money."

His money was what had funded Cort's failing business eight years ago. They'd gone in together, and Luke had funneled all his savings into the business under Cort's name, so there would be no paper trail. The only link to Luke was a clause in Cort's will naming Luke the heir of the business if Cort died. To say the business had a very well-performing stock portfolio was an understatement.

They had a gentleman's agreement that the money was Luke's, and Luke had never doubted he could get it back whenever he wanted, even though it was all under the name of Cort's business. Luke's house, his truck, everything he owned was under the name of the business.

Luke Webber had a pilot's license and was registered on their insurance, and other than that, he didn't exist. Adam Fie had been completely wiped out.

And somehow . . . they had found him.

Or rather, Isabella had found him. What had he missed? He'd had no time to figure it out, but he needed to before he disappeared again. No mistakes this time.

Kaylie gave him a tired look. "It's blood money, isn't it? The money you put into the business?"

A hardness settled in Luke's chest. No lies. Not anymore. "Some of it."

Kaylie made a noise of disgust. "Take it. We don't want it. We'll be fine without it. Wipe yourself out of our life."

"Cort needs it—"

She gave him a cold look. "No one needs money that badly." She winced and set her hand on her large belly. "Good-bye, Luke."

He leaned forward, sudden urgency making him sweat. "Is the baby okay?"

She turned her back on him. "It's not your concern."

"Shit, Kaylie, if something's wrong—"

She whirled on him, her eyes blazing. "Yes, something's wrong! You brought hell into our lives and you made us pay for being your friends. I've already lost so many people I love, and now *Cort* might die! How can you ask me if something's wrong? I love him and I might lose him because of you! Get out! Just get out!"

Luke was unwilling to defend himself or ask for her forgiveness. "I owe you that." He walked to the door, then paused to look at his friend. Cort's face was ashen, his body sunken next to all the machines. And suddenly, all Luke could see was Isabella's face lying there. Like his mother. Like Anna. Like Cort.

Isabella would be next.

Nate had seen them embrace. Nate knew she mattered to him.

Whatever danger Isabella was already in, he'd just made it worse.

Unless he stopped fucking around, Isabella was going to die.

His hands curled into fists, and a thread of violence began to weave through his body.

Staying out of the game hadn't worked. Alaska hadn't worked. Playing by his rules had gotten Cort shot. The game was on, and he was ending it now, the way he should have eight years ago.

He yanked on the door and headed out into the hall to find Isabella.

He was going back to Boston.

He was going back there for one reason: to take his life back and to protect those he'd sucked into his sphere. To protect Isabella from the fate he knew was heading right toward her: death. And he was doing it on his terms: as Luke Webber.

But as he strode down the hall toward Isabella's room, a ruthless chill closed around his heart, and he knew what it meant.

Adam Fie was waking up.

And the closer Luke got to his old life, the worse it would become.

If he went back, Luke Webber might die forever.

Murdered by Adam Fie.

But as Luke thought of Kaylie, Cort and Isabella, his soul hardened. The part of him that loved Alaska and had bonded with the people, the part of him that had fought so hard to be the man he'd wanted to be . . .

It died.

CHAPTER TWENTY

"Now there, hon, you just need to stop being so active." The friendly nurse finished bandaging Isabella's shoulder. "You're already going to have a nice little scar, and if you rip them again, it's going to be a mess." She patted Isabella's cheek. "You're far too pretty for that."

Isabella's cheeks heated at the compliment. Pretty was about being dressed up with perfect hair and makeup. Not being bedraggled, injured and wearing someone else's faded black sweatshirt, but she could tell the nurse meant it. Things were different in Alaska.

It made her feel good.

Her mom had spent a lifetime trading on her looks for survival, and Marcus prided himself on being surrounded by only the most beautiful and the most desirable. He'd made sure her wardrobe and her hair reflected it.

No one saw beauty in dirty, borrowed clothes.

But here . . . Luke had nearly made love to her when she was a soggy, muddy, shivering mess. She was still shocked by that whole episode. By his story about his mother's death. The memory made her throat tighten, and her emotions from her own mother's death blended with Luke's. Maybe Luke would understand what her mother's death had cost her.

Maybe, for the first time, someone would get it.

But then she thought of how Luke judged his own father, and her spirits fell. What if Luke was like all the others and saw her mother only as a hooker who had bought an early demise, and not as the wonderful, loving, nurturing mom who had given her daughter so much? If he couldn't forgive Marcus for the choices he'd made, how could he possibly forgive Isabella for what she'd done the night her mother died?

On some levels, she was no better than Marcus.

She couldn't handle it if Luke rejected her the way he'd done with Marcus.

The door opened, and Isabella jumped, but it was only another nurse poking her head in with a question. Not someone from Marcus's team.

The second nurse left, but Isabella didn't relax. All she could think about was how they'd left Nate and the others alive when Luke had jumped into the plane to fly Cort to the hospital.

Yes, there were state troopers outside her door and Cort's, but she was beginning to suspect that wouldn't stop Nate and Leon. It might slow them down, but they wanted her, and they would have her.

At any cost.

Isabella felt the lump of the necklace against her thigh. Still there. Her chip for bargaining for Marcus's life, and the reason she would never be safe.

A curse and a blessing. Still out on which attribute ruled the day in the end.

But after today's events, the necklace felt like the kiss of death.

She couldn't stop thinking of Cort lying there on the ground. Of Luke's anguish when he'd realized what had happened. Or Kaylie's raw panic and terror when she'd rushed into Cort's hospital room.

It had reminded Isabella of how broken she'd been when her mother had died. The loss. The loneliness. The pain. The disbelief. The brutal reality.

The nurse patted Kaylie's leg, jerking her back to the present. "Okay, sweetie, you're all set. I'll be back with the doctor's okay to release you in just a minute."

The door shut behind the nurse, and Isabella was tempted to lock it behind her.

Instead, she walked over to the window, as she had already done ten times since she'd been deposited there. She felt like Luke, continually scanning her surroundings for threats. The parking lot was relatively empty, which had given Luke plenty of space to land his plane.

She almost chuckled at the sight of the plane in the middle of a parking lot. Only in Alaska. She liked the craziness of this state. There was something liberating about strangers fishing strangers out of the river and handing over their own clothes. About wearing a ratty old sweatshirt and having no one care.

And Luke was here. Isabella's smile faded as she thought of him. She had no business thinking fondly of him. They weren't a fit. He rejected family, financial security and Marcus, all the things that were so important to her.

But he was strong. He'd dived into bullets to protect her. He'd beaten Nate and his cronies without firing a gun. He wasn't like them. He was, but he wasn't. He'd been tender with her. He made her feel brave. And she envied his ability to disregard all pressures as to how he should live. Granted, she couldn't eschew all monetary blessings as he had, but there was an honesty in how Luke lived and operated that she appreciated.

She leaned her forehead against the window and

thought about how they'd almost made love. It had been good they'd been interrupted. Really, it had. She would have done it, and then she would have had to deal with the fact that he was going to walk away. She had no doubt that he was going to get her out of Alaska, and then leave her to fight for Marcus herself.

Marcus.

Tears filled her eyes. Dear God, she couldn't lose him, too. Luke, Marcus—

A black car swung into the lot and eased up behind Luke's plane. Isabella tensed as she watched it idle. Then the passenger door opened, and a man in a suit got out.

She was too far away to identify him, but it was clear he was holding a gun.

Another man got out and they stalked the plane, stealthily approaching from the rear, guns out.

Isabella's fingers dug into the windowsill. How long until they made it into the hospital? She couldn't wait for Luke anymore. She had to go back to Boston and make a deal for Marcus's freedom. She didn't know how much of what Nate had said was the truth, whether Marcus had faked his own kidnapping and it had gone out of his control, or whether he had been kidnapped by Leon. Either way, she needed to go home and make sure he was all right.

But even as the thought occurred to her, she thought of Nate's words. Of Luke's claims about his dad. What if Marcus wasn't innocent on any level? What if he'd sent the goons after her? What if the necklace and earrings were so important that Marcus had given Leon permission to shoot her? "Dear God," she whispered. Nausea churned in her belly, and she closed her eyes.

She wouldn't allow her mind to go down that path.

Marcus would not betray her. Unlike Luke, she believed in those she loved. The world was not the black and white place Luke believed it to be, and she would not allow him to take away her belief that flawed people could still be worth loving.

She opened her eyes. "I am going to save him," she whispered. "And I'm doing it now—"

"Isabella."

She turned as Luke stepped inside her room. He had dark circles under his eyes, and his face was gaunt and heavily whiskered. His shirt was covered in blood from carrying Cort. It was smeared up his arms and over his jeans. On his face. Three hours later, he still wore his friend's blood.

"How is Cort?"

He shook his head once. "Hasn't woken up since the surgery. No predictions." His voice was hard. Cold. His face impassive.

Isabella knew what that was like. She'd done the same thing after her mother had died. Blocked the pain. "It wasn't your fault, Luke."

He flinched as if she'd stabbed him, and she saw a brief flash of hollow pain in his eyes. Then it was gone, replaced by the same steely flint she was accustomed to seeing on Marcus's face.

She shivered under the cold assault. "It's my fault," she said.

His eyebrows shot up. "Yours? How the hell do you figure that?"

"I came here. I brought them here." She gestured at the window. "And they won't leave."

Luke strode across the room and peered out the window. He scowled as he watched the men scavenge his plane. "They know now."

"Know what?" She moved beside him, watching the ruthless predators dissect the world that was Luke's. "What's left to know?"

"That Luke Webber is Adam Fie." His voice was hard. "No one Luke Webber knows will be safe once that's out."

Isabella closed her eyes. "I'm sorry," she whispered. "I'm so sorry for bringing this back to you."

"No." Luke caught her arms and turned her toward him. His face was furious. "This isn't your fault, Isa. It's me. And I'm going to take care of it."

She shook her head. "No, I will. I'm leaving. I'm going back to Boston. I'm going to face them and—"

"I'm going with you."

She stared at him, unable to believe what she'd just heard. "What?"

His grip tightened on her shoulders, and his face was hard. Ruthless. "I'm going to Boston, and you're coming with me, where I can keep an eye on you and make sure you're safe. We're taking this down."

His gaze was unwavering, and his jaw was hard with determination. He was in. She wasn't alone. Not anymore. Tears filled her eyes. "Thank you," she whispered.

He shook his head once. "It's not like that—"

"It is!" She launched herself at him, and he caught her around the waist. She threw her arms around his neck and buried her face in his shoulder. "You are a gift," she whispered.

Luke wrapped his arms around her and squeezed tightly, crushing her against his body. He held her as if he would never let her go. As if she were the only thing left in his world to cling to. As if she could keep him from sliding into the dark abyss trying to consume him. She sensed the desperation in the frantic beat of his heart, in the cords of tension in his neck, in the way his body was trembling against hers.

Her savior, her man of strength, needed her.

"Oh, Luke," she whispered. She pulled back slightly so she could see him. His eyes were haunted, so full of the pain he'd been suppressing. There were years of agony weighing on him. A lifetime of regret, of pain, of loss, of resistance. And she knew in that moment that saving Marcus wasn't her only goal.

Luke needed to be healed as well, and she could do it. She could bridge the crevasse between Luke and his roots. With her help, they could rebuild the connections. She could give him back the family that had been eating away at him for so long. Return his friends to him. It would be safe for him to care again.

She laid her hands on either side of his face. "The pain ends for you now," she whispered. "It's time."

Luke searched her face for a long moment, and she saw the resistance in his eyes. The denial. The rock he'd always been coming back to the surface.

She kissed him before he could argue.

Her kiss was the only thing that could have broken through the grief hammering at him, through the vision of his best friend lying in that hospital bed. Her kiss was the only thing bright enough to penetrate.

And the minute her mouth touched his, Luke was desperate for it.

He fisted her hair with one hand, then took over the kiss. He was ravenous for her, for the softness and innocence that she was. Not innocence, not exactly. He knew she'd been through tough stuff. It was evident in every word she spoke and in the way she fought for what she believed in.

Isabella clung faithfully to the innocent belief that it could have a happy ending. She could see the good in the world and will it to life. That was a gift, a treasure, something he'd never run across in his entire life. It should have scared him. It should have made him turn his back and snort with derision. But it didn't. It just felt so good to feel that sunshine on him.

She made a small noise of desire and his body went hard. He growled in response and angled her head so he could kiss her deeper. He needed more than a kiss, no matter how passionate. He needed to be inside her. To be consumed by that side of her that he'd never run into before he'd met her.

He didn't want a lifetime from her.

Not even a month or a year.

Just now. Today. Maybe tomorrow.

He had long ago learned not to look ahead.

The feel of her back beneath his hands, of her body pressed up against his, of her tongue dancing with his . . . it had created a need in him that burned so hard and so deep.

He broke the kiss and trailed his lips down her neck. He licked the salt off her, inhaled her unique scent, and he let himself drown in her essence. She knew about his past, knew what hell he brought to the table, had seen him get his own friend shot, and yet she stood here, in his arms, clinging to him as tightly as he was holding her.

This woman who was such a hardcore believer in love, in family, in being good to those you cared about . . . she knew all about him, and yet she still wanted him.

He didn't get it.

He didn't want it.

And he couldn't afford to suck her into the black hell that he brought with him.

He'd make sure to divest himself of her when it was done. He would disappear into the night and take his hell with him. He would leave her behind so she could live without being under the shadows that haunted him.

But for now . . . since they had to be together, he was going to get the most out of every minute he had. He'd inhale her life and her energy into his soul and let it carry him.

Her hips were soft and full, perfectly curved beneath his hands. A woman. Not just any woman. A woman who touched something inside him that made him want to be soft. Just holding her and kissing her made some of the darkness inside him fade, overwhelmed by the gentle nature of her soul. An abatement that made Adam Fie lose his grip on Luke Webber. Parts of his soul flickered back to life again. The parts that made him human.

Isabella Kopas was going to be his secret weapon to keep Adam Fie at bay once Luke went back into Adam's world.

Isabella Kopas was going to be his salvation.

And it began now.

He scooped her up and carried her toward the bed.

CHAPTER TWENTY-ONE

Luke set Isabella on the bed and straddled her, never breaking the kiss. She clung to him, her hands wrapped around his neck as he settled her into the white hospital sheets. Need raged deep inside him—

A rustle sounded outside the door, and Luke froze.

Isabella went still beneath him, her dark eyes focused on his.

"The guard was there when I came in," Luke whispered, as he eased himself off the bed and went to the door.

A quiet murmured conversation outside the door.

Footsteps retreating.

A light knock.

Luke watched the doorknob rattle lightly, and he swore.

He strode across the room and grabbed Isabella's hand. "Come on." If it were just him, he'd stay and fight if he had to, but he couldn't afford to risk Isabella's safety. He'd learned his lesson with Cort. Besides, whoever was at the door was just an ancillary tentacle.

He needed to take down the king, and the king was in Boston.

The doorknob stopped rattling, and Luke knew the person at the door was working on other options to get it open. A minute, maybe two, was all he had to get Isabella out of there. "Out the window."

He jimmied the window open, then thrust Isabella out onto the fire escape.

As soon as she was on her way, he went back into the room and grabbed a pen and a paper towel from the sink. He scrawled a note, then dropped it in the middle of the bed on his way back to the window.

Isabella was already hustling down the bottom flight of stairs by the time he'd gotten the window shut and rigged it so it wouldn't open. Yeah, they could break the glass, but any delay would help. And with any luck, the note would be all he needed.

Luke caught up to Isabella just as she reached the last rung. She hung from the end of the ladder, then dropped the last few feet to the ground. He swung down and landed beside her, just as their window began to rattle.

"Get back." He yanked Isabella against the side of the building, so they couldn't be seen from the closed window. He led her along the brick wall, heading toward the back lot where his plane was parked.

"What took you so long?" Isabella asked as she ran along beside him.

"I left them a note." They reached the edge of the building and he pulled them back against the wall before inching his head around to inspect the lot.

"A note? What kind of note?"

The black car was still there, but the three men were leaning against the trunk, chatting and smoking. They weren't paying attention. Arrogant fools, thinking their mere presence would be enough to discourage him from taking what was his. "Come on." He began working his way around to the plane from the other direction.

Isabella hurried quietly beside him, and they made it

quickly around the lot. He paused behind a pickup truck, taking a moment to listen to the conversation. They were talking about beer they'd had at a bar recently. All three were participating in the discussion. No one was listening for a sneak attack.

He gestured toward the plane. "Ready?"

Isabella's eyes widened. "We're just going to walk up there?"

"Yep." It was a huge risk, because if one of those men saw them before they got close enough, they'd be completely exposed. It was the only chance they had, and he needed his plane.

Besides, he was better than they were.

Isabella swallowed. "Do you have a gun?"

"Nope."

"They do."

"Yep."

"Okay. Just wanted to make sure you knew." She wiggled up next to him and set her hand on his arm. She was watching the men as intently as he had been. Her face was pale, but there was a firm set to her jaw.

She knew what they had to do, and she was right there with him.

Damn, he could love a woman like that—

Jesus. He rocked back on his heels, stunned by that thought. He'd have to be the stupidest son of a bitch on the planet to fall in love with another woman. And he wasn't stupid.

But shit, just the thought made him feel like he'd left his brains back in the river.

Focus, Luke. "We're going to head right for the plane." His lips brushed against Isabella's ear. He could smell her fantastic scent as he breathed the words, and his cock went hard. He was getting a boner *now?* What was he, fifteen? "If the men see us, run your ass off to the plane. I'll be right behind you. They don't have a plane to follow us if we can get airborne. Got it? Don't stop no matter what."

She leaned back against him, so her back was pressed against his chest. "Even if they shoot?"

"Even if they shoot. Just run for the plane."

A tremor ran through her body, and she squeezed his forearm. "Let's do it."

They moved from behind the truck together, right into the open, and ran across the parking lot. It was a fifty-yard exposed sprint that seemed like a marathon. Luke kept his body between Isabella and the men, slowing to stay even with her.

They reached the plane, and he hoisted Isabella up. Her foot caught the seat belt and she tumbled forward into the gears. Her turquoise necklace clanked against the shift, a noise that seemed deathly loud in the cockpit.

One of the men started to turn, and Luke ducked out of sight. "Buckle up," Luke whispered.

He settled in the pilot's seat and saw the reflection of a man in one of the gauges. Someone was coming. Slowly. Not sure if he'd heard anything. But easing over to the plane to assess.

Luke took a split second to narrow his concentration, then started the plane and yanked the door shut in one motion.

"Hey!" Shouts rang from outside. Luke ignored them as he readied the plane for flight. It was the kiss of death for a bush pilot to get airborne without doing a safety check. He'd never neglected it, no matter what the circumstances had been, and skipping it after the jokers had been in his plane would be sheer idiocy.

He almost grinned as someone yanked on the door handle, and he threw the plane into gear. Taking off without a safety check in this situation was something Cort would do. He *had* done it, in fact. And the poor bastard had nearly died for it.

Lesson learned?

Yeah. He'd get luckier than Cort. That was the lesson.

A man jumped in front of the plane and aimed his gun right at Luke.

"Duck."

Isabella bent over and Luke revved the engine. The man jumped out of the way, and a bullet flew harmlessly past. Luke taxied the plane to the end of the parking lot, spun around and straightened it for takeoff.

Facing him down were the three men, guns up, a blockade across his path.

"Good God," Isabella said. "We'll never make it."

"It'll take a perfect hit to keep us on the ground."

"Marcus hires only the best."

"Yeah, well, I'm pretty good as well." Luke jammed the plane into gear and headed right for the guns.

The men started firing instantly, and Luke held his course, bearing right down on the men. He heard a few pings of metal hitting, but the plane kept picking up speed.

His windshield cracked, and he pressed harder. And harder. Until the men were right in front of him, guns flashing like crazy.

Then they were behind Luke, and he gunned the plane. The roar of the engine was so loud he couldn't hear the gunshots he knew were following him. The plane bucked and Luke swore. But then she recovered. Another fifty feet and the wheels lifted off.

Three more seconds and they were up.

Out of reach.

"Dear God." Isabella leaned back against the seat and closed her eyes. "That was close."

Luke did a thorough and rapid scan of his controls. "We're leaking fuel."

Isabella's eyes snapped open. "How long do we have?"

"Not long." He ran over their options in his mind, then decided how to proceed. "We'll give them a false lead. We'll land at the airport and switch planes. We'll leave this one there for them to find. We'll buy tickets to Seattle, and they'll think we caught a ride to the Lower 48."

The plane was vibrating now, and he knew more vital parts had been hit. Twenty minutes to the airport. Was that too much to ask of his damaged aircraft? No way. He was making it.

"You're so confident they'll think we went to Boston?"

He nodded. "Yeah."

Her expression became suspicious. "What exactly did you put on that note you left them?"

"I wrote, 'See you in Boston.'"

"You did?" She sat up. "Why would you do that?"

"I don't want them around here anymore. I want them in Boston, away from Cort and Kaylie." His fingers tightened on the controls. "It's my game now, and they're playing by my rules."

"And having them waiting for you when we get to Boston is what you want?"

He shrugged. "It's what we've got. We'll make it work."

Isabella grabbed her harness as the plane bucked. "I have to ask you something. I want an honest answer."

"Ask."

"Are you trying to get us killed?"

It riled him that she had to ask. "Fuck, no. You're staying alive, and so are Cort and Kaylie. No other option is acceptable."

She met his gaze. "And you think you can take them on head to head?"

He ground his jaw. He'd lost every other time. But this time would be different.

The lives of three innocents demanded he get it right this time.

"Luke?"

"Yeah, I can."

She leaned her head back. "I hope you're right. I really, really do."

So did he.

They'd landed at the airport on fumes, but Luke had made quick work of borrowing another bush plane and checking them on to a commercial flight bound for Seattle. In less than twenty minutes they were airborne in another bush plane, but even that brief time on the ground had made both of them antsy.

Once they were on the way to Luke's house to pick up supplies, Isabella finally relaxed. Only in the air did she feel truly safe right now. In Luke's capable hands, high above the spray of bullets, being airborne was her respite, and she was asleep almost instantly.

By the time Luke was preparing to land his borrowed plane, Isabella had woken up, but she was still so tired she could barely keep her eyes open. She watched as he did the third flyby of his property. "You really think it's safe to land?"

"Yeah. We can crash here for a few hours while I get

stuff together. There's no way for them to find out I own this property. "

"Even Leon?"

Luke didn't hesitate. "Even Leon."

"Okay." She sighed and rubbed her shoulder. It was throbbing, and she felt like she had been run over by a couple of cars and a motorcycle.

After fighting so hard to get Luke to go back to Boston with her to save Marcus, she'd finally succeeded, and it was as if her body hadn't been able to keep going a moment longer.

It was nearing dusk, and as Luke banked the plane to land, he said, "Check out the sunset."

Isabella turned her head and gasped. The sky was filled with the most vibrant oranges, yellows and reds she'd ever seen. Purple clouds hung low in the sky. Brilliant orange coated the trees in a haze of color. Huge mountains stood in the distance. A vast expanse of nature's beauty in a way she'd never seen in her life. "It's unbelievable," she breathed, as she leaned forward, trying to get closer to the magic.

Marcus tried to create beauty in his house, and she'd always thought he succeeded, but it was nothing compared to the vista before her. This was untainted. Pure. Unlike anything her life had ever been.

"First time I saw it," Luke said, "I was on a run for Marcus that he'd piggybacked on an expedition I had up here. Alaska won me over that very minute, and I knew I'd end up here someday."

Isabella was surprised by the regret in his voice. He was watching the sunset intently, as if drinking it in for the very last time.

"I'll miss this," he said.

"Why do you have to miss it? We won't be in Boston

forever." She cleared her throat. "I mean, you won't be." Because Luke wouldn't be staying with her.

Luke straightened up and turned the plane again, and the vista vanished from sight. "Can't come back. Too many roots. I won't endanger them."

"So you'll just leave again? Like you left your dad?"

He shot her a hard look. "Yeah. Just like it." His sarcasm was evident, as was the fact that he had no interest in discussing it. He landed the plane on a bumpy clearing and taxied the plane around. "That's my place." He nodded at the magnificent log cabin in front of them.

His house was two stories high, with massive windows that faced the sunset. A giant curved pane of glass spanned the entire west side of the second story, and a deck stretched around the whole house, sporting beautiful carved furniture. It was refined and elegant but rustic as well.

Not a decrepit log cabin.

A beautiful, beautiful home that was honest in its beauty. "Who built this place?"

"I did." He stopped the plane and leaned on the dash. "Nice, isn't it?" He pointed slightly to the right. "There's a lake down there you can see from the edge of the clearing. I fish there sometimes, but mostly just breathe it in. Have you ever experienced the purity of air that surrounds a pristine lake? You can practically breathe the lake into your lungs. Incredible."

He stopped the plane, and Isabella stepped out. The air was crisp and fresh, her breath clouding in it. She felt as if she were inhaling pure cleanliness into her lungs. "It's incredible."

"It is." Luke walked up beside her and brushed his shoulder against hers. "I'm glad you appreciate it."

"I do." For a moment, they stood in silence, simply

enjoying it together. Her throat tightened, and she had a sudden urge to lean into him. "It feels like peace out here," she said quietly. Never had she experienced anything like this. It was an oasis of nature and safety. There was no noise of civilization. No cars. No clutter. Just soothing quiet.

"This is where I come to find peace," Luke agreed. "Cort's the only one who has ever been here. It's my sanctuary. I don't share it."

He was gazing over the valley, a look of utter relaxation on his face. She'd never seen him so at ease, and it make him look so much younger. Almost boyish. She understood it, because being here, in this moment, she felt the same way. As if all her problems were surreal and distant.

She could see for a hundred miles. Acres and acres of woods. The lake down below, cast into a golden glow by the sunset. Total freedom.

Everything her mother had ever wanted and never had. She'd come so close to her dream, and it had been jerked out from under her at the last second. Killing her.

Tears filled Isabella's eyes. "Too late, Mama," she whispered. "It came too late."

"What did?" Luke began rubbing Isabella's shoulders.

"God, that feels good." She closed her eyes as his fingers dug into her back. He was staying away from her injury, but her body was so tense from trying to compensate for it, and from all the stress. It felt so incredible to have his thumbs working away at the knots in her shoulders.

"Figured it would." He rubbed her neck. "Tell me about your mom."

She tensed at his persistence. "I don't want to talk about it." If he knew the truth about her, she wasn't sure he'd still come to Boston. Luke wanted those he loved to be pure and perfect. If he couldn't love his own father due to some shady dealings, how would he possibly stay with her if he knew the truth?

But a part of her wanted to be wrong. She wanted to tell him what she'd done and give him the chance to show he was more than she had initially believed. Maybe she should give him a chance. Maybe—

A faint roar made Luke stiffen, and she followed his gaze across the valley toward a small plane barely visible in the distance. "We need to go." Luke caught her arm and hustled her back up toward the house.

Isabella hurried along beside him. "Do you recognize that plane?"

"Yeah, it belongs to a bush pilot named Titus Fector. He always flies this route. Shouldn't be anything to worry about." But Luke kept an assessing eye on the horizon as he unlocked the front door.

He shoved her inside, and she barely had time to gape at the magnificent interior of the not-so-rustic cabin with its panoramic windows and two-story ceiling with exposed beams, before Luke herded her toward the kitchen. "Get some food, then crash in the bedroom." He looked at his watch. "It'll take me a couple hours to get everything together, and you need to rest."

The kitchen had granite counters and hand-carved wood cabinets. She loved its traditional clean lines. There was a thick rug on the wood floor, and she wanted to pull her shoes off and dig her toes into it.

The place felt like home, and she'd never been in such a cozy house. That felt so right.

It was the place of her dreams. A dream that had always been vague and fuzzy, unclear, because she'd never actually seen or experienced what it was she wanted. But this house, the way it made her feel, it resonated.

This was her dream. To feel this way. And now that she felt it, had found a building that made her feel like she was home, she knew that it existed. Really and truly.

Her dream could come true. Someday. Somehow. She would have this. And Luke, he was her enemy, and she could never trust him, but he was going back to Boston with her to help her. On this mission, for this moment, she wasn't alone. On some levels, he was the personification of her dream as well: a wonderful, passionate, powerful man who could protect her and keep her safe, just because he wanted to. Not because she paid him or had some other leverage over him.

Luke was helping because he'd decided he wanted to, and she knew nothing would shake him.

Her throat tightened, and she was suddenly overwhelmed with emotion.

"Isa." Luke caught her arm and turned her toward him. "Are you listening? You need to catch some sleep. Do you understand?"

She threw her arms around his neck. "Thank you."

His gripped her waist with his hands, and his eyes went dark and stormy. "For what?"

"For showing me your house. For going back to Boston with me to save Marcus."

Luke's face became grim. "Isa, I'm not going back to save—"

She kissed him.

Chapter Twenty-two

She didn't want him to ruin the moment with some negative talk about his father. She wanted to engrave the feel of it into her cells so she could re-create it, so she could pull the memory out in the future when life got tough, as a reminder that she had once felt this way and she could feel it again.

Luke fisted the back of her hair and took over the kiss almost instantly. His kiss was ravenous, as if he'd been stalking her, waiting for the moment to attack. His tongue plunged between her lips, a hot, wet probing that made chills shoot down her spine. He grabbed her hips and in one motion, hoisted her up and forced her legs around his waist, never letting up the assault on her mouth.

It felt so good to be against his hard body and to be held in his arms. He was strong, he was hot, and his kiss was so demanding, as if he couldn't live another minute without her. The way he held her and kissed her made her feel wanted and beautiful. Sexy.

He kicked open a door, and she opened her eyes as he carried her into a bedroom. Against the right wall was a huge king bed with a light maroon comforter. The walls were soft beige, the ceiling raw wood, and windows stretched along two full sides of the room.

Scenic paintings decorated the walls, and big, comfy throw pillows filled half the bed.

The bed was lived in, loved and personal. It looked like a bed that had been chosen because it made him happy, not because it would be impressive when *Architectural Digest* did a story on the house.

The room was probably completely different from the one in which Luke had grown up.

She remembered the story of his mother's death, and her heart tightened. Like her, Luke had never had a home. He'd created one here for himself. She might hate the way he judged his own father and the fact that his love was conditional, but at the same time . . . they were the same. At their hearts, at their cores.

He might, just might, understand her and what she'd done. She framed his face with her hands as he carried her across the room. She wanted him to know the truth about her. "Luke—"

He kissed her again. The kiss was so intense, so passionate, filled with such fire she forgot what she was going to say and got lost in the emotions rushing through her. She felt the mattress beneath her back, and then she was tossed into the pile of the pillows. She had no time to sink between them before Luke was on her. His weight pinned her to the bed, his kiss teased down the side of her neck, and his hands caressed her waist.

Excitement pulsed through her, and she threw her hands around his neck and pulled him toward her as she kissed him back, desperate to get closer. She wanted to bury herself in the gift he gave her: the sensation of being safe, of being home, of being protected.

Luke was going to Boston.

He hated Marcus, and yet he was going for her.

"Luke." She arched her back as he tugged her shirt out of the waistband of her jeans, and then gasped when he kissed her bare stomach. The kiss was so tender and passionate, but it was also aggressive and dominant, exactly how Luke was.

She ran her fingers through his hair and he kissed his way up her body to her bra, and then he caught the waistband of her shirt and lifted. "Sit up, hon. I don't want to hurt your shoulder."

She did as he instructed, startled by the intense passion on his face. He didn't take his eyes off hers as he pulled her sweatshirt off, but he was so gentle as he guided her injured arm through it that she almost felt like crying. He was intense, he was passionate, and he was also tender. Gentle. Caring.

Everything she wanted. Everything she'd craved.

Except he would leave her if he knew the truth about her.

Her stomach turned and she pulled back. "No, Luke, I can't—"

He kissed her again, and this time it was pure tenderness. Deliberate. Seductive. A kiss that made her feel like a treasured lover, like a best friend. It was how she'd always wanted to be kissed. She didn't want it to end. She couldn't bring herself to walk away.

Maybe there was a way it could work between them. Maybe Luke could be healed. Saved. Maybe he would kiss her like this forever, not just once. Maybe—

He cupped her breast, and Isabella gasped with pleasure. God, she wanted it. She wanted him to touch her. To kiss her. To make her a part of this amazing house. To bring her into his pain, pain she shared and understood. She could help him. He could help her.

And he could destroy her as well. If she let herself

care, if she trusted him too much. If she forgot that he believed love should be conditional . . . She wasn't perfect. He wouldn't be able to cope with her past. "Luke!" She caught his head as he began kissing his way down her belly. "Stop!"

He looked up at her, but his hands kept working on the fly on her jeans. "What's wrong?"

"I'm not the woman you think I am."

He raised one eyebrow at her as he unzipped her jeans. "How do you know?"

"I—" She caught her breath as he began to tug her jeans down her hips, following the path of her pants with his mouth. A kiss over her belly. Another kiss lower. And lower. And then on her inner thigh. He had such intense passion on his face, she couldn't bring herself to speak. She couldn't force herself to blacken her image in his eyes. She didn't want him to look at her with revulsion. To—

"I think you're courageous." He pulled her jeans over her feet, and then ripped off his shirt. "I think you're a survivor." He unbuttoned his fly and began to slide his jeans over his hips. Slowly. "I think you love unconditionally, and that's pretty fucking incredible."

She stared at the expanse of skin he was revealing. Dark hair, narrowing to a V, and then . . . He was erect. Ready. Wanting her.

"It's naive, and it drives me nuts that you love Marcus." He moved over her, a deliberate tease, giving her the chance to stop him.

She couldn't do it.

All she could do was watch in nervous anticipation as he moved between her legs. He lowered his hips between her calves and wrapped his arms around her thighs. He kissed the tuft of hair at the top of her cleft.

"I think you overestimate your ability to deal with the people after you, which could get you killed. That annoys the hell out of me." He kissed lower, and her body clenched. "I think you try to be so tough."

His tongue swept between the folds, and she closed her eyes. Dear God, it felt so amazing. "I'm not tough," she whispered. "I'm scared all the time. Scared of losing everything that matters to me."

"Which makes all you do that much more amazing." He kissed her again, and her whole body shuddered as his words resonated in her. He thought she was courageous. Tough. Beautiful. And he recognized her need to love. And thought it was incredible.

This man . . . he was broken. But not irrecoverably. There was so much good stuff beneath the surface, beneath the pain . . .

He upped his assault. God, she wanted him. Wanted this man to be inside her. Now. To feel close to him. To reach him. To bring him closer to her heart and her soul. It was foolish, but she didn't care. She needed him. She needed what he gave her. And this was her moment. "Make love to me, Luke. Please."

He shifted position, kissing his way up her body as he wedged his hips between her thighs. He nudged at her entrance, and she was filled with the need for him to be inside her. To connect with him. To turn the bond she felt with him into something physical.

He kissed her lightly and moved his hips. Teasing. Nudging. "Are you sure?" His voice was tight with the effort of restraint, and tendons were taut in his neck. He moved his hips again, pressing a little deeper. "You say yes, and I'm going to take you at your word."

She knew the answer. She was utterly committed to wanting him in whatever way she could have him. He filled that void in her heart she'd been struggling to fill her whole life. Luke had the home, he was strong, he could protect her and she wanted him.

The future didn't matter. It couldn't matter. She had to take what she could get.

His hips began to move faster. Press a little harder. "Isa?"

She met his intense gaze and trailed her finger over the tense set of his jaw. "Yes," she whispered. "I want you to make love to me."

"*Isa.*" He whispered her name so reverently she felt like a goddess to whom he was paying homage, and then he kissed her. A hot, passionate kiss that shattered all her restraints. She was suddenly desperate for more, to kiss him deeper and—

He plunged deep inside her, and she gasped at the sensation of him entering her, of her body adjusting to fit his, of them coming together in the way that bound a man and a woman forever.

"Jesus, Isa." He caught her face as he withdrew and sank deeper again. "You feel amazing."

Her heart tightened at the raw passion in his voice, and then he was kissing her again, and she was swept up in the sensations rushing through her. His weight pressing her to the bed was erotic and sexy, not a threat. Her skin felt like it was on fire, radiating heat, so sensitive to every touch as he kissed her, touched her, drove deeper and deeper, again and again, until her whole body was shaking and trembling, until she couldn't think of anything but him, couldn't feel anything but his body against hers, inside hers, until the pressure built inside her so much she felt like her skin was going to explode and—

"Let it go, hon. Just melt into me." Luke's husky

whisper went right to her core, and her whole body went rigid as the orgasm shot through her.

Luke drove deep and then let out a shout. His body vibrated and his muscles went utterly taut as he buried his face in her neck, his body convulsing against hers. She clung to him as the orgasms rolled through them both, together. He wrapped his arms around her and held her so tightly she could barely breathe, his body still convulsing as he whispered her name again and again against her skin.

It wasn't until they were both still that her tears began to fall.

CHAPTER TWENTY-THREE

Luke didn't want to ever let Isabella go.

Ever.

Her body felt so right beneath him, and he couldn't bring himself to loosen his grip on her. Making love to her had been unlike anything he'd ever experienced. Even being with Anna hadn't been this intense. And since Anna, he hadn't let himself care about anyone he'd been with. He hadn't been able to afford to.

But Isabella had gotten under his skin. He pulled back to look at her face. Tears were rolling down her cheeks. He swore. "Did I hurt you?"

She shook her head once, and laid her hand over his jaw. It was such a tender gesture, and he pressed his face into her touch. "I need to know something."

He raised his brows. "Sure."

She brushed her thumb over his whiskers. "Why did you leave Marcus?"

Luke stiffened. "I told you. My mom—"

"No." She shook her head. "That happened when you were eight, but you didn't leave until you were thirty. Why did you finally leave? What happened?" She caught his face. "I need to know exactly what it is about Marcus that you can't forgive."

With a groan, he rolled onto his side and pulled her

up against him. She snuggled into him, and he closed his eyes to enjoy the feeling of skin to skin . . . but at the same time he kept listening for the sound of approaching planes.

Not that he thought there was a chance they'd be found, but he was keeping alert. He'd give himself five more minutes to enjoy Isabella, and then he'd get up. It simply felt too good to have her skin against his, to feel the heat of her body, the softness of her hair . . . "After the incident with my mom, Marcus brought me back and kept me tight by his side. Before her death, he kept me out of his business, but afterward, he sucked me in as much as he could. He taught me to shoot within three months, sent me on missions, taught me about the business."

Isabella began tracing circles on his chest, and he concentrated on that sensation, making sure to keep his emotions partitioned from the story he was telling. "His business became somewhat less violent after my mom's death, but it was still heading in that direction. His ethics were questionable at best, and I wanted out. I cut bait after college and I figured if I got a PhD, I'd be able to have my own career and ditch him."

"But he co-opted your degree for his purposes."

"Yeah." Luke lifted a lock of Isabella's hair and rubbed it across his cheek. "So damn soft," he murmured.

Isabella scooted on top of him and propped herself up on his chest with her elbows. "Then what?" Her face was intense, her voice demanding. He could read her desperation for answers in the determined set of her body.

"Then I met Anna."

She blinked in surprise. "Who?"

Luke tucked Isabella's hair behind her ears. "She was a fellow grad student. Brilliant. From a good family. Her dad was a college professor and her mom was a minister. A minister. I loved that. Freaking loved the fact they said grace every night and that no one in the family would consider killing a business partner who tried to screw them."

Isabella's lips tightened. "She was the antithesis of your life. An immaculately clean existence and background. No skeletons in her closet, I assume?"

"Anna had never uttered a curse word in her whole life, let alone killed anyone. I think her purity was part of why I was so attracted to her." Isabella tensed, and he squeezed her more tightly against him. "Anna and I started to date, and it got serious." He kept tunneling his fingers through her hair, needing the touch of her body to stay in the present. "We got engaged."

"Did you love her?" Isabella's voice was tight.

Luke shrugged. "I loved what she represented at least. I dated her for three years before I finally asked her to marry me. When she said yes, I finally told Marcus about her. I'd worked hard to keep Anna under the radar, and I'd succeeded. Marcus was furious when I told him." He couldn't keep the bitterness out of his voice at the memory of how Marcus had lit into him when he'd come into his office, riding the high of the new engagement. "The bastard couldn't afford to share me."

Isabella cocked her head and gave him a thoughtful look. "Did it occur to you that maybe he was angry because loving your mother had gotten her killed, and he was afraid the same thing would happen to you? Maybe he was trying to protect you and Anna."

Her comment made Luke freeze for a second. Was

she right? Then he thought of the man Marcus had been, and he dismissed it. "Marcus wasn't that sensitive."

"But—"

"Two days later," he continued, "I got a request from my father to go to South America to retrieve the earrings that went with the necklace you stole. I refused. He said if I didn't go, Anna would get hurt."

Isabella frowned. "He threatened her?"

"Sure did."

"What did you do?"

"When Anna found a photo of my mother in her locker at the gym, I realized it was my dad's way of saying he could get to her anywhere. So I went." The same anger began to fester inside him again. "He gave me three days, but I took my time, just to piss him off. On my way back after a week, I got a call from Anna's father." He worked his jaw, feeling that same fury and disbelief that had nearly destroyed him eight years ago. "She'd been critically wounded in a hit and run while she was jogging."

Isabella stiffened. "Dear God."

"She died two days after I got to the hospital." He felt a raw satisfaction in the shock he saw in Isabella's face. Maybe now, she would understand. "It was my punishment for taking too long." He worked his jaw. "I sat through her funeral and watched them bury a beautiful young woman who had done nothing but fall in love with the wrong man. Afterward, I drove to Marcus's house. I walked in there with a gun. I was planning to kill him and Leon. To end it all. Nate was with me, and we were going to do it together."

"Oh, Luke." She set her hand on his arm.

"The place was empty. No one to shoot." His body was trembling now with that same fury and betrayal.

Seeing Anna in the coffin had made something inside him snap. "Nate and I sat there all night waiting for someone to come home, pounding back Marcus's finest scotch. When the door to his office finally opened in the morning, I shot right through the wood. I didn't even give a shit who was on the other side of the door. Anyone involved with Marcus deserved to die."

Isabella sat up, her hand over her heart. "Who was it?"

Luke fisted his hands to keep from pulling Isabella back toward him. If she wanted to go, he would let her. "It was the interior decorator dropping off samples on her way to the gym. My bullet hit her in the chest, two inches from her heart."

Isabella's jaw dropped. "Dear God, Luke!"

"As I stood there, in my half-drunk state, watching her clasp her chest and fall to the floor, everything came crashing down on me. I realized what I'd become, that I was willing to trade a life for a life, that I'd turned into a man who would murder in cold blood." He stared at the ceiling, remembering the sensation of the world crushing down on him, unwilling to see the recrimination on Isabella's face. "So, I hid the earrings and I walked out. I was done with that life, and I was getting out before Marcus could wreck me and use me to destroy others."

Isabella was still staring at him as if he were a freak. "What about the woman? Did you even stay to see if she was all right?"

"Fuck, Isabella, of course I did. She recovered just fine, and Marcus paid her a fortune for her troubles. She quit her job and now splits her time between her flat in Paris and her mansion in the Florida Keys." He knew, because he'd tracked her for years. It wasn't until he'd read she'd married some rich entrepreneur and had two kids that he'd finally allowed himself to accept she was okay. That he hadn't stolen her life from her.

"Oh." Isabella sank back down onto the bed. "Wow." To his surprise, she snuggled up against his side, as if he hadn't just told her he'd shot a woman in cold blood. "I understand now," she said quietly. "You had to leave."

"Yeah." He shuddered as she set her hand on his chest and gently stroked him. He hadn't been expecting Isabella to reach out to him after his story, but he should have. He'd never met anyone who stuck so firmly to those she had decided to believe in. He wrapped his arm around her and hugged her close, pressing his lips to her forehead. *Thank you, Isa.*

For the first time in his life, he didn't feel dirty. Isabella made him feel like he had a chance to cleanse the rot from his soul. He rubbed her earlobe between his thumb and forefinger and rested his cheek against her hair. "Once I got out, I swore I would never aim a gun at another living soul again," he said quietly. "I also promised myself I would never get in a position where I could be manipulated again, and I would never endanger anyone by letting them get close to me."

She propped herself up so she could see him. Her brow was furrowed with understanding. "But then your friendship with Cort got him shot."

"Yeah. I can't do this again." He framed her face and pulled her down so he could kiss her. "You will stay safe, Isa. I swear it. The cycle breaks now."

Tears filled her eyes. "Luke," she whispered. "I didn't understand why you left."

"I know."

She touched his jaw, a brush so gentle and tender he

wanted to grab her wrist and never let her go. "I didn't know how you suffered," she said. "I had no concept of how going back there will make you suffer."

"Fuck that." He brushed his thumb over her cheek. "It's long overdue. I'm ready to end it."

She shook her head. "Before you go back there for me, I need to tell you something."

"No, hon." He held her gaze. "I'm going back for me. Keeping you alive is an added bonus. Nothing you could say is going to change my mind."

She put her hands on his wrists. "I have to tell you something."

He raised his brows at the urgency of her tone. "Okay."

"I killed a man."

CHAPTER TWENTY-FOUR

Luke's face went from compassionate to utterly impassive instantly. Almost cold. Isabella realized he was hiding all his emotions. "What happened?" he asked.

She swallowed, afraid to continue, but knowing she had to. Luke had confirmed her hopes, that there was more to the story than him simply judging his father for being imperfect. A woman had died because of him, and he'd almost crossed a line for which he could never have forgiven himself. Despite the fact that he'd pulled himself out of it and changed who he was, his blame and self-recrimination was relentless, and it broke her heart.

For that, she would trust him with her secret. Because she had to. His story had opened her heart to him even more, and so had making love. She couldn't go any further, wondering if he would ultimately reject her. She needed to know now. "My mother was a prostitute," she said.

She kept her gaze pinned on his chest, unwilling to see the possible censure in his eyes. "It was the only way she knew to earn money to provide for us. But when I was fourteen, she got a job as a secretary and quit working the streets." She still remembered when she and her mother had burned her mother's wigs in a small fire in the alley behind their apartment. "My mom was so happy that day," she whispered. "It was the first time I'd ever seen a grown-up cry with happiness."

Luke began to stroke her hair, and she leaned into his touch.

"For three years, she worked at that office. She made me promise I'd go to college. No matter what. Nothing less than an A was acceptable, because she wanted me to have the future and the choices she hadn't had."

"She sounds like a great mother."

Isabella looked up at the softness of his tone. His eyes were dark, and kind. "She was."

He smiled. There was a tinge of sadness in his expression, and she realized he was remembering his own mother. "What happened?"

The warmth in her heart faded, replaced by tightness as she tried to block the pain of the memories. "She met a man. A wonderful, amazing guy named Stanley Henderson. He had money and could take care of her. He treated her like the princess she'd always wanted to be. They fell in love and he proposed to her." She smiled at Luke. "You should have seen her dancing around the apartment. I'd never seen her like that in my whole life. She was practically radiating joy. We would dance and sing and run down the street screaming, just to be silly."

Luke returned her smile. "She deserved to be happy."

"She did." Isabella's joy faded, and she toyed with the hair on Luke's chest, unable to meet his gaze as she continued. "The night before the wedding, my mom decided she had to tell him the truth about her past."

"Oh . . . hell."

"Stan walked out the minute she told him." Isabella

brushed the back of her hand over her damp cheek. "He told her he could never touch her again, knowing how dirty her body and her soul were."

Luke swore. "Son of a bitch."

Isabella blinked back tears. "My mom was devastated. Just crushed. It hadn't even occurred to her that his love was conditional."

Luke began stroking her hair again, and his touch felt so wonderful. It chased away some of the pain and loneliness that had held her heart hostage for so long. "I was at the library studying, and she called me up, absolutely hysterical. I tried to talk her down, but she was insane with grief. She told me she was going back to a life where the men never rejected her."

Luke's fingers tightened in her hair. "Shit."

"I screamed at her not to go, but she hung up on me. I raced home." She wiped the back of her hand across her damp cheeks. "I ran as hard as I'd ever run, my heart screaming for her, but when I got home, she was gone." The grief and horror from that night welled up hard and fast, just as painful as they had been in that moment. "I was too late. I called her pimp and I had to threaten him with the cops before he told me where he'd sent her."

Luke was rubbing her back now, but it didn't stop the pain, the tears. "It was some high-class club. They wouldn't let me inside. I kicked one of them in the shin and then ran inside, searching for my mom. I couldn't find her. I looked everywhere. The dance floor. The tables. The lap-dance rooms. I looked and looked and there were so many people and then I found the other rooms. The ones with beds. I pounded at each one, and no one would help me, everyone was just doing their thing and too busy to care, and then I reached one and

I heard my mom screaming." She covered her ears at the memory of that sound. "She was screaming, an awful, awful noise. I got the door open, I don't know how, I don't remember, but when I got in there, my mom was on the floor and this man was beating her, and I couldn't stop him, and he grabbed me and tried to touch me and I got away and he went back to my mom and I hit him with the lamp again and again and again and then he finally stopped and he fell to the ground . . ."

She shuddered. "There was so much blood," she whispered. "Mine, his, my mom's . . ."

"Isa." Luke wrapped his arms around her and hugged her against him. "I'm so sorry, hon."

Isabella buried her face in Luke's chest. "I called an ambulance and then crawled over there to hold her. She was so broken and battered. I held her on my lap and told her I loved her and that it would be okay and that the ambulance would be there soon . . ." Sobs caught her off guard, and Luke's arms tightened around her. "It took an hour to come," she whispered. "They said afterward that the internal bleeding was just too bad and too fast. By the time the paramedics were there, it was too late. If they'd come right away, they might have had a chance. But no one came for her. She wasn't worth it."

"Oh, babe." Luke pulled her tighter and rocked her gently back and forth. "I'm so sorry." He kissed her head, his face pressed in her hair. "I'm so sorry, hon."

"Stan didn't come to her funeral," she whispered. "I called and left him a message, and he didn't come. He didn't love her, and he wasn't worth my mother, but she gave him the power to kill her."

Luke rubbed his cheek against her hair, and she concentrated on the feeling of his skin against hers, the heat of his body, the reassurance of his arms wrapped around her.

"I was tried for murder," she whispered. "He was an important man, and his murder had to be addressed."

Luke swore and pulled back. "It was self-defense," he snarled.

His outrage brought a teary smile to her face. "I know. And it was dismissed for that reason. The case was sealed because I was seventeen when it happened." She spread her hands. "There was no record of my involvement, but they never bothered to try him for the murder of my mother. They were both dead, but he was the one whose murder was investigated. Not my mother's. There was no point in tarnishing the man's pristine reputation for the sake of a hooker, not when they were both already dead."

"No justice." His voice was angry.

She shook her head. "No justice," she whispered.

"Oh, babe." Luke pulled her up on his chest so he could look at her. "Why didn't you tell me this earlier?"

She was stunned by his gentle tone. By the kindness in his voice. He hadn't judged her. Hadn't shut her out. Something in her heart began to melt, something hard that had been there for as long as she could remember. Even Marcus didn't know about her past. "My mother was a prostitute and I murdered a man," she said quietly. "It's not exactly first-date conversation." She couldn't believe he was holding her so tightly after her revelations. But he was. He was rubbing the small of her back, and his lips were pressed against her temple. It was intimate and cozy. He knew the truth about her, and he accepted it.

He accepted her as she was.

Tears threatened again, and she blinked them back. *I found him, Mama. I found the man worthy of us. You would like him.*

"Yeah, I guess it is a little heavy for first-date intros." Luke rubbed her shoulders, his touch gentle and reassuring. "That's why you worked for Marcus," he said thoughtfully. "Security. A man with enough darkness in his past that he wouldn't judge you by yours. A man who could fill in for the parent you'd lost, giving you the home you'd never had."

"I took the job with your dad because he's a good man," she corrected sleepily. It felt too good in Luke's arms, and she was so tired. She was so exhausted, and now that he knew the truth, all the strain had just fallen away. "He's not perfect, any more than my mother was. But that doesn't change that he's a good man. He loves me, and he loves you and—"

"No." Luke pressed his index finger to her lips. "Your mom was a good woman, and she did what she had to do to protect you. Marcus is about greed and wealth and power. He's had plenty of other options his whole life, and he's chosen a lifestyle that hurts others. It's not the same thing. *He murdered my fiancée.*"

His sharp tone penetrated Isabella's sleepy state, and she lifted her head so she could see his face. She simply couldn't believe Marcus would do that. "How do you know? Did he tell you he did?"

Luke snorted. "Hell, no. He denied the whole thing. He claimed it was an accident."

"So how do you know? Maybe it was. He's not the monster you've created in your mind—"

"Isabella." Luke gripped her arms. "My father taught me to shoot to kill. He had Leon teach me how to live with the ramifications of taking a life. He tried to make me into a man who would murder my own father. For God's sake, you got a bullet in the shoulder already. Do you have to die before you understand what he's like? Before you realize he's a bastard who will use you and throw you away when you're no longer necessary to him?"

Isabella shuddered at the coldness in Luke's voice. "You can't really believe that," she protested. "Not if you're going back to Boston to save him. It's okay to admit you love him, despite his flaws—"

"No." Luke interrupted. "I'm not going back to Boston to save him. I'm going back there to destroy him. To wipe out his business. To do whatever I have to do to end this shit forever. To finish what I didn't have the courage to finish before. I held back, and more people have been hurt." He tightened his grip on her. "I'll do whatever is needed ensure you, Cort and Kaylie are never threatened."

His words were cold and hard. No love. Just ruthless mercenary. The sharp knife of betrayal pressed against her chest and she sat up, suddenly feeling raw and exposed in her nudity. "You're going to kill him?"

He flinched, but then nodded. "If I have to."

She couldn't believe it. After his story, she'd been so certain the trauma of that night had been too much, that he'd never let himself become that man, no matter what. "But I love Marcus. His business is my career. It's my life. His home is mine. You can't destroy it. I came out here to get your help to save him, not kill him!"

She scrambled away and grabbed her sweatshirt, clutching it to her chest. Her stomach turned with the pain of betrayal. She'd trusted this man with her heart, her body and her deepest secret, and he was repaying her by stealing the only thing in her life she cared about, the only human who kept her heart alive, the man who had plucked her out of the gutter and given her a chance at a new life.

"Luke, for God's sake," she cried. "Stop talking like that! It will break you if you hurt him. He's your father! Give him a chance to explain what's going on. For all we know, it's Leon driving this whole thing and your father is an innocent pawn, just like you were."

But there was no mercy in Luke's face. No sympathy. Nothing of the man who had just held and comforted her. She saw only a man who had reached the end of his tolerance. A man who saw his father in black and white.

A man who was prepared to kill.

Dear God, what had she unleashed?

CHAPTER TWENTY-FIVE

Luke felt like shit.

And it wasn't simply that the pilot had just announced they would be landing shortly at Logan Airport in Boston. A place he never thought he'd set foot again. And he was doing it with the lives of people he cared about at stake. Again. But that wasn't all that was grinding at him.

No, what was dragging him down was the hostility emanating from Isabella ever since he'd admitted to her the reason he was going to Boston. That haunted look in her eyes, that utter betrayal, the disbelief. It had hit him right in his core, and then she'd turned her back on him.

She hadn't spoken more than the bare necessities on the entire journey from Alaska to Boston, and they'd slept in separate rooms at his cabin. No warmth in the morning as they'd prepared to leave. She'd tried to convince him not to accompany her once they'd gotten to the airport, but she'd stopped protesting when he'd booked the tickets using one of several fake identities he kept in a safe in his house, safeguards he'd created eight years ago in case Marcus found him again. She realized he had resources to help them slide through the airport without alerting Marcus and Leon, but he knew she was going to ditch him at the first opportunity.

"Oh, God, we're home," Isabella whispered, putting her hand over her heart. Her voice was reverent with a joy he simply couldn't relate to. "I missed it."

Luke leaned over and peered out her window. He tensed at the sight of the Boston skyline. How many times had he seen that on his return to the city after another run for Marcus? It had never been home for him. It had always been hell. The eight years of absence fell away, and he was back in that moment, returning from that last trip to South America. He could almost feel those earrings burning a hole in the pocket of his jeans, Anna's blood on his soul.

He swore and leaned back against the seat. It was time to focus.

Isabella had to lose Luke.

Now.

There was no way she could allow him to go after Marcus.

But what chance did she have without his help and support?

He had his hand on her elbow and he was guiding her swiftly through the airport crowd. He was constantly surveying their surroundings. His handgun was tucked away in his checked baggage, not that he could use it there anyway.

She knew Leon probably had men canvassing all the nearby airports, watching for them.

But facing them down by herself was a risk she had to take if she had any chance at saving Marcus. Bringing Luke with her would be like putting a bomb in Marcus's business and possibly his life. It was time to separate. "I'm heading to the bathroom." She pointed at the ladies' room she knew had two entrances. "Back in a second."

Luke scowled, but he nodded his agreement and leaned against the wall to wait for her. He was large and powerful, his dark jacket and broad shoulders making him appear intimidating and lethal. But there were shadows beneath his eyes, and she knew he'd been distracted since his announcement that he was going back to take out his own father.

Regret?

No. She couldn't risk her life or Marcus's on the off chance Luke would suddenly develop familial bonds. She understood his fury over Anna's death. She knew what guilt he'd been carrying after shooting an innocent woman. For the first time, she really understood why he'd left and rejected Marcus. But that didn't change that what he wanted to do would strip her of all she had.

Luke's eyes narrowed. He checked out her clenched hands and her nervously tapping foot, and he shifted ever so slightly.

She knew then he had already figured out she was planning to run. "Luke—"

He tapped the face of his watch. "I want to be at the baggage claim in three minutes. We need to retrieve our bags and get out before we're tracked."

She hesitated. He wasn't going to stop her? "Okay. I'll hurry."

He gave her an assessing look. "Go. I'll wait."

She knew he wouldn't wait long. He was going to allow her go. Of course he was. She was his conscience, so he wouldn't want her around when he went into his assault mode. They both needed to be free to do what they wanted. Did that mean he was worried she could change his mind? If there was a chance, she had to try. "Luke?"

He raised one brow at her, but his attention was on the crowds around them.

"Every night after dinner, Marcus takes a bourbon into his office. He picks up a picture of your mom and you on a beach, and he sits at his desk studying it until he finishes his drink. Every night."

Luke's gaze swiveled toward hers, but his expression was unreadable. "What beach?"

"I don't know. But you look like you're six or so, and you're wearing an orange hat that has stripes like a tiger."

She remembered the photo so clearly, and she would never forget the look on Marcus's face the day she'd caught him looking at it. The photo had been on the desk, and he'd been leaning his head in his hands, staring at it. When she'd opened the door and walked in, he'd jerked his head to look at her. Tears had been streaming down his cheeks. They'd looked at each other for the longest time, and then Isabella had quietly left. It had taken Marcus six months before he'd pulled out that photo and showed her what it was. "Your mom has an American flag bandana in her hair, and she's wearing a black one-piece suit. He keeps it in a locked drawer in his desk."

A muscle twitched in Luke's neck. "Fourth of July on the Cape," he said quietly. "I was seven. Marcus took that photo. One of the few vacations he'd come on with us."

Hope flickered at the lack of anger in his tone. It wasn't soft, but she felt the emotion beneath it. Was he reachable? "He cries over that photo, Luke. He loves you."

His face hardened again. "He should cry. He killed my mother. The bastard should cry every fucking day of his life."

"But—"

Luke glared at her. "If he truly regretted what happened to my mother, he would have changed his life. He would have taken his son and disappeared to a world where we were both safe. But his response was to amp up the business and bring me fully into the situation. He didn't need the money. He wanted it. Big difference."

Anger glittered in his eyes, and Isabella couldn't deny the truth of his words. They did make sense . . . on some level. But she'd seen Marcus's grief and his regret, and she knew the situation was more complex than Luke gave it credit for. "I'm sorry you see it that way."

He shrugged. "I'm not. Better to be smart than dead."

Isabella sighed. "Okay, I'm going to the bathroom. I'll be back in a sec."

He raised his brows. "Will you?"

She couldn't meet his gaze. "Yeah." Without a backward look, she slipped inside the bathroom.

She paused just inside the door, her heart aching at the thought of leaving him behind. But she had to get to Marcus before he did. She had to stay true to her own heart, because the more Luke talked, the more he made her doubt her own convictions about Marcus. She would not let him take away what she'd worked so hard to create for herself.

She had to do it.

Isabella hugged her purse under her arm and jogged

past the stalls. She ran out the other entrance, then pressed up against the wall to survey the crowds the way Luke had. So many people. How could she possibly determine if someone was stalking her? The man by the phones in a suit. On his phone. One of Leon's new cronies?

The man in jeans lounging by the gate. A magazine was open on his lap, but he was watching the crowd. He turned his head and made eye contact with her.

She tensed, and then he moved on with his survey.

Dear God. How could she do this by herself? For a moment, she considered going back through the bathroom, to Luke. For what purpose? She had to do this on her own. She was the only one who cared.

Cautiously, she moved away from the wall and began walking down the corridor toward the baggage claim. She didn't have time to get her bag. She'd have to skip it—

Someone bumped her and she jumped to the side as a woman in a suit hurried past.

"Okay, Isabella, you need to chill." She took a deep breath and hunched her shoulders. She tucked her head down and began to walk fast, trying to keep up with the crowds hurrying toward their flights. All she had to do was make it to—

A hand caught her elbow. "Welcome to Boston, Isabella."

She went rigid at the sound of the harsh Boston accent she knew so well, and her shoulder began to burn. She jerked her head up and stared into the pitch-black eyes of Nate Sampson. His nose was swollen and bruised, and there were dark purple and black bruises around both eyes. How could she possibly not have noticed him?

He smiled, a flat, unemotional smile that didn't reach his eyes. "Where's Fie?"

Isabella shook her head. "I don't know. I left him."

Nate looked past her and surveyed the airport. "No. Fie wouldn't have let you go. He's watching you." Nate took her arm and began to haul her through the crowd. "You're working just fine as bait."

"Bait?" Isabella had a sudden realization as Nate dragged her along. "I'm bait? Have I been bait all along?" She stopped and ripped her arm out of Nate's grip. "Was the whole thing a setup?" Her mind started racing through everything that had happened prior to her going after Luke. Had she been played all along?

If she had, then that meant Luke had been the ultimate target all along.

Why? Why would they want him so badly? And why now? After eight years? What had Luke not told her? If it had anything to do with Marcus—

"In here." Nate steered her toward an exit door. Not the main one. A small side one. Like the one Marcus had used many times to slip out to his private vehicle that would whisk him away without anyone knowing.

If she went out there, it was over.

He punched the key code on the door.

"No!" she screamed and started fighting him. "Help! Help! Let me go! Someone help!"

"Goddammit, Isabella!" He slammed his hand over her mouth and shoved her outside. The door locked behind her and she heard someone crash into the door, yelling for the police.

She slammed her elbow back into his gut, and he bent over with a bark of pain. She whirled around and palmed his broken nose with her hand. He screamed and fell to his knees.

There was a shout, and two men got out of a black car and ran toward her. "Shit!" She quickly punched in the same code Nate had used and then yanked on the door.

It opened.

"Get back here!" Nate lunged for her. He caught her purse, and Isabella dropped it as she ducked in the door. She ran right into a security guard. "He's out there! He stole my purse!"

The uniformed guard charged past her and Isabella was caught by another guard. "No, no, let me go!" She tried to squirm out of his grasp, knowing it would take mere seconds for Nate to talk his way out of it. "Let me go!"

He dragged her to the side. "You're under arrest."

"Me? Why me?" But she didn't need the answer. It was an airport, and she'd been screaming. Of course they would be cautious. But she knew Leon had to be nearby and if he found her—

There were shouts from outside and her captor swore. He edged closer, and she saw the security guard was fighting to subdue Nate, who was demanding they check his ID. Shit! Of course he would have some sort of ID to get him out!

"Hey!" There were more yells and suddenly more armed guards swarmed down on them. They shoved through the crowds, and her captor started shouting at them, directing them outside. Mass chaos—

Someone jerked her arm and yanked her backward, hard. Her captor lost his grip on her and she tumbled backward, hauled into the crowd.

Dear God, had Leon found her?

CHAPTER TWENTY-SIX

Isabella twisted around to fight the man holding her, and gasped with relief when she saw it was Luke dragging her back into the crowd. He hadn't left her. "Luke!"

"Hey!" her original captor shouted and charged after her.

Luke jerked her to her feet. "Go!"

He tripped their pursuer, and Isabella turned and sprinted through the crowded corridor. Isabella didn't look back, but she heard footsteps and knew she was being chased. Frantic, she ran harder, following the exit signs. Just to get out. To get to a cab. To—

"Come on!" Luke was suddenly beside her. He caught her hand and dragged her through the masses, dodging people as they ran.

"They'll never let us go!" She was breathing hard now. Two more armed guards ran past in the direction of the melee.

Luke yanked her sideways toward the women's bathroom. It had two entrances, one that came out in the next hallway. "Go through and meet me on the other side. Ditch your coat and change your hair. Ten seconds!"

He didn't wait for her. He just sprinted into the men's bathroom.

Isabella ran through the same bathroom, and she peeled off her coat. "Trade!" She tossed it at a group of teenage girls. "Can I have your hat and sweatshirt? I'm hiding from my boyfriend!"

It took a minute of negotiation and a bit of cash, but one of the girls finally agreed.

Minutes later, Isabella, wearing a glittery pink sweatshirt and a matching hat, stepped outside the bathroom.

Luke was already waiting, in a white T-shirt and a Red Sox baseball hat. He caught her hand and began a brisk saunter toward the gate. "Glitter is a good look for you."

Her breath was wheezing in her chest. "You like the hot pink? I feel like it's a good combination of sophistication and attitude."

"Agreed." Luke put his arm around her as they neared the exits that led to the baggage claim. Two armed guards were standing there, watching everyone who went by.

"Oh, God."

Luke tightened his grip and pulled her over for a kiss. His mouth was wet and hot, and her belly clenched as his fingers caught her hair, forcing her against him as he continued the kiss. Not just a kiss. The kind of kiss a man gave a woman when he was thinking about getting her naked and beneath him.

He snuggled her closer and moved his hand. "I apologize in advance for being crude."

"For—"

He cupped her breast just as they reached the guards. Isabella sucked in her breath to protest, and then realized both guards were gawking at Luke's hand on her breast. Neither of them could tear their gazes away to inspect her face. "You men are all such pigs," she whispered into his mouth, as he guided them past the stunned guards.

"I know." He kissed her through his grin. "It comes in handy."

He removed his hand and Isabella relaxed . . . but at the same time, she missed it. She had loved the way he'd touched her in Alaska, and his caress in the airport had been blatant and annoying . . . but it has also been a tease of the physical connection she craved so much.

They moved quickly down the stairs and toward the back door near the baggage claim.

"Do you want your bags?" she asked. His gun was in there.

"Yeah." Luke glanced over at baggage claim three, which was the one their flight attendant had directed them to. He nodded toward the belt. "Yankees hat."

Isabella followed his gaze and tensed at the sight of the man hunched against the pillar near the baggage claim they'd been heading toward. He had a navy blue Yankees cap pulled low over his eyes, but his body language was alert and ready.

As if he'd felt her gaze, the man turned his head sharply, and Luke yanked her around for a hot kiss before they could make eye contact. Isabella threw her arms around him and drank in the feel of his mouth on hers, of his arms around her, holding her tight. He was so strong, and this was his element.

"Did he see us?"

Luke grabbed her butt and began to massage it. "Still watching us." He kissed his way down her neck.

Goose bumps shivered down her body and she gripped his shoulders. His lips feathered along her skin, and heat pooled low in her belly. Her legs began to tremble.

"He's moving on." Luke nibbled on her earlobe. "I want to try to get my bag." He slipped a handful of bills into her hand. "Bribe the attendant for the first cab in line, then make him sit there and wait for me. If someone else comes after you, go." He kissed her temple and then pulled back. "But I'll be there. I want more of your body."

She swallowed at her answering shudder. "This isn't the time for sex."

"No shit." He kissed her again, hard and deep, then pulled back just as she was reaching for him. "Go." He shoved her toward the door.

Isabella hurried for the revolving door, but as she neared it, she looked over her shoulder. Yankees hat guy was gone, and Luke was nowhere to be seen. He'd melted into the crowd. A man who knew how to play this game.

She shivered, and this time it wasn't from the hormones he had stirred up. It was for the man Luke was, the world in which he was comfortable. She ran outside, saw the livery stand and began to work her way along the sidewalk toward it.

A hundred bucks and a smile later, she was ensconced in a black Lincoln.

Isabella twisted around to peer out the rear window, but there was no one who looked familiar. No guards racing after the car.

She was safe. For now.

No Luke yet.

She could leave now. Leave him behind. Take it on by herself. He knew that. He'd given her money and sent her for the cab.

She'd already run once. Now was her chance.

She should go. Luke would only help her for as long

as his goals coincided with hers. But that wouldn't last forever.

There was nothing she could do to make him need to stay with her . . . but her heart ached at the thought of leaving him behind.

She couldn't trust him, and she was a fool for keeping him around. He would never love her back the way she wanted, because he simply would never allow himself to feel that intensely. And yet every kiss, every touch, they all sucked her in more deeply.

He was going to break her heart and destroy her life . . . she knew it. She did. The only smart thing to do was to cut him loose and protect herself, as she'd been doing her whole life. Replace him with a situation she could control. With—

She noticed the guy with the Yankees cap on the other side of the street, and he was eyeing her car.

Shit! Where was Luke?

Isabella hunched down, watching him over the rim of the seat. Her heart started to race as he crossed the street and began to walk down the sidewalk toward her.

Luke had told her to go. But she couldn't leave him. She just couldn't.

"Can you start the engine, please?" Her voice was trembling. Where was Luke?

The engine roared to life. "Ready to go?"

"Just one more minute." The Yankees hat was closer now. He paused to talk to the taxi line attendant. She had to go. Had to go. Couldn't wait. But Luke—

The Yankees hat guy looked right at her car, and their eyes met. Slowly, he raised his phone and spoke into it, and she realized he was reading the license plate.

And then he sprinted toward her.

"Go!" Luke jumped into the cab from other side. He

tossed his bag on the floor. "A thousand bucks if you can break the speed limit and not get stopped!" he barked at the driver.

Yankees hat slammed his hands against the window. She jumped and grabbed for the lock as he yanked the door open.

Luke lunged over as the man shoved his head into the car, and he slammed his fist into the man's jaw. The man stumbled backward and Luke jerked the door shut. "Go!"

The cab lunged forward, someone yelled at them, and Isabella covered her head as they darted in front of a bus. Somehow they squeezed through without being crushed and she whipped around in her seat in time to see the Yankees guy hail the next cab.

He leapt in, and another man jumped in beside him. Then the cab took off after them, dodging traffic to catch up.

Luke leaned forward. "See that red and white cab behind us?"

The driver checked his rearview mirror. "Yeah."

Luke shoved a wad of hundreds through the window. "It's yours if you lose them."

The cabbie snorted. "Is this for real?"

"Yeah."

The driver pulled the cash out of the tray and thumbed through it. He whistled softly. "The guys are never going to believe this."

"You in?"

"Yeah." The cabbie checked out his mirror again. "Okay if I do it after we get into the city? Got some tricks in those alleys."

"Have at it. Just make it happen fast, then pretend to drop us at Park Street Station."

The cabbie frowned. "Pretend?"

"Yeah. We'll be sneaking out beforehand, but your money depends on you keeping up the charade. By the time they realize we're not in the cab, we need to be long gone. You fail to keep up with the race after we get out"—Luke read the man's ID tag hanging from the mirror—"I'll find you."

The words were simple, but they were uttered with such coldness that Isabella actually shivered. It was the way Marcus occasionally spoke, and the cabbie nodded quickly. "Okay, okay. I get it."

Luke leaned back in his seat and tossed her bag to her. "Ditch the pink. We're going over the railing soon."

She eyed the guardrail on the edge of the highway. "You sounded exactly like Marcus when you threatened the driver."

Luke scowled. "I'm not Marcus."

"Maybe you are." She unzipped her bag and pulled out a black turtleneck sweater and a fleece. It was going to be cold in Boston without her jacket. "Maybe you're more like him than you think, and that's not a bad thing." She looked over at him. "If you can have some of his same traits and still be a good person, then maybe he can as well. Did that ever occur to you?"

He glared at her. "Cut the crap, Kopas."

She had to stifle a smile as she pulled off the pink hat. He hadn't denied it, had he? Maybe there was hope. Maybe, if they all survived this, Luke would discover truths he'd denied his whole life.

She caught sight of the gun in his duffel.

Or maybe they would all die.

CHAPTER TWENTY-SEVEN

Luke carefully inspected their surroundings. Their driver was weaving through the North End, which was the Little Italy of Boston. The roads were narrow and crowded, and they couldn't go quickly. The other cab was less than half a block behind them, and it was proving impossible to shake.

"We need to get out."

The cabbie nodded. "There's a hard right turn up ahead. You'll be out of their sight for about thirty seconds. There's a narrow alley on your right. It puts you out on the next street, which is one way the wrong way. They won't be there. I'll take them back out of the neighborhood and toward the train station."

"Good." Luke had made sure he and Isabella were both sitting in front of the head rests, so their heads wouldn't be missed when they ducked out. He glanced over at Isabella, who was dressed in a couple of sweaters and a pair of boots.

Her hair was tousled, and her cheeks flushed. Her face was pale, but her jaw was firm and her hand was clenched around the handle of her bag. She looked determined. A fighter.

"Now!" The cabbie slammed on the brakes.

Luke shoved the door open, and he and Isabella

vaulted out of the cab. She didn't hesitate, sprinting straight toward a narrow alley between two old brick buildings. The alley was barely big enough for a person to pass through, maybe about twelve inches wide. Luke turned sideways and followed Isabella into the passageway.

Their cab roared away with a screech of tires, leaving them on their own.

Isabella was hurrying sideways, and Luke stayed next to her. He watched the narrow gap of the street until their pursuers' cab sped past.

He listened carefully, and the engine didn't idle. Unless the occupants had jumped out at full speed, they were still in the cab.

"Did we make it?"

"Maybe." Luke kept moving behind Isabella, and he watched the opening ahead of them. If they were hit from both ends, there was nowhere to go. They were trapped. "Hurry."

She rolled her eyes at him. "I guess I'll stop fixing my hair and just worry about my nails tomorrow, then."

Her comment took him by surprise, and then he grinned. "Your hair looks great. Don't change it."

Her cheeks flushed and she averted her gaze to look ahead. "You need to go away."

"From what?" He heard the screech of tires and he caught her arm.

"Me." She leaned back against the brick, then wiped a cobweb off her shoulder. "Boston."

"No chance." He watched as a red and white cab like the one that had been tailing them raced past the opening they were heading toward. Shit.

"Seriously, Luke." Isabella was also watching the

street. "You're too judgmental, and you're going to destroy yourself, Marcus and me. Is that what you want?"

No one emerged in pursuit of them, and Luke was antsy to get out of the alley and into an area he could defend. He nudged her forward. "I want you and Cort and Kaylie to live."

"At what cost?"

He peered past her into the street. Just some locals. "Any cost." He pushed her outside and guided her down the street. They passed a restaurant that had the scent of roasting garlic and baking bread emanating from it. God, he'd forgotten what it smelled like to be in the North End. To be in a city that offered a thousand different food options in every ethnicity on any given day.

He scowled as he saw a coffee shop up ahead and caught a whiff of its scent. He hated Alaskan coffee, and it was nothing compared to the rich, heady aroma of fresh ground.

Damn.

He'd missed Boston.

"I know him." Luke leaned against the windowsill of their hotel room as Isabella riffled through her bag, looking for something to wear to bed.

"Who?"

"The guy in the Yankees cap." Luke paced the room, trying to think. Yankees hat hadn't worked for Marcus, but Luke remembered him from somewhere. "You recognize him?"

Isabella sat down on the bed. "I think I do, but I don't know where."

"He works for Marcus, but I'm not sure what role." They'd driven past Marcus's house this evening, and the lights had been blazing. Guards had been pacing along the fence, and it was clear that Marcus's house was the active location. "I need to go back to his house."

Isabella looked at him sharply. "For what?"

"To get my insurance." And he needed answers about what was going on. Despite Luke's belief that Marcus was guilty as hell, Isabella's constant pressure had cast enough doubt in his mind that Luke had to go see what was really going on before taking action.

He was prepared to do whatever he had to do, but he would not make a half-cocked choice as he had eight years ago. This time, he was going to plan every step of the way, and do what he had to do.

She frowned. "What are you talking about? What insurance?"

Luke sat down on the edge of the bed and finally told her the truth. "Eight years ago, I stashed the earrings in the house. I thought it would be funny that they'd be right under Marcus's nose, but he'd never be able to find them. I want to get them. That's why they want me. Now that they have the necklace within their grasp, they need those earrings, and I'm the only one who knows where they are." He didn't add that he needed to get inside and find out what was going on. Who was playing whom? Who was running the shots? He was pretty certain of the answers he'd find, and he didn't want to get Isabella's hopes up.

Isabella stood up. "I'll go with you."

"No." He walked over to his bag and pulled out his gun. "This is my deal."

"I lived there for six years. Marcus showed me every passageway in that building," she said. "I can get in and out as easily as you can."

He held up a gun. "Are you prepared to shoot someone to save yourself?"

Isabella's gaze went to the weapon. "I—" She stopped. "I don't know," she finally said. "I've never tried to shoot someone before."

"Then don't start. It's not worth it." Luke shoved the gun into his holster.

"I don't trust you." Isabella was sitting on the bed, her knees pulled up to her chest.

Her words bit at him. "Trust me to do what?"

"I don't trust you to go in there and not kill a man I love."

A man I love. Marcus. Not him. "Don't be a fool, Isabella. Don't put your lot in with him."

She levered herself off the bed and walked over to the door. She leaned against it and folded her arms. "Please don't go."

He couldn't help but grin at the sight of Isabella blocking the door with her small body. She was so petite, he could toss her aside. But he liked that there was no fear in her eyes. He wasn't a nice guy, and she knew that, and she didn't fear him.

He walked over to her and stopped inches away.

She lifted her chin.

"You are incredibly sexy when you try to boss me around."

She blinked. "This isn't about sex."

"I'm a guy. It's always about sex." He didn't give her the chance to stop him. He figured she probably would, and he wasn't interested in being stopped. What he needed was a solid dose of her spirit before heading into the hellhole that raked his soul raw. The world where Adam Fie liked to play. So he grabbed her around the waist, hauled her against him and kissed her.

She melted into the kiss instantly, and a sense of arrogant satisfaction pulsed through him as he deepened the kiss. He didn't let up his assault, needing to leave his mark on her before he left. Needing to feel her softness against him. Her touch eased the tension within him, and he felt a sense of calmness settle over him. He knew he wasn't in danger of going in there trigger-happy, not with Isabella still in his soul.

He finally broke the kiss and pulled back.

"You're an ass," Isabella said.

He grinned. "Yeah, I am."

She shoved him back. "Promise me you won't do anything to Marcus? That you'll just get your earrings and come back."

He shook his head. "I'll do my best, but I can't promise anything. I don't know what I'll run into."

Isabella fixed her dark eyes on him. "How much would it break you if Cort died?"

He felt his jaw harden. They'd called the hospital upon arrival in Boston, and there was still no change. The jury was still out on the man who'd somehow become Luke's best friend over the last eight years, despite his efforts to stay aloof.

Isabella's face softened with empathy. "That's how I'll feel if something happens to Marcus. You fear the guilt if I die, but if you take Marcus and that life from me, my soul will die, just as yours will if Cort dies."

Luke heard the torment in her voice and he knew she spoke the truth.

It haunted him all the way to the house that he had once called his own.

* * *

Isabella stood at the hotel window and watched Luke stride toward the black pickup truck he'd bought with cash two hours ago. It was registered to Luke Webber, but the hotel room was under a fake name, again paid for in cash.

She braced her hands on the rough wood of the sill. His shoulders were so wide, his body strong and lithe as he headed toward his truck. He was wearing jeans and hiking books, the same clothes he wore in Alaska. He was all Alaska, but at the same time, he was a fit for Boston as well.

She'd seen him look around with wonder and surprise when they'd passed a landmark from his youth. She'd seen the way his hands had clenched the wheel when they'd driven past his old house.

His pain was deep, and she understood that. She knew what pain was. Regret. Loss.

She got it.

But she couldn't let him destroy what was most dear to her—and to him as well, if he could simply admit it.

He'd gotten her this far, and now she was taking over.

Luke got in the truck, and the engine roared to life.

Isabella opened her phone and scrolled down.

Luke didn't pull the truck out, and for a moment, Isabella waited. Hoping. Then he put the truck into reverse and backed out of the spot.

Isabella sighed, and hit send.

"Black and White Cab Company," a friendly voice said. "May I help you?"

"Yes." Isabella watched Luke pull out onto the main

road and head toward the highway. "I need a cab." She gave the gal her address and then hung up.

Her heart was racing, and she had no idea if her plan would work.

But she was going to try.

Luke parked the car two blocks down from his old house, then walked into the garage of a small gray Cape at the end of the road.

He unlocked the door and stepped into the dim interior. Parked inside was the same old Chevy. It even had the same mud splatters that had been there eight years ago. The same half-used can of gasoline sat on the shelf, with a pile of dirt and a couple of flowerpots, as if someone were in the middle of potting some new plants.

Same pots had been there for eight years.

This was his spot. Even Marcus hadn't known about it, and he knew Isabella couldn't have.

Isabella.

He couldn't shake the look of betrayal on her face when he'd walked out the door. He'd wanted to promise he wouldn't hurt Marcus, but he couldn't. Tonight was about going in and out and setting up his plan.

But if shots were fired, he was doing whatever it took.

No more holding back.

Too many people had died because Luke hadn't stood up for what he believed in, and he wasn't making that mistake again. As much as he wanted to alleviate Isabella's stress, he wouldn't lie to her. He believed Marcus had been lying to her all this time, and she deserved the truth. He would never insult her with empty promises.

Luke punched the seventeen-digit alarm code on the door between the garage and the house. The steel door opened easily beneath his touch. It was faced in decrepit wood, but beneath that was solid steel.

He stepped into the small archway between the house and the garage, but instead of going into the house, he crouched and felt through the layers of dust to a small chink in the corner of the cement floor. He pressed the cement in specific spots, in an order long memorized. Then the entire floor began to slide back. No trapdoor to see, because the whole floor moved.

He swung down the ladder the minute the door began to slide. The opening was so tight his shirt caught on the cement, but the moment he was through, it snapped shut over his head. Open for less than three seconds, then gone.

Motion-sensitive lights gave the tunnel an eerie glow, and Luke landed quietly in the dirt. He flipped the switch he'd rigged on the wall. The security cameras inside Marcus's house would start looping tape now. They'd be on the fritz for twenty-seven minutes.

Then he turned to the lock box on the wall that contained all his weapons. He unlocked it and swung the door open. "Jesus."

It was the arsenal of an assassin.

He ran his hand over several of the guns. Tested the blades of the knives. Sharp as hell.

He'd forgotten.

He took down one of the knives. It felt natural and right in his hands. Not so different from the knives he always kept in his planes, except those were for nasty furry creatures and sawing through frozen rope. Not for people.

Luke turned the knife over in his hands, then pivoted and hurled it across the tunnel. It pierced the wall with a solid thunk, right between the eyes of the target he'd scrawled a decade ago.

Dark satisfaction pulsed inside him. "Your payback will come for shooting Isabella, Leon." His voice was cold. Lethal. Emotionless.

A voice he hadn't heard in eight years.

For a moment, Luke didn't move.

Then he slammed the locker shut and headed down the tunnel.

He left the knife behind.

CHAPTER TWENTY-EIGHT

It was almost dark by the time the cab pulled up in front of Isabella's old apartment building, the one where she'd been living during college when Marcus had found her. The same one she'd lived in with her mother for so long.

The exterior paint was peeling, and the first-floor windows were still covered with metal grills. She stared up at the gray cement building with a sinking heart. Had it been that depressing and decrepit when she'd lived there?

She knew it had.

She just hadn't been able to let herself see it. But now, after having been out of it for so long . . . it didn't make her homesick for her mother as she'd expected. It made her want to get out. And it reinforced her need to save Marcus, the man who had pulled her out of this life.

"You sure you want to get out here?" the cab driver asked.

"Yes." Isabella handed him some money. "Please wait for me."

"Yeah, okay." The cabbie pocketed the cash and pulled out a newspaper.

Isabella pushed the door open and stepped outside.

The sidewalk was cracked. Littered with trash. A couple of kids were tossing a basketball in the street. She paused, having a sudden memory of playing ball with her mom the same way.

Her throat tightened, and Isabella hurried up to the front door. Her key still worked, and the rusted door opened slowly.

The stench was of mildew and body odor, the walls yellowed and stained. She hurried up the stairs, her chest tight. The second door on the right. Apartment 21.

Her key ground in with a rough protest, and she held her breath as she pushed the door open. For six years, she'd paid the rent on this apartment, afraid to let go of a safety net. Needing to keep a backup in case her situation with Marcus went south.

She felt an overwhelming sense of depression as she stepped inside. The place was trashed, and the odor told her someone had been using it as a place to sleep. The window was broken, and cardboard was taped over it.

The bed she and her mother had shared was still against the wall, next to the kitchenette, and even the sheets were the same. Faded roses. But it was stained and filthy, the blankets half on the floor.

Tears filled Isabella's eyes. Had her mother really given her life and her soul to provide *this?* What an unfair life her mom had had.

Isabelle bit her lip and picked her way across the carnage. She pushed the bed aside, and nearly gagged at the stench. Beneath the bed was the same floorboard she'd taken the screws out of when she was eleven, after seeing someone do the floorboard stash in a movie.

Isabella pulled the board up. In the cavity was a

black cell phone. New and shiny. Exactly where Marcus had promised it would be. An untraceable phone, linked to his own emergency phone. Put there for her, just in case. In case she ever had to run.

The night he'd asked her to suggest a place he could stash an emergency phone for her, she hadn't understood why he wanted to do it.

But after Luke's story about his mother having to take off in the middle of the night, about not being able to call Marcus . . . she understood.

Despite what Luke thought, Marcus had learned from that experience. He'd taught Isabella to shoot, he'd taken her to the garage and shown her the SUV for a quick escape, and he'd followed through on his promise that there would always be a phone here for her. He had done what he could to keep her safe.

Tears filled her eyes and she carefully reached past the cobwebs and picked up the phone. "You did it, Marcus," she whispered. She held the phone to her chest. *I won't let you down.*

She tucked the phone into the pocket of her jeans, then reached farther beneath the wood. Inside was a box with a carved lid. She still remembered the street vendor who'd given it to her. An old man, hunched over, smelling faintly of stinky clams. She'd been eight and in awe over the beauty of the flowers engraved on it.

He'd given it to her. No money. No thanks. Just a gift.

Isabella pulled out the box and opened it. She thumbed through the pictures of her and her mother. And then the ring.

She picked up the diamond ring Stan had given her mother. Isabella had found it on the floor the night she'd come back after her mother had died. Thrown there by her mother after Stan had left?

She'd kept it, as a reminder not to count on anyone. Not to give anyone the power to hurt her.

Isabella turned it over in her hand. The diamond was small, and it had a yellowish tint. And yet to her and her mother, it had been the most beautiful thing they'd ever seen. It had represented freedom, a new life, a gift.

And it had been the biggest trap of all. It represented all the vulnerability her mother had exposed herself to by falling in love.

But Isabella didn't want a life like Luke's—isolated from everyone, unable to trust. She'd seen inside his soul, and she understood the pain that drove him. She'd seen his heart and knew it was broken. But it was a good heart. A heart she loved, just as she loved Marcus's.

Flaws and all.

Even if they both broke her heart, she refused to keep from offering it. They had taught her that love was out there, that the life she wanted was out there, and she would find it.

Isabella set the ring back in the box and placed the box in the middle of the bed. Maybe the person sleeping there would use it as a chance to start over.

Then she tucked the photos in her purse, double-checked to make sure she had the phone, and then she headed for the door.

She shut it and locked it behind her, then paused to look at the dirty, worn key. This was the security blanket she'd held on to? The home she could always return to if her new life fell apart?

No longer.

She would never come back.

Even if everything with Marcus went south, she was no longer the girl who would return to this world. She simply wouldn't. This home . . . it wasn't a security. It was her past, and she wouldn't return. She had come too far, and she'd done it on her own. She didn't need this anymore.

Isabella squatted and slid the key under the door.

And as she ran down the decrepit stairs, there was a lightness in her heart that had never been there before.

Luke was startled to see his old bedroom was exactly as he'd left it. His graduate diploma still leaned against the wall under the window where he'd stashed it, never bothering to hang it up. His favorite pen was still on the ornate desk he'd bought himself. The bookshelves were lined with his reference books.

Had Marcus thought he would come back?

Was the old man that naive? Marcus changed the decor of the house every six months, and yet he'd left Luke's room untouched for eight years?

It made no sense.

But as Luke strode across the room toward the door, Isabella's story popped into his mind. About how Marcus had sat there with that beach photo every night. Something tightened in his chest, and he quickly pushed it away. There was no room for wishful thinking.

Luke eased into the hallway and made his way silently down the corridor. Security cameras winked at him from every corner, but he ignored them, fully confident they weren't working. Footsteps raced down the hall, and Luke melted against the wall, almost hoping someone would come his way.

He heard someone yell that the security system was down, and then the footsteps thudded down the stairs, no doubt toward Marcus's office, where everything was controlled.

He reached Marcus's bedroom suite at the other end of the house with only a couple of close calls with a guard. Twenty-one minutes until the cameras would be engaged again.

Luke knocked on the door.

No answer.

He silently opened it and stepped inside. The room was unrecognizable from the last time he'd been there, which fit with Marcus's need to redecorate constantly. Another massive bed, huge dresser, ornate blinds that blocked out the sunshine.

Overdone.

Luke shook his head, almost amused at Marcus's awful taste. He'd forgotten how unappealing his father's style was.

Luke walked across the room and slid open the trophy case holding Marcus's most prized possessions. He removed the autographed Red Sox game ball from its case. He turned it over, carefully inspecting the stitching. He grinned when he saw that the coloring of the stitching of a two-inch section was still slightly off. He'd left it that way on purpose. A challenge to see if Marcus was smart enough to notice someone had tampered with his ball.

Marcus had failed.

Luke tossed the ball, but the earrings stashed inside didn't rattle. There was no indication they were inside. That would have made it too easy for Marcus.

Luke felt a faint hint of sadness that Marcus was so clueless. The man put on such a good show of being dominating, but Luke knew how weak his father was. He counted on those who surrounded him to back up the persona of power he carried. Inside, Marcus was weak. How did the man expect to survive in this business if he couldn't notice things like his most prized possession being tampered with? Of course he would have failed to notice signs Leon was planning a take-over . . .

Luke smiled ruefully at his thought. Isabella was clearly getting to him if he was actually contemplating the possibility that Marcus was innocent and Leon had set it all up. More likely, Leon had floated the idea of shooting Isabella for financial gain, and Marcus had clapped his hands in delight.

But for Isabella's sake, he needed to find out the truth before he took any action.

The answer would be in Marcus's office. Leon knew about the passageways leading to the office, and no doubt would have them rigged. It would be impossible to get down the back way. The only option would be the frontal assault, which Leon wouldn't be expecting.

But there was a hell of a risk of running into someone and being forced to act before he was ready. Luke paused on the landing of the main staircase and listened to the muted sounds of voices from below. Seventeen minutes until the cameras went back on.

Despite the risk, he needed to know what was really going on. For Isabella. For himself.

The baseball in hand, Luke headed straight for the men who'd been trying to kill him.

Isabella hurried up the stairs to their motel room, her heart pounding at the thought of using the phone Marcus had left for her. Would Luke think of it as a betrayal for her to call Marcus directly?

But Luke could be hurting Marcus even now. She had to do something.

She slid the key card in the lock. Would Luke really hurt his own father? In her heart, she didn't think so. She knew how much he valued human life, and she couldn't believe he would sacrifice his own standards. He'd suffer forever.

But what would he do to save his friends?

That was different.

She opened the door and stepped inside. "Luke?" She almost hoped he was back, so she wouldn't have to make the choice now. She wanted him to step out of the bathroom and tell her Marcus was safe, that all was well.

But the room was empty.

She threw her purse on the bed and walked into the bathroom. Flipped the light switch, but it didn't come on. She tried again.

It took the third attempt before she realized the lightbulb had been removed and was sitting on the edge of the sink. She stared at the white globe, and became aware of a faint breeze ruffling her hair.

She spun around to see that the window was open and the curtain was drifting in the breeze. The window had been closed and locked when she'd left. Luke had made dead certain the place was impenetrable.

And now it was open.

Her muscles twitched with the urge to race for the door, but she didn't move. She didn't know if someone was waiting for her in the room, preparing to pounce the moment she raced for the door.

Isabella swallowed, hooked her toe on the bathroom door, and ever so slowly began to pull it shut. There was a good lock on it, and Luke had augmented it when they'd arrived. If she could get it closed, she might be safe.

There was the faintest whisper of movement from the room, and Isabella slammed the door and threw the deadbolt.

The metal latch hit the casing and bounced back open.

Shit! The door wasn't closed all the way!

"Come on!" She slammed her hip against the door, and then the door flew open. She was flung into the opposite wall.

Leon stepped into the bathroom. "Welcome back to Boston, Isa."

CHAPTER TWENTY-NINE

Luke eased down the hall toward Marcus's office. He could hear voices coming from within and recognized one as Nate's.

But no Marcus.

The office door opened, and Luke ducked into the next room. He shut the door and waited.

Footsteps hurried past, but no one came in.

Luke's eyes adjusted to the interior and he frowned. This had been his office, right under Marcus's nose. But it had been completely redone. It was still an office though . . .

He quickly moved to the desk and sat down at the computer. The dim glare from the streetlight outside cast a small glow across the desk, and a photo of Isabella and another woman was propped right next to the monitor. He realized he was in Isabella's office, and he scowled when he saw the camera was still mounted in the corner. He didn't like the idea that Isabella had been kept so closely under Marcus's thumb. Had she known her every move had been on camera?

He didn't want her to come back here. He wanted her to be free.

He picked up the photo and peered more closely at it. Isabella appeared to be around sixteen, and the other woman didn't look much older. They were clearly related, with the same dark coloring and the same smile.

Her mother.

Isabella's eyes were dancing, and she had her head on her mom's shoulder. She looked young and vibrant. No makeup, no hardship in those beautiful eyes.

Her T-shirt was faded, and she was wearing big, gaudy earrings that looked as though they'd come from a street vendor. The peeling wallpaper behind the women was an ugly beige. The kitchen cabinet didn't fit quite right, and the counter was old linoleum.

But the two women were holding on to each other as though they were best friends, and nothing else mattered.

Isabella's mom wore ratty clothes similar to Isabella's, and there were lines around her mouth. But there was a sparkle in her eyes, a liveliness, and Luke suspected the picture had been taken while Isabella's mom was in love with Stan.

Around her mom's neck was the turquoise pendant Isabella always wore. Luke ran the pad of his finger over the necklace. The two women had had nothing but each other, and it was clear from their faces that had been enough.

Until Stan had ripped them apart.

Anger rumbled inside Luke, and he set the photo down. Isabella's childhood hadn't been so different from his: a loving mom taken away by a cold bastard who didn't appreciate what he had. Isabella deserved better than to put her lot in with the kind of man who would do it to her all over again. She needed someone who would stay by her side and love her, someone she could count on.

In another life, in a world where he didn't have hell

on his heels . . . who knew? Maybe he could try to be that man—

Shit. What was he thinking? *Pull yourself together, Webber.*

Luke pried his attention off the photo and began to inspect her desk. Countless folders on various artifacts, but nothing of interest. Her computer was on, as if someone had been using it. Had her notes on Luke been in there?

He checked his watch. Six minutes until the cameras kicked back on. It would take him four minutes to get back upstairs to the tunnel. Shit. He didn't have time to spend poking around her office. He moved to the door again. Listened. Heard nothing. Slowly, he opened the door and eased out into the hall.

The door to Marcus's office was open, and Luke crept toward it. He reached the doorway and crouched so he was below eye level. Then he peered around the corner.

What he saw made anger roil deep inside him.

Marcus was sitting behind his desk, wearing a suit. Ruling the fucking show.

So much for the kidnapping theory.

But Luke couldn't take his eyes off Marcus. The man looked *old*.

Luke was shocked by the slump of Marcus's shoulders, by the heavy lines on his face. Yeah, he still had his classy haircut, expensive clothes and a coldness to his face. But there was something else he hadn't remembered. Weight. Burden. Illness? Why hadn't Isabella told him there was something wrong with him?

Marcus wasn't the powerful man he used to be. Luke could see it in the weariness of his expression, in the sagginess of his skin. It was as if the weak man Luke had always known he was had finally broken through the facade Marcus tried to carry off, as if the spirit were too heavy to be disguised anymore.

Hell, he almost felt sorry for the old man.

Luke worked his jaw. *I will not care.* Marcus was still a ruthless bastard who deserved whatever harshness life had dealt him.

"You have three minutes to get those cameras working," Marcus snapped at a tech guy sweating it out over the security system.

Ah, yeah. The tone was the same. So much for Luke's brief moment of concern about poor Marcus. Spirit intact. Probably just up too late celebrating the fact that he'd lured Isabella and Luke back to Boston.

Nate was slouched in a chair, looking pouty and tired, while three other men stood around the office. Men who were clearly armed. One was the New York Yankees guy from the airport.

"So, start over, and tell me exactly what happened at the airport," Marcus said to Nate. His voice was harsh and laced with anger. "When you lost Isabella and my son." He gave Nate the cold stare that had made Marcus Fie legendary in his business circles. The stare no one ever fucked with. "Need I remind you exactly how long I spent planning that before you screwed it up?"

Son of a bitch.

It *had* all been a setup. Marcus had betrayed Isabella to try to get to Luke.

"You bastard," Luke whispered.

The betrayal sliced like a knife in his gut.

Not for himself.

For Isabella. He thought of the love in her eyes in that photo with her mother, and he finally understood why she'd latched on to Marcus. Isabella needed to love, and Marcus had filled that void in her life.

And the bastard had used her.

Luke set his hand on his gun. One move now, and it would be over. He pulled out his weapon, a dark coldness settling over his body.

No one was ready for him. He could simply walk in there, and they would all be dead within a minute.

Isabella would be free.

Then he closed his eyes. Jesus.

This was why he'd left. So he wouldn't become the cold-blooded murderer Nate had become.

"You will not win," he muttered. Killing Marcus in cold blood would leave the old man dying with a smile on his face because his son had finally joined his team, and Luke wouldn't give him that satisfaction.

Marcus would pay.

Marcus would suffer.

But not now. Not by the Fie method. It would be Luke's way.

He holstered the gun. "I'll be back for you."

Marcus stopped talking and looked toward the door.

Luke stepped back out of sight. Just before Marcus's gaze landed on him.

Isabella scrambled to her feet, and Leon grabbed her hair and yanked her across the bathroom. She yelped and dug her nails into his wrists, but he didn't release her. "Let go of me!"

Leon dragged her across the room and threw her on the bed. Before she could move, he was straddling her, his gun in her throat. "Where's Fie?"

Isabella closed her eyes so she couldn't look into the face of the man she used to trust. "Why are you doing this?" she asked. "I thought you were our friend."

"Shut the fuck up, Isa. This isn't about you." He pressed the gun tighter. "I need the necklace and the earrings. Where are they?"

Screw that. She wasn't going to make this easy for him.

She opened her eyes and stared into Leon's blue ones. She wanted to force him to see whom he was pointing a gun at. They'd been friends for so long. "Luke has them," she lied. "He has them all. He's going to trade them for Marcus."

Leon's eyes narrowed. "Don't lie to me."

Isabella's heart began to pound. "Fine. He went to Marcus's house to kill everyone. He's pissed."

Leon swore, and she knew he believed her. This was the man who knew Luke from his old life, and he actually believed Luke would go to Marcus's house and murder everyone? She felt a sudden sadness for the man Luke had once been.

"Give Luke a message for me," he said.

She shrank back from the coldness in his eyes. "What message?"

"Tell him I want the necklace and the earrings. That this time, I'm calling the shots."

Isabella tensed, already guessing Luke wouldn't respond to threats. He wasn't in victim mode. "He won't care—"

"He will." Then Leon flipped the gun around and slammed the butt into the side of her face.

Luke was halfway up the stairs when he realized the door to their hotel room was ajar.

Cold dread seized his gut. "Isabella!" He whipped out his gun and vaulted up the steps. "Isa!"

He sprinted for the door and slammed it open with his shoulder. Gun up, ready.

Wind was whipping through the room, and it was pitch-black. "Isa?"

He heard a whimper.

"Fuck!" His heart was pounding, but he didn't dare run for her. Gun still up, he edged over to the light switch and flicked it.

Light filled the room, and he had to fight not to close his eyes against the sudden glare. He kept his weapon up and ready, listening intently for any movement.

His eyes adjusted within a split second, and the first thing he saw was Isabella on the bed. She was bound with a cord, arms and feet tied behind her. Blood streamed from the side of her face and over her shirt.

"Jesus." His heart nearly stopped, and he forgot about any possible threats.

He just lowered his gun and tore across the room to her. "Isabella!"

Her left eye was swollen. There was a gag across her mouth. She made another desperate sound that cut at Luke like a dagger.

"I'm here, baby, I'm here." Luke grabbed a knife from his belt and sliced through the gag. He pulled the torn pillowcase from her mouth.

"It was Leon," she gasped.

"Leon?" His body went cold at the thought of Leon in the same room, and he shot to his feet, gun up. "Is he still here?"

"No. He went back to the house to keep you from killing Marcus."

"Good girl." How the hell had she kept her cool enough to think of the one thing that would have gotten Leon away from her before he had time to kill her?

Kill her. Jesus.

Anna's face flashed in Luke's mind, and he was suddenly frantic to cut the binds that held Isabella. He needed to free her. To take her away. "Hey, baby, I'm here now. I've got you. It's over."

"Luke." She groaned as he freed her arms, and Luke caught her as she rolled over. She was trembling and he pulled her into his arms. He crushed her against him, his mouth so dry he could barely talk. How close had he come to losing her? It was Anna all over again. His mother. Dead. Both of them. His mother bleeding to death—

"Shit!" He pulled back and frantically began to touch her. "Where are you hurt? Where's the blood coming from?"

She touched her face. "He hit me with his gun."

"Son of a bitch." Darkness rooted deep in his core, and Luke knew Leon had to die.

Luke Webber couldn't do what needed to be done. But Adam Fie could.

He cradled Isabella to his chest as he carried her to the bathroom to clean off the blood, and he opened his heart and invited Adam Fie back to life.

CHAPTER THIRTY

Isabella leaned her head against Luke's chest as he carried her into their new hotel room. It was almost twenty minutes from the one Leon had tracked them to, and Luke had made certain this one wasn't traceable.

"Hey, baby, we're here." Luke set her on the bed, then dropped their bags on the floor. He'd carried them all at the same time, refusing to leave her alone to go back to the car.

Isabella wearily rolled onto her side to watch him as he checked the room and set up safeguards on the doors and windows. He kept looking over at her, and there was such worry on his face.

And guilt. So much guilt.

She knew about that emotion. How many years had she tortured herself for not knowing the right words when her mom had called her? The words that would have kept her mother at home that night, that would have kept her alive.

"Let me get you some ice." Luke dumped the bucket of ice he'd retrieved on the way up into the sink, and then wrapped a handful of it in a towel.

He eased onto the bed next to her. He helped her adjust so she was using his thigh as a pillow. He lightly set the ice on her cheek and stroked her hair. She closed her eyes at the tender touch.

"Luke."

"Yeah."

"What happened? Did you find the earrings?"

"Yeah." He nodded at his bag. "They're in a baseball that was in Marcus's bedroom."

She tensed. "Is he okay?" She could barely bring herself to ask, so afraid of the answer.

Luke said nothing.

She pulled the ice pack off her face and sat up. "What happened?"

A veil dropped over his face, and she knew he wasn't going to tell her.

"Luke!"

"I didn't touch him. He's fine."

She knew there was more he wasn't telling her, but the way he bit out the words told her what he said was the truth.

Luke hadn't betrayed her.

From the tension on his face and in his jaw, she knew how hard it had been to walk away. And she knew he'd done it for her. Her throat tightened. He'd spent a lifetime hating his father, and yet for her, he'd left him alone. She leaned over and pressed her lips lightly to his. "Thank you, for leaving him alive." *For being the man I believed you were.*

He said nothing, but his eyes were dark and stormy as he searched her face. He kept stroking her hair, his fingers tangling in her curls. So much intensity in his face. So much complexity. So much hurt.

So much strength.

Something welled deep in her heart, and she knew she had no more defenses against him. His leaving

Marcus alive had broken through the last barriers she had around her heart. "My dear Luke." She placed her hands on either side of his anguished face, needing to take away his guilt over the fact that she'd gotten attacked. "You are an amazing man. You make me feel safe. You give me a place I've never had before."

He caught her wrists and held tightly, searching her face. "I fucked up." His voice was anguished. "I should have realized Leon would find us—"

"No." She placed her hands over his lips. "You need to stop. You need to forgive yourself."

"Jesus, Isa." He caught her shoulders. "When I saw you on that bed with all that blood? It was my mother and then Anna and—"

"I love you."

He stiffened. "No!"

"Yes!" She straddled his lap and leaned close to him. "Don't you get it? You can't keep the world out, and you can't protect us all by keeping us away. I love you, and you're a good man. I loved my mother despite her past, I love Marcus no matter what he's done, and I love you. Because all of you have good souls and are worth loving."

He searched her face, and she saw his disbelief, his struggle. "I—"

She kissed him.

For a split second, he tensed, and she had a sinking feeling he was going to push her away.

And then his arms snapped around her and he yanked her against him. He took over the kiss. Turned it from a gentle kiss designed to convince him she loved him to a kiss of raw need, of raw passion, of such burning force that heat seared through her.

"Yes," she whispered. "Kiss me."

"Isa." He growled her name, a fierce possession that made chills rush down her spine. He grabbed her shirt and ripped it over her head. His mouth was frantic on her skin, his hands desperate as he nearly tore her bra off. Then his shirt, his pants, hers, until they were skin to skin. His mouth never left her body, his hands never stopped touching her, as if he couldn't get enough of her, no matter how hard he tried. Her throat, her collarbone, her breasts, her ribs, her hips, her legs, every inch of her was his, and he was taking her. His touch was firm, a statement of ownership, as if he needed to prove to himself that she was his, that he really could have her.

Isabella's heart ached for his need, for his intensity. The man who had strived so hard to separate himself from friends and family, who had isolated himself for the protection of others . . . it had all been a lie, and his need for her was so evident in his kisses, in the way he whispered her name against her ear, in the way he buried his face in her hair. "God, Isa, I thought I'd lost you—"

"You can't lose me," she whispered. "I'm a survivor. Life can't beat me."

He paused to search her face. "You are a survivor, aren't you?"

She smiled. "I am. You don't need to worry about me. No matter how much you love me, it won't kill me."

He swore. "You have no idea what you're facing."

"Oh, but I do." Isabella grabbed his hair and pulled him toward her. "I know exactly what I'm facing, and I know that with you by my side, we can do anything."

He resisted her attempts to kiss him. "My life is hell—"

"It's my life already. I got shot by Leon before I even met you." She smiled. "All you can do is make me safer. I already get in enough danger on my own." She lightly pounded her fist on his chest. "Don't you get it, Luke? I'm already involved with the demons who stalk you, and there's no way I'm going to walk away, no matter how hard you try to make me. The danger I'm in is my choice, and has nothing to do with the fact that I love you. *It's not your fault!*"

His eyes darkened with acceptance, with awe. "*Isa.*" He fisted her hair and kissed her.

A ruthless, demanding kiss. A kiss of such intensity and passion that she realized he'd been holding back before. Now there was nothing between them but their own need for each other. She clung to him, kissing him back as fiercely as he was kissing her. Needing him. Embracing him and all he was. She wanted more. Craved more. Couldn't live without more. "Make love to me, Luke." Not sex. Love.

Without breaking the kiss, he rolled her onto her back and moved between her legs. He plunged deep instantly, and she cried out at the sensation of him making her his. Of him moving deep inside her. Of their bodies intimately entwined. Ripples of fire raced through her body, and her heart ached with love, with passion, with everything she had ever wanted to feel for another human, but never had.

"God, Isa." Luke caught her mouth in a heady kiss that shredded what little inhibition she still had, taking over her mind and body until she was consumed by him. By his kiss, by his hands, by his body protectively pinning her beneath him, by the sensation of his moving in and out of her, faster and faster, intensity growing and growing, until she couldn't think, couldn't breathe, just needed more and more and more—

The orgasm ripped through her like an explosion of heat and fire and scorching passion. Luke shuddered above her, and then he was pounding deep, holding her so tightly against him she felt like no one would ever be able to rip her away from him. Again and again, and then he shouted her name and his body went rigid, his grip on her never relenting.

She clung to him as the orgasm rocked him, holding him tightly and supporting him while he surrendered himself to her. When he was spent, he simply dropped on top of her, and pressed his face to her neck. Not moving, not speaking. Just holding her tight, almost desperately.

Isabella wrapped her arms around his head and kissed his hair. The man who stood alone had completely capitulated to her. He'd let down his shields and let her in.

Tears filled her eyes at the gift he had given her. *I won't let you regret it, Luke.*

Without lifting his head from the curve of her neck, he laid his hand across her bruised cheek. He stroked lightly, and his muscles began to tense.

"Luke, don't—"

"Don't try to stop me, Isa. It has to be done." His voice was cold, his fingers still methodically stroking her face, as if he were feeding his rage with her injury.

He was planning his revenge. He was planning his assault to take out the threat against her. It would destroy them both, on so many levels, but she knew he saw no other choice.

It was up to her to repay the gift he'd given her. To save him from the man he used to be.

She knew what she had to do.

Isabella waited until Luke was asleep. He was tucked up behind her, his arms and legs pulling her into the protective shield of his body. His face was nestled in her hair, and he had her wrapped up so tightly she couldn't tell where her body ended and his began.

She felt cherished, loved and protected. Everything she had ever wanted. And she knew it wasn't conditional. Marcus had loved her because she had insinuated her way into his business. Her mother hadn't loved her enough to stay alive. But Luke was willing to sell his soul to keep her, and his friends, safe. All she offered him was difficulty and stress, and yet he'd still given himself to her.

She'd done nothing to make Luke stay, and yet he was staying anyway. Just because of who she was. She treasured him for the gift he'd given her, and that was why she had to save him. But she knew he might hate her forever for what she was about to do. "I love you, Luke."

His only response was the deep breathing of sleep.

Her heart aching with regret, Isabella tried to wiggle out of his embrace. He muttered something and tightened his grip on her. "I need to go to the bathroom," she whispered. "I'll be right back." When he didn't respond, she lightly tapped his arm. "I'll be three feet away from you," she whispered. "Let me up."

This time, he loosened his grip enough for her to slip out. She paused to look at him once she was free. His face was tense even in sleep, and she had to resist the urge to smooth his brow. That wasn't the way to give him true peace.

She forced herself to turn away. In the corner was her bag with the cell phone she'd retrieved from her old apartment. Padding silently across the carpet in her bare feet, Isabella grabbed her purse and took it into the bathroom. She shut the door and turned on the shower to drown out her voice.

The phone powered right up. There was one stored number—the one Marcus had programmed into it. "I hope you will forgive me, Luke," she whispered.

And then she hit send.

No one answered, and she got a recording that her party was unavailable.

Marcus had always sworn he'd answer that phone. Something was wrong. Luke hadn't lied about Marcus being okay, had he?

She dismissed the idea before it had time to take root. She believed Luke. She trusted him.

So she dialed again. Again, she got the recording.

A third time she tried.

One ring. Two rings. Three rings.

"Isa." His voice was low, as if he were trying to keep himself from being overheard.

"Marcus!" She couldn't keep the joy out of her voice. "You're okay!"

"Why are you calling me?"

"I want to make a deal to get you free and to keep Luke safe."

He sighed. "My dear sweet Isa, don't get involved. I—"

"I have the earrings," she interrupted. "And the necklace."

She heard Marcus's sharp intake of breath. "You really have the earrings?"

"Yes! Will that be enough to get Leon and Nate to let you go? To get them off Luke's case?"

A long pause. "I think it might."

She gripped the phone. "Tell me what to do. Tell me how to handle Leon."

Marcus was silent for a long moment, and then he started giving her instructions.

CHAPTER THIRTY-ONE

Something was wrong.

Luke jerked awake. He grabbed his gun off the floor and jumped up.

No Leon.

What the fuck?

Then he saw the bed. Empty.

"Isa!" He vaulted over the bed to check the bathroom, but he knew what he'd find.

Empty.

"Isabella!" He bellowed her name, and the only answer was silence. "Fuck!" He bolted for the door, then noticed a paper with his name on it taped to the door.

Something froze deep inside him.

They had her.

He snatched the paper off the door and flipped it over. It took him a minute to realize what he was reading. It wasn't from Leon. The curly, delicate script was from Isabella.

> *My dearest Luke,*
>
> *Forgive me. I couldn't let you destroy yourself or us. I am meeting with Marcus to give back the necklace and the earrings, and to negotiate your freedom. I love you. Isabella.*

Luke crushed the note in his hand, a vise closing around his heart. He'd tried to protect her by not telling her the truth about Marcus, that he was clearly still running the operation. That he'd been using Isabella and had probably even given Leon the green light to hurt her.

And in return, she'd betrayed Luke on every level.

She'd put herself in danger. She'd stolen the earrings that had been his insurance policy for eight years. She'd stripped him of his leverage, and she'd dismissed all of his expertise on the situation and her safety.

He knew damn well Leon's attack of Isabella had been to show him he could get to Isabella any time, any place, just as he had with Anna. It had been a warning not just to return the earrings, but to get back in the game. A statement that Adam Fie belonged to Marcus and his empire.

And now she'd gone and delivered herself into their hands.

Because she hadn't trusted Luke. She hadn't believed his analysis of the situation, had refused to trust his judgment on how to deal with it.

Isabella had chosen to align herself with Marcus instead of Luke.

A dark cloud wrapped around him, and he hurled the paper aside. He'd trusted her. He'd put himself out there, and she had walked away, taking everything he had.

Taking the earrings . . .

Jesus. Had she been in on the setup all along? Marcus had to have known Luke would never have turned the earrings over to him. That he would have jumped ship at the first hint he'd been found. But Isabella's arrival had changed everything.

Isabella had gotten Luke to play ball.

And now, she'd taken the earrings and left him in the middle of the night.

An icy lethality gripped him. He stalked across the floor and grabbed his phone. He called Kaylie.

She answered on the first ring. "Cort's dying."

Luke closed his eyes. "He's not dying," he snapped. "Cort's too tough to die."

"He's in a coma. He had a brain bleed from the surgery. He's dying, Luke." Sobs took over and she hung up the phone.

Luke shut his phone off and shoved it in his pocket.

He'd lost it all. By trying to be Luke Webber, he'd lost it all.

There was nothing left to lose.

Adam Fie began to assemble his weapons.

Isabella paused just down the block from Marcus's house. There were two guards inside the front gate, dressed like doormen, but she recognized their stance and knew they were armed. Marcus had never employed guards. He didn't trust strangers enough to bring them in to keep him safe. He built his own safeguards and developed his own inner circle of those he trusted.

She hesitated, fisting the strap of her handbag.

For the hundredth time, she went over Marcus's instructions in her mind.

To her surprise, he hadn't wanted her to stash the jewelry somewhere else and come without it. He feared they would simply torture her into giving it to them. He wanted her to simply hand it over and give them what they wanted.

Capitulation had never been Marcus's style, and it broke her heart to hear how subdued he sounded. She'd expected some innovative plan, not a simple delivery.

But she trusted him, and she just wanted it to end. She wanted to take Marcus out of there and to get Luke his life back. It wasn't about winning or losing or pride. It was about getting out, and maybe Marcus finally understood that. Maybe Marcus had finally understood the lesson he should have learned when his wife was murdered.

She took a deep breath, then walked up to the front gate.

Her shoulder started to burn from the bullet wound, and her face was throbbing from where Leon had hit her. "I'm here to see Leon," she announced. "My name is Isabella Kopas."

One of the guards nodded and unlocked the gate. "He's expecting you."

Isabella stepped inside the gate, and it swung shut behind her with a loud clank. Then she marched up the front steps of the place that had been her home for so long.

Nate opened the front door as she walked up the steps. His nose was swollen and he had two black eyes. "Nice of you to make it easy for me."

Isabella swallowed. "I'm here to see Leon."

"Yeah, I got that." He slammed the door shut. "You got 'em?"

She licked her lips as she heard the lock engage behind her, trapping her. Dear God, what if Marcus were wrong? "Where's Leon?"

Nate leaned into her. "You made me look bad, and I don't like that."

Isabella ducked under his arm and bolted down the hall toward Marcus's office. Nate's taunting trailed after her, and she immediately forced herself to slow down. He was just messing with her. Leon was in charge.

Nate would never touch her. "Trust Marcus's judgment," she whispered.

She wished she'd brought Luke with her to keep her safe . . . But no, the whole point was to free him. She could handle this.

She was poised and controlled by the time she strode into Marcus's office.

The first thing she saw was Marcus sitting at his desk, wearing a suit. He appeared tired, but not as if he'd been locked up in a hostage situation for the last few days. Leon was leaning against the desk, his arms folded across his chest.

Isabella tightened her grip on her bag. "Marcus?"

"Do you have them?"

"What's going on?"

Marcus sighed, and she saw the weariness in his shoulders. The strain in his eyes. Something was wrong. "Just give them to me, Isa."

Slowly, she pulled the necklace out of her purse and set it on the desk.

Leon picked it up and inspected it. "It's the real one."

As if he could tell! She was the only one here who could make that kind of call. But Leon was speaking as if he were the voice of authority. Marcus would never let Leon have first inspection of it. Marcus controlled everything . . . what was going on?

"The earrings."

Isabella took the ball and tossed it at Marcus. He caught it before Leon could intervene. "My baseball?"

"They're inside. They always have been."

A small smile played at Marcus's mouth. "That's so like Adam," he said, his respect evident in his tone. "A sense of humor and a little bit of attitude."

Leon pulled out a knife. "Give it to me."

Marcus hesitated, then handed it over. "Be careful with it. It's valuable."

Isabella frowned as Marcus let Leon dig into the ball. "Marcus? What's going on?"

He met her gaze, and she saw the regret. "I'm sorry, Isabella."

Oh, God. What had he done? "About what?"

Marcus nodded to someone behind her. "We're done with her."

She spun around to see Nate standing behind her. He was grinning. "I saw the way Adam is with her," he said. "He'll definitely come after her. We have him."

"What?" Isabella backed away from Nate. "Why do you need Luke? You have the earrings—"

"Marcus fucked up," Leon snapped.

Isabella's heels hit the baseboards, and she realized she couldn't back up any farther. There was nowhere else to go. "What are you talking about?"

"Marcus's reputation took a major hit when he didn't deliver those earrings eight years ago," Leon said. "And profits have been spiraling ever since. It's time to turn it around, and we can't do it without Adam on the payroll. We've got new requests our current field staff don't have the expertise to handle. No one is as good as Adam when it comes to antiquities, and some clients won't work with us unless he's on their case."

"But he quit the business—"

"As long as he has you to protect, he'll do whatever we want. Sending you after him worked out exactly as we figured it would." Leon grinned.

Isabella stiffened. "You sent me after Luke?"

Leon snorted. "You think it was a fluke you ran straight to Adam after that night? We needed the earrings and we knew Adam would disappear again if we went after him. But he's never been able to turn down a pretty girl."

Isabella wrapped her arms around her stomach. "Marcus? Is that true?"

He shook his head. "It wasn't like that, Isa."

"What was it like?" She felt sick. "Did you set me up to go after him?"

"Just for the earrings!" he said wearily. "All this other stuff wasn't supposed to happe—"

"Tell her the rest," Leon interrupted.

Marcus swiveled toward the younger man. "There's no more—"

"Tell her about last time. We made a mistake last time. Tell her the mistake, Marcus."

Isabella stared at Marcus, her heart aching. "Tell me what?"

Marcus looked beaten. So destroyed. "I tried to control Adam through Anna. It didn't work."

"Once she was dead," Leon said, "we had no way to manipulate him. And now we do, thanks to you."

A cold chill settled around Isabella's heart. Utter betrayal. "You killed Anna?" she whispered.

"No!" Marcus sat up. "I didn't mean for that to happen! I just needed those earrings—"

"Stop." Isabella shook her head, feeling sick to her stomach. "I don't want to hear it. I trusted you, Marcus. I believed in you." She had to get out of there. Had to get away from him.

"Isabella! You have to listen—"

"No! I don't owe you anything!" She turned and stumbled to the door. She'd trusted him with everything, and he'd betrayed her on every level. And he'd betrayed his own son.

Nate caught up with her at the door and grabbed her arm. "You're not going home, Isa. You're here for good."

She didn't bother to resist as he dragged her down the hall.

She'd blown it. She'd betrayed Luke. Instead of freeing him, she'd trapped him forever. Instead of two men who loved her, she had none.

Nate shoved her into her old room and locked the door behind her.

She stared numbly at the lush drapes, at the massive ornate bed, at the hand-woven Oriental carpet on the floor. The room that had once been home. It seemed like a stranger's room. It was cold and impersonal. Too perfect. No touch of herself in there. Just Marcus's decorator's opinion.

It was nothing like Luke's home in Alaska. That had been a home.

She'd had her chance. And she'd thrown it aside.

She'd lost it all.

Luke tossed his weapons in the passenger seat of the truck and climbed inside.

He was focused. Intent.

He had one goal: to make it end.

It didn't matter how it had to happen. He was willing to take it all the way. He was taking his life back, and he was avenging his mother, Anna and Cort.

As for Isabella . . .

Darkness settled around his heart as he jammed the truck into gear.

Isabella had lost.

CHAPTER THIRTY-TWO

Isabella peered out her window, assessing the distance to the ground.

It was a second-story window, but it was high, and the drop to the brick patio was too far. But she had to find a way to get out and warn Luke—

"Isa!"

She whirled around as Marcus slipped into the room. "What do you want?"

"Shh!" He shut the door behind him and leaned against it, exhaustion making his shoulders droop. "Do you know how to reach Adam?"

She narrowed her eyes. "Why?"

"They're waiting for him. Leon knows about his access tunnel from another house. Adam's got no chance. Can you warn him not to come?"

"He won't come for me—"

"He will." Marcus levered himself off the door. "I found out what happened in Alaska with his friend. He won't let it go, and he won't let you go."

"I betrayed him!"

"Doesn't matter. He'll come. He's been pushed too far." Marcus sighed and walked over to the bed. He sank onto the thick mattress like an old man.

"But you tried to trap him!" She wouldn't fall for him again, no matter how exhausted he appeared.

Marcus shook his head, and he gave her an imploring look. "I don't expect you to forgive me, but you need to know the truth. Ever since Adam left, my reputation has been dicey. I've been trying to recover it, and Leon has been instrumental. I've given him more and more power, and it's gotten out of control."

Isabella pressed her lips together.

"When he found out I'd located the necklace several weeks ago, he wanted a piece of the money. He found a buyer for the whole set, and he committed us to it." Marcus rubbed his hand over his eyes. "It's for a tremendous amount of money, and once Leon arranged the deal, he snapped. He will do anything to make sure it comes through, including murder. I had to give Leon those earrings, and I knew Adam still had them."

Isabella sank down onto the high-backed chair in the corner. "You really sent me after him?"

Marcus nodded. "I let Adam go eight years ago. I hadn't meant for Anna to get killed, but Leon arranged it, making sure it looked like my doing. If I tried to turn him in for it, it would have come back to me. But I knew it was my fault, and I saw it was breaking my son, so I let him go. I helped cover his path, and I was never going to bother him again."

Did she believe him? He sounded so broken, but she didn't know what to think anymore. "Then why go after him now?"

"I had to. Leon will kill for them, and he'll kill Adam if he has to. I was hoping to get the earrings back without compromising Adam."

Isabella dug her fingernails into her palms to keep from responding to his visible anguish.

"Leon decided to go after Adam and force him to come back." Marcus wiped his hand over his brow. "The thought of Leon hurting my son makes me sick. I couldn't let him do it. I thought he only wanted the earrings, so I convinced him if Adam found out we were after him, those earrings would disappear forever. I thought you would be able to get the earrings from him and bring them back. Then Leon would never have to know where he was and Adam could continue with his new life."

She had to admit Marcus had specifically instructed her not to keep records of her search for Luke, so no one else would be able to find him. She wanted to believe him so much, but she was afraid to trust him again. She didn't know what to think.

"But Leon somehow found out where Adam was, and he took over." Marcus's face grew even more solemn. "He knew how much of an asset to the business Adam always was, and he had apparently made a deal with the new client for future business, that Adam would be his sole employee. That convinced the client to hand over a sizeable retainer." Marcus rubbed his head. "Jesus, this got so out of hand, but I don't have any options, Isabella. Everything is in danger if we don't follow through. He'll kill me, and probably you and Adam as well."

Isabella sagged against the chair. "How could you stay involved in something like this? After it killed your wife?"

Marcus shrugged. "I was young and stupid. Obsessed with more. I thought I could avenge her death."

Isabella went cold. "Did you?"

Marcus met her gaze. "Yes. I did. Leon was with me, but I took out everyone."

"So that's it, then." Understanding finally dawned.

"That's what Leon has over you. He'll turn you in for that if you don't behave."

"I killed seven men that day. In cold blood. I was insane with grief and anger." Marcus stood and walked to the window. "All I could think of was my lovely Rebecca, so sweet and innocent. I'd been working so hard to give her the life she deserved." His voice grew hard. "I wasn't even thinking. I just had to destroy those who had killed her. Leon helped me find them and he gave me the guns. It was the first time I'd ever killed, the only time." His fingers dug into the wood. "That night changed me forever. I became hard. I stopped feeling."

"And you stopped loving your son."

Marcus turned his head. "I stopped feeling anything until you came into my life. You woke up a part of my soul that had died with my wife." He gestured at the door. "And I'm in too deep to get out. If I try to leave, you'll die. Adam will die." He snorted. "I don't care about myself, but I won't let anyone else die because of me."

"So then why didn't you stop them?"

"Because I had to get those earrings or you both would have been dead anyway!" Marcus snapped. "I was hoping the earrings would be the end of it."

"But it's not."

"No." He levered himself off the window. "I'm sorry, Isa. I truly am. I don't expect you to forgive me. But at least you are both alive. That's all I can offer you." He tossed her a cell phone, and she caught it. "Call Adam. Warn him. Tell him to disappear." He walked toward the door and opened it. "You're too valuable for them to kill. I'll make sure they understand that. I'll do my best. But my son must come first. I owe him that."

And then he was gone.

Isabella closed her fist around the phone. Did she

trust Marcus or not? Would calling Luke be the final nail in his coffin? Or had that been a true olive branch from Marcus?

Was Marcus really a good man who was just too weak to stand up for himself? A man who had been broken after the death of his wife? Or was he so ruthless that he would hang his own son out to dry?

She clenched the phone and knew she had to make a choice.

Now.

And there would be no going back.

Luke pulled up in the driveway of the same house he'd used earlier to access Marcus's house. He grabbed his duffel bag and swung down out of the truck. He strode across the lawn toward the garage door. There were explosives in his bag. Guns.

Marcus's empire would be dust by the time he finished with it. Artifacts destroyed. Records annihilated. Marcus, Leon and Nate would be dead.

It was the only way Adam Fie knew.

Luke stopped walking and closed his eyes. Luke Webber would walk away from all of this. He would just disappear and let the bastards drown in their own filth and inner mutiny. Luke Webber wouldn't let himself be destroyed by his past.

But how many times had he walked away? And it hadn't ended. It had just gotten worse and more people had gotten hurt.

He ground his jaw. There was only one way to make sure people like Cort and Anna never suffered again. He had to play their game.

He tightened his grip on his bag, and he committed himself.

People would die today, and he was going to be the one to pull the trigger.

Luke reached for the doorknob, and his cell phone vibrated in his pocket. He jerked it out and saw the number was blocked. The hospital? *Come on, Cort.* Luke answered the phone. "Yeah."

"It's a trap!"

He stiffened at the sound of Isabella's voice.

"I'm so sorry, Luke, I really am. I thought I was doing the right thing to save you. But I was wrong! I mean, I was right that Leon is manipulating Marcus. He is basically blackmailing him. They're using me as bait to force you to come, and they're waiting for you."

Luke jerked the door open and stepped into the garage. The agitation in her tone hammered at him, and he had to fight to ask if she was all right. If they'd hurt her. *She betrayed you.*

"Luke! Don't come. Just walk away."

He walked across the garage toward the small passageway that led to Marcus's house. "Why should I trust you?"

"Because I love you."

Luke closed his eyes at her declaration, and something turned in his chest. He couldn't trust her. She'd made her choice.

"I know you have no reason to believe me," she said. "I understand that. But I believed in Marcus, and I believed I could convince him to let you go. I found out he sent me after you to get the earrings, and then Leon took over. But I swear to you, I didn't know. I took the earrings only to save you. To free you. I love you, Luke. If you come here, you will be trapped forever in this life. They'll never let you go. Don't come!"

Luke crouched on the floor to unlock the trapdoor.

Her words made sense. And God, he wanted to believe her. But he didn't believe in anyone anymore. Marcus had stripped that from him. For all he knew, it was just her ploy to keep him from hurting Marcus.

"Luke? Are you there?"

He wanted to take her words to heart. He wanted to know she was on his side, no matter what.

But he couldn't.

He didn't have the ability to trust anymore. "I don't know what game you're playing." He triggered the floor and it began to slide open.

"They know about your access point through that house! Don't use it!"

"My—" Luke had one second to register what she'd said, and then a gun emerged from the tunnel below and Leon rose through the opening.

"Welcome home, Fie."

Luke froze. His duffel was too far away to be of use. Sweet Jesus, Isabella had been telling the truth. She'd actually tried to keep him safe. Instead of trying to get him to rescue her, she'd tried to get him to run. Second thoughts after betraying him? Or was she telling the truth about everything? Had she really tried to save him the whole time?

The moment the thought passed through his mind, it felt right, all the way down to his core. The part of him who was Luke Webber knew, with absolute certainty, that she hadn't betrayed him.

She'd shown him that all along, but he'd let his bitterness rule him. He'd let Adam Fie rule. Isabella had tried to teach him how to have faith, and he hadn't listened. Hadn't let her in.

He'd fucked up, and now they were both screwed.

CHAPTER THIRTY-THREE

Leon had a gun to the back of Luke's neck when he forced him into Marcus's office.

Marcus was no longer sitting at his desk.

He was tied to an armchair with a gag in his mouth. A dark bruise was forming on his right temple, and blood trickled from the corner of his mouth. His head sagged forward, as if he would have fallen over without the ropes holding him up. Jesus. "Marcus?"

The old man's head jerked up and their gazes met. For the first time, Luke noticed the pain etched in Marcus's eyes, in the lines of his face. He didn't look like a ruthless businessman. He looked like an old, beaten soul who had lost the will to live.

Luke jerked his gaze to Leon. "What did you do to him?"

"Caught him sneaking out of Isabella's room." Leon shoved Luke into another chair. "Now that I've got you, I don't need him anymore anyway. It's time for the new generation to take over." Leon grinned. "And that would be you."

"Fuck that—"

"Luke!"

He spun toward the door in time to see Nate yank Isabella into the room. Her face was a dark purple and black from Leon's assault on her, and her eye was still puffy. He leapt up. "Isa!"

Nate shoved her at Luke, and Luke caught her as she fell into him. Her body was soft and warm against his, and some of his tension eased now that he had her. It was as if his soul knew this was where he belonged. The mere feel of her in his arms cleared his mind and brought him into focus.

"I'm so sorry, Luke." Her anguish was genuine.

He shook his head and kissed her temple. "It's my fault. I was an ass not to listen to you." If he hadn't been so caught up in hating Marcus, maybe he would have figured out what was going on. He was a scientist, a man built on analytical assessment, and he'd totally blown it.

She blinked, and she realized he wasn't angry with her. Her face crumbled and she threw her arms around him. "I love you!" she whispered fiercely.

Luke tensed at her words, and Leon exchanged smug looks with Nate.

Carefully, Luke peeled her off of him. For a split second, Isabella looked confused, but then she glanced over at Nate. Immediately, she stepped back from Luke. Her face was taut with the realization that she'd just revealed too much to the enemy.

Nate grabbed her and yanked her back over to him. He set his arm over her shoulder and pulled her close. Then he nuzzled her neck.

Son of a bitch—

Leon cocked a gun and pressed it to Isabella's temple.

Luke forced himself not to react. He needed to be smarter than he had been for the last eight years. He had to find a way to tap into the skills he'd ditched when he walked away. He channeled his adrenaline into focus, into a lethal-assault mode.

"I was wrong eight years ago," Leon said.

Luke scanned the office, taking quick inventory. Books. Computer. Chairs. Nothing to use against a gun. But he knew Marcus had guns hidden. Or he used to. One had been in the wall safe. Not reachable. Another in a coffee table that was no longer there. The whole room had been redone. None of the old hideaways still existed. What new places would he have chosen?

"I thought killing Anna would make you mine," Leon continued.

Luke's attention snapped to Leon. "You killed Anna." He kept his voice flat. Emotionless. Giving away nothing.

"I did." Leon rubbed the nose of the gun against Isabella's neck. She tensed, and Luke had to take his gaze off her to keep his focus. "Marcus instructed me not to kill her. I figured he was wrong."

Luke jerked his attention to Marcus. The old man was watching Luke, and he nodded once in acknowledgment. Jesus. Marcus had been telling the truth? He hadn't had Anna killed?

"Turns out, you take off when the women you love get killed. I thought you'd do me the favor of killing your old man and taking over the business." Leon wiggled the gun against Isabella. "So this time, we'll just hurt your girlfriend. We'll make her suffer whenever you aren't a good little boy. It's time for you to come back to work for us."

Luke shifted his attention back to Leon, his mind rapidly processing everything Leon had said. Trying to sift the truth from the lies.

Leon handed his gun to Nate, who immediately pointed it at Luke.

Then Leon pulled out a hunting knife and pressed it to Isabella's injured shoulder. She winced and couldn't quite stifle her gasp of pain.

Blood began to pound in Luke's head.

Leon moved behind Isabella, as if using her as a shield. Then he tossed a gun at Luke.

Luke caught it and immediately aimed it at Leon. "Stupid fuck."

"One bullet." Leon bent down so Isabella was blocking all but one side of his head. "You shoot me, you risk hitting the girl. If by some dumb luck you manage to hit me and not your girlfriend, Nate still has his gun and will delight in taking you out."

Luke took aim at Leon's eye, then swore when Leon pushed Isabella. She stumbled right into his line of fire and he jerked the gun aside. Fuck.

"Kill your father," Leon said.

Luke stared at him. "What?"

"Marcus. Kill him." Leon pressed the knife into Isabella's shoulder, and she let out a small gasp of pain. "Every minute you delay, she gets cut again."

Kill Marcus. The gift he'd been waiting for. Luke aimed the gun at the man who had once been his father.

Marcus raised his head and looked right at the barrel of the gun. There was no fear in his eyes. No resistance.

Just relief.

Relief? To die?

He must be mistaken. Luke set his finger on the trigger. "This is for my mother."

Marcus nodded.

Luke hesitated at Marcus's immediate acquiescence. "And for Anna."

Marcus nodded again, which didn't make sense after Leon's declaration that Marcus wasn't responsible.

"Do it now," Leon ordered.

Marcus's gaze met Luke's, and Luke was shocked when he realized his father wanted to be shot. It was a face begging for relief of a lifetime of guilt and anguish. A man devastated by guilt. Not a ruthless mogul. A broken man.

Luke swore, and the gun started to tremble.

"Now!"

"Don't kill him," Isabella shouted. "He loves you! He—" She screamed and Luke whirled around in time to see Leon yank his knife out of her shoulder. His arm was tight around her neck, forcing her to stay in front of him and shield him.

Fury roiled inside him at her suffering. She raised her chin and met his gaze, and his heart tightened for her courage, for her refusal to capitulate. For her unconditional love of those who mattered to her. He hadn't been worthy of her.

It was time to change that fact.

Slowly, Luke raised his gun. "I love you, Isabella, but this will never end. I can't let you live like this."

Her eyes widened. "Luke? What are you doing?"

"I saw in Marcus's eyes that he wanted me to kill him to free him from the suffering. He doesn't deserve that gift. You do." He let her see the love in his face, in his heart. That he would give up the world for her. "I give you the gift of freedom." Then he pointed the gun at Isabella's forehead and pulled the trigger.

Isabella realized Luke's intention a split second before he fired.

She slammed her elbow into Leon's gut and dropped

out of his arms the moment his grip loosened. She was still falling to the floor when gunfire shattered the silence of the room.

Leon collapsed beside her on the carpet, a precise bullet hole in the center of his forehead. Nate raised his gun to fire at Luke, and Isabella flung herself at his leg to knock him off balance. His gun went off as he stumbled, and Luke clasped his side and dropped to his knees. Blood stained his shirt almost instantly, and Isabella screamed, "Luke!"

She lunged to her feet, but Nate grabbed her and flung her to the side. She crashed into a coffee table and went tumbling over it. A porcelain vase crashed to the floor, and Isabella rolled to her side as Nate raised his gun at Luke, who was hunched over on the floor.

Luke dove behind the desk and shoved his hand beneath it as he went. The carpet exploded from Nate's bullet, right where Luke's head had been. Nate charged across the room, and then Luke rolled out on the carpet.

Isabella had a split second to register he had a gun, and then he fired.

Nate's gun went off at the same moment, and the explosion was deafening.

Nate crashed into the desk and bounced off of it. He rolled to the floor and landed on his back, blood oozing from a small circle right in the middle of his forehead.

Luke was up on his shoulder, his face pale. "The guards. Free Marcus. He needs to call them off."

"But—"

"Now!"

Isabella heard shouts and immediately went to Marcus, who was sheet white and gaping at his son. She grabbed Leon's knife and sliced through his gag.

"Adam!" His voice was raw with anguish. "Adam!"

Luke was down on his side now. "The guards," he rasped. "Call them off."

The door was flung open and guards poured in, guns up.

Marcus pulled himself upright. "Leon and Nate tried to kill us," he snapped. "Untie me. Make sure they're dead. Call an ambulance for my son. Now!" His voice was authoritative and demanding, his posture rigid.

He had become the Marcus of old, and the guards obeyed immediately.

Isabella raced across the room and dropped to her knees beside Luke. His hand was pressed to his side, and sweat beaded his upper lip. "Oh, God, Luke!" His face was ashen, and his mouth was twisted in pain. "Don't you dare die on me!"

She ripped her shirt off and wedged it beneath his hand. "Let me do it."

He groaned as she pressed the shirt against his wound. "Jesus, Isa. Are you trying to kill me?"

Tears filled her eyes. "Of course I am. You tried to shoot me in the head. I owe you."

His eyes slitted open. "I knew you'd duck."

The tears spilled over and streamed down her cheeks. "What if I hadn't?" Her shirt was saturated with his blood now.

He raised one hand to touch her face. "I believe in you, Isa. I knew you would."

"Adam!" Marcus knelt beside her and opened a first-aid kit. "Don't be an ass and die on me." He pulled out a stash of gauze. "Here, Isa."

She switched the shirt for the gauze, and Luke let out a sharp gasp as she pressed it to his side. "Oh, God, Marcus. He's bleeding so much."

"The ambulance is on its way." Marcus cut more gauze. "Press harder!"

"I'm trying!" She realized Luke's eyes were closed. "Luke! Wake up!"

His eyes flickered open. "I love you," he whispered.

"Oh, God, I love you, too! Don't leave me!"

"You're better off—" He coughed, an awful gurgling sound. "It'll never end if I live—"

"No! Don't you dare give up! I'm not better off without you. You make me whole, for God's sake, Luke! I need you!"

Luke's eyes closed.

"Oh, God, Marcus!" Isabella hammered at Luke's chest with her free hand. "He's letting himself die. Do something! Luke!"

Marcus grabbed Luke's arm. "Leon's dead, Adam. It's over. You can have your happily ever after with Isabella, dammit. It's fucking over!"

Luke's breathing became shallower.

"Luke!" Isabella shouted, sobs ripping through her chest. "Stay with me. I love you. You're such an ass to pull this martyr shit right now."

Marcus bent over so his mouth was next to Luke's ear. "I love you, son. You need to live so you can make me suffer for the rest of my life. If you die, who the hell's going to make me pay?"

For the longest moment, there was no response.

Then the corner of Luke's mouth turned up ever so slightly.

And she knew he was going to fight.

CHAPTER THIRTY-FOUR

Luke watched Isabella pace his hospital room restlessly. Her hands were on her hips, and her hair was shoved into a careless knot on top of her head. She was wearing jeans and a pair of sneakers. None of the perfection of when she had first arrived, and yet she carried it off perfectly.

Around her neck was the pendant from her mother. A symbol that had been a threat when he'd first met her, because it had been an indication that she was the type of woman who cared too much. But now, he saw it only as his anchor, a reminder of the importance of believing in those you love. "Isabella."

She spun around. "You're awake!" She ran across the room and flung herself onto him.

Luke grunted and caught her, well aware she had been careful not to come near his injured side. "You do realize I'm only a few days out of major surgery, don't you?" He caught her face and kissed her. It was the first time he'd had the energy to do more than a light peck, and he cherished the feeling of her body on top of his, of her lips against his.

She made a small noise of pleasure, then pulled back. Her eyes were dancing. "Kaylie called. Cort woke up.

He still pretty weak and has a lot of recovery ahead, but he's going to be fine."

Something stung Luke's eyes. "I knew that bastard was too tough to die." He hugged Isabella fiercely. "Hot damn!"

"I know." She grinned at him. "Kaylie says to tell you that you owe them, though."

Luke nodded. "I know." It was time to bring up the topic he hadn't been willing to address until now. "Leon and Nate are dead, but as long as Marcus is alive, I won't be safe, and those I'm with won't be safe."

Isabella propped her elbows on his chest and rested her chin on her hands. She gave him an impatient look.

"What's that for? I'm being serious."

"You really think you can scare me with all that mumbo jumbo? I am already involved."

"No." Luke trailed his hands through her hair. "I can't go back to Alaska. I need to disappear again, and I can't ask that of you."

"Ask anyway."

Luke scowled. "Isa. This isn't a joke."

"Do you love me?"

He didn't hesitate. "Of course I do."

She grinned, a brilliant smile that made her face light up. "I love you, too. Thank you for not killing Marcus."

"It was my only option. I had to take out Leon first."

"Was it?" She cocked her head. "I don't think you wanted to kill him. I think you've finally realized he's not a bad guy."

"Isa—"

There was a light knock at the door. Luke turned his head as Marcus walked into the room. The bruise on his face had faded somewhat, and he looked more like the Marcus of old. His suit was immaculate, his hair perfectly coifed, and he had that persona of confidence and power.

Luke stiffened. What? Had he expected the humbled Marcus to still exist now that his oppressors were eliminated?

"My son."

Isabella rolled off of Luke, and Luke forced himself to let her go. There was no way he was showing how he felt about her in front of Marcus. "What do you want?"

Marcus gestured at the seat next to the bed. "May I?"

Luke shook his head. "I'd rather you not."

Marcus sat anyway.

Luke scowled, then some of his tension eased when Isabella took the seat on his other side. She rested her elbows on the bed so her arms were brushing against Luke's shoulder. The slightest contact, but it felt good.

"Adam—"

"My name is Luke."

Marcus nodded. "Luke. I want to apologize."

"For what?"

"Your life."

Luke couldn't hide his surprise. "What are you talking about?"

Marcus removed a framed photo from his briefcase and handed it to Luke.

It was the photo Isabella had described. Luke and his mother on a beach. "Mom." He hadn't seen a photo of her in so long. His chest tightened and he ran his finger over her laughing face. "I forgot how beautiful she was."

"I haven't." Marcus leaned forward. "I don't know if

Isabella told you, but after she died, I went after the men responsible. I killed every single one in cold blood."

Luke shot a surprised look at his father. "You didn't even seem to care."

Marcus managed a tense smile. "I was raised to believe that men didn't show emotion. I responded by taking revenge. Leon helped me. He was at each killing. I didn't know it at the time, but he videoed them, and he later used them to force me to run the business as he wanted. After your mother's death, I decided to leave the business. I wanted to take you and walk away. Leon had other plans."

Luke set the picture on his lap. "You could have disappeared."

"Like you did? You can be found, Luke. You should know that. I'd murdered seven men. If the feds found out, how long do you think it would have been until they took me away? And then what about you? No one to take care of you. You'd have ended up in foster care at age eight."

"Maybe that would have been better," Luke muttered, then regretted his words when he saw Marcus flinch.

"Perhaps." Marcus leaned forward. "I couldn't get out of the business, and so my choice was to make you so strong that it couldn't hurt you. That's why I brought you in and taught you everything. I wanted you to be strong enough to survive what I brought into your life. When you left, I covered your trail. Leon wanted to find you and get the earrings back, and I protected you."

Luke frowned at the earnestness in Marcus's face. Felt the truth of it. But he couldn't accept it. "Why?"

"Because I wanted you to live." Marcus shook his

head. "When Leon killed Anna . . . I couldn't stop thinking of Rebecca." His voice cracked, and he pulled out a handkerchief. Wiped at his eyes.

Luke averted his gaze to give Marcus privacy.

"I realized the past would keep repeating itself. I felt your anguish at the funeral. It was like mine. I had visions of you reacting the way I had, of ruining your life forever by doing something rash, and then you did it. When you shot that decorator and I realized you were becoming like me—" He swore softly. "I would have done anything to get you out of there, to give you a chance to start over. I realized I had utterly failed to keep you safe. So, when you left, I let you go. I prayed for you to get a chance to start over. It was what your mother would have wanted. I was so glad when you got out."

Luke shifted, suddenly feeling uncomfortable and trapped in the small bed. He wanted to get up, get away from the tightness in his throat.

"The buyer was furious, but I negotiated a substitute." Marcus gave a tired smile. "Then a few weeks ago, we found the necklace, and Leon made a deal for the whole set. He thought I'd been holding on to the earrings all that time. When he learned I didn't have them, he gave me a deadline to get them back."

Luke held out his hand, and Isabella put her hand in his. "So you sent Isa after me."

"She didn't know."

"I know." Luke squeezed her hand. "I know she didn't."

She smiled.

"I figured she could get the earrings from you and bring them back. She was the only one who knew where you were, or your new name." Marcus shook his head.

"I was so naive, thinking I could trick Leon." Marcus looked at Isabella. "When I heard he'd shot you . . ." Tears welled up again. "Jesus, Isa. I'm so sorry."

"Oh, Marcus." Isabella released Luke's hand and ran around the bed. She threw her arms around him and hugged him. "I love you."

"I love you, too." Marcus hugged her fiercely and didn't bother to hide his tears. "I had to hide my feelings for you when Leon was alive, because I knew he'd use you against me, just as he'd done with Anna." He pulled back and framed her face with his hands. "You were my shining light these last six years. You gave me hope that maybe there was still some good in the world. No one had loved me since Rebecca, and I'd forgotten what it was like."

Luke was stunned by Marcus's obvious love for Isabella. He hadn't thought Marcus had the capacity to feel like that, but it was so apparent Isabella had broken through his veneer.

Still holding on to Isabella, Marcus turned to Luke. "I'm shutting down the business. The public announcement will be that with Leon and Nate dead, I can't continue. I have enough money to retire, and I'm going to walk away."

Too many years too late. "Congratulations." Luke couldn't keep the bitterness out of his voice.

"No." Marcus touched his arm. "What I'm trying to say is that it's over, Luke. You don't have to hide anymore. No one is left to come after you or your friends. I've already sent a bunch of money to Alaska to pay for your friend's care, and I will continue to support him. It's over, Luke. You're free."

Luke stared in disbelief at the old man as the implications of Marcus's words settled on him. Jesus. Marcus was telling the truth. He was free. After a lifetime of looking over his shoulder, *he was free.* He couldn't stop the grin from spreading across his face, and he wanted to stroll down the middle of the city of Boston in broad view, just because he *could.*

"And you." Marcus turned to Isabella, who was beaming at Luke from her place on Marcus's lap. "I owe you, as well. For that reason, I'm turning over the legitimate side of my business to you. The store, my connections and all the contracts with the museums and universities. They're yours, plus I'll fund all your start-up costs."

Isabella was visibly stunned. "Are you serious?"

"Yes. My house is yours as well. You can redecorate it. It's your home now, Isa." He smiled. "I just hope you'll let an old man come by for dinner on Sundays, just so he can tell you how much he loves you."

Isabella's eyes filled with tears, and she flung her arms around Marcus. "Thank you!"

Luke ground his jaw and pulled his gaze away from Isabella. Marcus had just given her everything she wanted. A home. A career. Financial security. And a father.

"But I can't accept it."

Luke jerked his gaze back to her.

Marcus was frowning. "Why not?"

"Because I want more."

Luke looked sharply at her, but she didn't acknowledge him. She removed herself from Marcus's lap and walked across the room. She sat down on the windowsill, resting her palms by her hips. She still didn't look at Luke. "I love you, Marcus, but I don't want to be a part of that world anymore. That house isn't home for me, and I don't want to spend my life searching for antiquities."

He frowned. "But I thought you loved it."

"I loved it because you came to me when I was in college and offered me a future. You offered me a PhD and a home and a career, and a place to call my own in this world." She smiled. "For that, I thank you." She finally looked at Luke, a passing glance that told him nothing. "But that was your dream, not mine. I want my own dream now, and I believe I can do it on my own."

Pride shone on Marcus's face. It was a father's pride to see his child finally stepping into her own skin. It was the look Luke had always wanted to create on his father's face, the one he'd never gotten. To see him give it to Isabella . . . no one deserved it more than she did. He wanted to thank his father for that, for giving her that gift. He knew how much it would mean to her.

"What are you going to do?" Marcus asked her. "Where are you going to live?"

Isabella shrugged. "I don't know yet, but I'm okay with that." She grinned. "I feel free now, and I know I can create the life I want. I'm not going backward." She held her arms up over her head and lifted her face to the sun creaking through the windows. "The world is mine."

"That it is," Marcus said softly, and Luke heard the envy in his voice.

And for the first time, he looked at his father as a man. Not as an enemy. Marcus had given Isabella the gift of his love, an incredible thing. Luke couldn't deny the pain his father had lived with for so long. He didn't forgive his father, but at the same time . . . he was tired of hating the man. He wanted to let it go. He wanted to feel the love that Isabella had so generously given to both of them. He wanted to learn from Isabella and her relentless pursuit of love and those worthy of it.

"Dad." The word stuck in his throat, but at the same time, it felt good. Really, really good.

Marcus shot a disbelieving look at him, and Isabella gasped.

"You get to start over as well," Luke said. "Where are you going to go?"

Marcus hesitated and his shoulders became hunched, as if he were a little, timid boy. "If Isa isn't going to be in Boston, then there's no reason for me to be here." He peered hopefully at Luke. "I was thinking of moving to Alaska. Learning how to fish."

Luke smiled, and something heavy fell from his shoulders. "Somehow I knew you were going to say that."

Hope flashed in Marcus's eyes. "You wouldn't kick me out?"

Slowly, Luke shook his head. "No. I don't think I would."

Tears filled his father's eyes, and Marcus didn't bother to hide them. "Adam—I mean, Luke. I have always loved you. I did a crappy job as a dad, I know I did." His voice became raw. "But I did the best I could, I swear."

Luke nodded. "I know."

Marcus started to raise his arms, then dropped them. Luke grabbed his dad's wrist and yanked him over.

And for the first time in thirty years, he hugged his father.

CHAPTER THIRTY-FIVE

Isabella pressed her hands to her chest as she watched Luke and his father embrace. The hug was so awkward, she almost wanted to laugh, but she knew if she opened her mouth, she'd start bawling.

She wrapped her fingers around her mother's pendant. "I love you, Mama," she whispered.

She and her mother had been stripped of their chance for a life together because an awful man had broken them apart. They hadn't had the chance to recover, to come back together, but Luke and his father had. They would have a lifetime of the love she'd lost.

But she had Marcus now, too. A father who would always be there for her, just because of who she was. There would always be a hole in her heart from the loss of her mother, but now, it was a little less empty.

The men stopped embracing, and Marcus stepped back. His face was flushed, but there was a light in his eyes she'd never seen before. "Well, I've got to run. If I'm not going to hand the business over to Isabella, I need to make arrangements to sell off everything." He grinned at Isabella. "I love you, sweet thing."

She smiled. "I love you, too, Marcus."

He gave a giddy little wave so incongruous with his staid suit, and then he turned and nearly skipped out the door. The door shut behind him, leaving Isabella alone with Luke. "How do you feel?" she asked.

He turned his head to look at her, and her heart nearly melted at the tender look on his face. "Come here."

She rose from the window and walked across the room, stopping just beside the bed. "I'm so glad you're letting your dad back into your life."

He took her hand and tugged her onto the bed. She eased beside him, aware that his injury was on that side. "I owe you for bringing my dad and me together again."

"Don't say that." She pressed her fingers to his lips. "I worked so hard to force Marcus to need me so much he would love me, but I don't want to do that anymore. I don't want anyone to owe anyone for anything. Let's just let the past go. Live in the present, because we want to."

"Fine." He rubbed his thumb over the back of her hand. His touch was gentle, but seductive at the same time. Her stomach tightened, and anticipation pulsed through her. "I don't owe you anything then. I just want to—" He swore suddenly. "I can't do this lying down. Move."

Isabella quickly stood as Luke struggled to his feet. She caught his arm and helped him up, and he didn't argue. The moment he was up, he pulled away. "Sit."

She raised her brows. "You're awfully bossy when you're hurt."

He winced with pain, and she quickly sat, not wanting him to push himself. "Okay, I'm sitting. What—"

He lowered himself to one knee, grunting with pain.

"Luke, don't hurt yourself—"

"Shh." He took her hand and pressed his lips to the

back of it. His dark eyes were fastened on hers. "When you showed up on my doorstep, you brought hell back into my life."

She nodded. "I know."

"You drove me nuts, with all your talk about how great my dad was." A small smile played at his lips. "You have to admit I wasn't wrong. The man's a bastard."

She inclined her head. "He did murder seven men," she admitted. "But *you* have to admit, he's also a good man."

"Weak." He thumbed her palm. "But he did the best he could. I see that now." He searched her face. "I thought my life was great in Alaska. I thought I had everything I needed. Then you showed up babbling about love and loyalty. You broke apart all I'd so carefully set up."

She smiled at his aggravated tone. "Do you want an apology?"

"Hell, no." He moved closer so he could wrap his hands around her hips. His body was warm and strong between her legs, even with his injury. "My soul died on that beach when I was eight, when my mom was killed. I worked so hard not to feel anything. Even with Anna, I never really let her in. I felt guilty as hell when she was killed, and I was pissed, but I wasn't broken." He tightened his grip on her waist.

Isabella stiffened. Anna, the pure and innocent daughter of a minister. There was no way Isabella could ever compare.

"But when Leon put that gun to your head, I knew the kind of rage that had made my dad murder seven men. Leon had to die, Isabella. So did Nate. They had to." He searched her face. "I didn't kill them just to save us. I killed them because they had to die for hurting you, and as much as I wish I felt bad about it, I don't. I'm not a good man, Isa. I'm more like my father than I want to be. Do you understand that? I tried to be Luke Webber, and I failed at it. I'm Adam Fie, down to my core. I—"

She placed her fingers over his lips. "I know there is some Adam Fie in you. But there is also Luke Webber. I love them both, just like I loved my mother and her flaws, as well as Marcus and his. I'm okay with all of you, Luke." She bent down and kissed him lightly. "I accept you as you are," she whispered. "Because I can see into your heart, and there is a good man in there. A man who is worthy of my love."

Luke caught her face and kissed her hard. Not a light kiss like she'd given him. An aggressive, possessive kiss that thundered through her soul. He pulled back, his hands still framing her face. "I love you, Isabella Kopas," he said fiercely. "Do you have any idea how much I love you?"

She nodded. "You became Adam Fie for me," she said. "You became the man you didn't want to be to save me." She knew what it had cost him, and she understood what it said. What it meant. She felt the strength of his love in every cell of her body.

"And I'd do it again."

She laughed. "God, no. I think nine dead bodies between the two of you are plenty."

He managed a small laugh. "I can't believe you can laugh about it."

"We have to laugh," she said. "It's the only way to survive."

"And that, my dear," Luke said, "is why I've decided I can't live without you."

Her heart caught. "Really?"

Luke pulled back so he was on one knee again, and he took her hand. "Isabella Kopas, I'm flawed, I have a crazy family and a strong affinity for living in a godforsaken state with crappy coffee, but I swear on my mother's spirit that if you'll have me, I will love you every day of my life. I want to make a home with you. I want to wake up every morning with you in my arms, and watch the sunset from our porch every night." He wrapped his other hand around hers. "I want to give you the home and the love you've always wanted. I'm not the fairy tale you dreamed up, but I swear I will love you every second of every day."

Isabella stroked his jaw, her heart feeling so full it seemed as if it would explode right out of her chest. The intensity of his voice, of his face, of his words . . . "The way you love me is exactly what I've always dreamed of," she said. "You *are* my dream. Every last bit of you."

Luke's mouth tightened, and his hand began to tremble where he held hers. "So, you'll marry me?"

She smiled. "You haven't asked me to marry you."

He stopped and took a breath. "Isabella Kopas, will you marry me?"

She beamed at him. "Yes, I will."

He finally grinned, his whiskered face stretching into a huge smile that lit up his eyes. He looked a thousand years younger than he had the day she'd met him. "Yeah?"

"Most definitely." She held out her arms and he came into them. She buried her face in his neck, in the strength of his arms as he held her tight, and she knew she had finally found the home she'd been searching for her entire life.

Her mother's turquoise pendant burned against her

skin, and Isabella smiled. *Thank for teaching me to believe, Mama. I love you.*

She'd found her place, and her new, wonderful journey was finally beginning. She lifted her face and smiled at the man who had finally brought love into her life, the kind of unconditional, pure love she'd always wanted. "I love you, Luke."

He smiled. "And I love you, Isa. Always and forever."

And then he kissed her, and it was the most perfect kiss ever.

And there were many, many more to come.

☐ **YES!**

Sign me up for the Love Spell Book Club and send my
FREE BOOKS! If I choose to stay in the club, I will pay
only $8.50* each month, a savings of $6.48!

NAME: _____

ADDRESS: _____

TELEPHONE: _____

EMAIL: _____

☐ I want to pay by credit card.

☐ **VISA**   ☐ **MasterCard**   ☐ **DISCOVER**

ACCOUNT #: _____

EXPIRATION DATE: _____

SIGNATURE: _____

Mail this page along with $2.00 shipping and handling to:
**Love Spell Book Club
PO Box 6640
Wayne, PA 19087**
Or fax (must include credit card information) to:
610-995-9274
You can also sign up online at **www.dorchesterpub.com**.
*Plus $2.00 for shipping. Offer open to residents of the U.S. and Canada only.
Canadian residents please call 1-800-481-9191 for pricing information.
If under 18, a parent or guardian must sign. Terms, prices and conditions subject to
change. Subscription subject to acceptance. Dorchester Publishing reserves the right
to reject any order or cancel any subscription.

GET FREE BOOKS!

You can have the best romance delivered to your door for less than what you'd pay in a bookstore or online. Sign up for one of our book clubs today, and we'll send you *FREE* BOOKS* just for trying it out... **with no obligation to buy, ever!**

Bring a little magic into your life with the romances of Love Spell—fun contemporaries, paranormals, time-travels, futuristics, and more. Your shipments will include authors such as **MARJORIE LIU, JADE LEE, NINA BANGS, GEMMA HALLIDAY,** and many more.

As a book club member you also receive the following special benefits:
- **30% off all orders!**
- **Exclusive access to special discounts!**
- **Convenient home delivery and 10 days to return any books you don't want to keep.**

Visit **www.dorchesterpub.com** or call **1-800-481-9191**

There is no minimum number of books to buy, and you may cancel membership at any time. **Please include $2.00 for shipping and handling.*